CATALINA CARNAGE

NANCY CHURCHILL

Raging River Press

Also by Nancy Churchill

The 7th Victim

Deadly Aftermath

A Deliberate Lie

E-Books are available on all titles

Copyright @2019 Raging River Press, Yorba Linda, California

ISBN: 978-0-9909030-2-4

Book cover designed by Jenny Ruvalcaba

Book cover model, Madison Kishineff

If you prick us, do we not bleed?
    If you tickle us, do we not laugh?
    If you poison us, do we not die?
    And if you wrong us, shall we not revenge?

William Shakespeare,
    Merchant of Venice, Act 3, Scene 1

Dedication

This book is dedicated to Robert L. Cunningham, deceased, WWII pilot, hero, and my boss at North American Aviation in Downey, circa 1960's. Feared by many, loved by me. He inspired me to reach for the stars, fostered my sagging self-confidence, paid for the plumber when I was poor and wrote a "sticky" note that I read each day with a smile. "God, I spoiled you rotten." Thanks for being my friend. I miss you.

People waiting to meet you:

The Penningtons
    Grace, the mother, former CIA
    Amanda, daughter, FBI
    Rachael, daughter, Bullhead City Police Detective
    Meg, youngest daughter trying to get a break

Josh Meyers, Catalina cop, Rachael's boyfriend

Dred, mercenary, gun-for-hire

The Spencers
    Elliott, serial killer, incarcerated in San Quentin
    Marisa, sister
    Derek, brother

The Walters
    Greg, Catalina cop, Josh's partner
    Stella, bipolar, schizophrenic, in love with Josh

Catherine, resident ghost

Chapter 1

AL SWIPED THE GRIMY RAG across the dented bar top, soaking up the remnants of condensation from his patron's beer. Hotel Catherine, known for the coldest and cheapest brew on Catalina Island, was showing her 110 years. Chipped paint around the windows, vinyl flooring worn through to the concrete and stained bar top. He checked his watch, and with aging gray eyes, glanced upward to the ceiling over the antique jukebox.

"That time of day, Al?"

"Yup. Any time now," he drawled, not bothering to look again.

When locals gathered around the bar at this time of day, they always engaged in the same conversation. "How long you two been hangin' out together? When you grab her does she slip through your fingers? Is it a spiritual thing?" Then they would laugh and poke fun at him for hours on end. There was no answer that would satisfy the questions.

He paused to watch, never tiring of the apparition, even after thirty years. Catherine's ghost was never late.

An almost imperceptible dribble of red appeared and then flowed across the cottage cheese ceiling, stopping only when a ghost-like apparition took shape.

"Right on time," Al mumbled. With a slight smile, that drooped to the left, he turned and finished wiping down the bar.

Chapter 2

RACHAEL PENNINGTON AMBLED into her sister's bedroom, a glass of Chardonnay in hand. "You going out? It's Thursday. You got tomorrow off?" She parked herself in the rattan chair and plopped her bare feet onto the bed. Leaning forward, she wiggled her toes and gave them a thorough examination. "God, I need a pedi."

Meg finished pulling her pony tail through a scrunchy. "And this is your business?"

"Oh, drop the 'tude." Rachael smirked at Meg's total look. "You're not going to pick up any handsome sailors in that get-up. Since when do you dress like a Victorian street walker?" She did a double take on the tight velvet bodice Meg was struggling to fasten.

Meg grunted as she wiggled and attached the last hook on the bodice and checked the mirror one more time trying to decide whether or not to grab some earrings. Plopping down on the bed, she gave Rachael her full attention. "I've got a new gig tonight." Her impish smile broke through.

"Oh, I thought you accepted that job at the Hotel Catherine… housekeeping was it?"

"Yeah, that, too." Meg jumped off the bed again, fiddling with the ties of the classic costume that accentuated her tiny waist. "Crappy job. I know I should have passed on going to Cal State last semester, but you know Mom. School, school, school. That's what I get. I was tired of fighting with her and finally gave in."

"She had your best interests in mind. You know that." Rachael grinned. School was an ongoing battle between Meg and their mother.

"I know, but..." Meg grunted, knowing that any further discussion with Rachael wouldn't change anything. "Bottom line? I went to school for a semester. Now, as a reward, I've got two shitty jobs here on the island. Thanks, Mom."

Rachael, ever the peacemaker in the Pennington family, didn't want to get her sister started on their mother, since that would undoubtedly lead to Grace's recent confession---a secret lover who was Meg's real father. While the confession seemed to be acceptable to Meg, Rachael knew that her sister still harbored some resentment. "But you also came away with your PI license. That's a good thing."

"Big wow. Had my office open six months, landed one big job and then closed it." Meg shook her head in disgust and pulled again on her pony tail.

"Hey. Wait a cotton-pickin' minute. You made a bunch of money on that case and brought the crooked governor of Arizona down in the process. Your memory is sure as hell short-term." Rachael never let Meg get away with too many negative generalities.

Meg's mind swirled back in time. She fought back a tear. "Yeah. But I didn't save Blaze's life. Not too successful there, was I?" She turned her back on Rachael.

"That was not your fault. But, back to college. That was your own decision. Don't be blaming Mom for that." Not wanting to get into a full-blown tiff with her sister, Rachael moved on. "You know Catalina jobs are always filled early by local kids. Your strong suit never was planning." Rachael handed her wine to Meg who took a sip. "College is never a waste." Rachael didn't want to dwell on the past year, but gave it one more shot. "You did need some R&R, and

Mom always supplies the best of that." She moved behind Meg and tucked a loose wisp of blond hair behind her sister's ear.

"We'll see." Meg knew an education was important, a fact that had been pounded into her mental schedule for years. Both of her sisters had degrees, but she was impatient to live her life, not read about someone else's life. This habit of taking the unknown fork in the road had resulted in a full year of mayhem which almost got her killed "So, how do I look?" She bounced on the bed and went air born into Rachael's back, spilling wine on contact.

"Brat." She let the wine dribble down her wrist. "Well, it's not your typical Meg outfit, but I guess you know what you're doing." Rachael shook her head, salvaged the rest of her wine and moseyed out of the room. "Oh, by the way. There's a letter on the kitchen sink for you. Looks like jury duty." A laugh joined her departure down the hall.

"What? Oh, great. Just what I need. Another exercise in futility." She decided against the earrings, grabbed her purse, and headed for the compact kitchen.

June had finally arrived on Santa Catalina Island, and the hordes of vacationers were streaming across the 26 miles from Balboa to the island's pristine shores, looking for a twelve hour adventure of swimming, boating, scuba diving or parasailing. Along with the vacationers came the college kids and Meg looking for jobs. Earning enough money to pay the rent and party with the leftovers was the plan The few remaining positions were grabbed by those willing to cope with minimum-waged stints and horrible working hours.

"Thought I'd get the scuba diving job, or even parasailing. But, no. Catherine's? One of those damn ghosts will probably grab me when I'm not looking." She executed two quick turns and ended up, nose to nose with her sister. "Well, what do you think?" She posed for Rachael.

"What a sight. Okay, I can't stand it any longer. What's with the costume? What are you doing tonight?"

"I'm the new guide for the ghost tours." She knew the laughter would come, and was not disappointed. "Gotta go." She grabbed a clipboard and headed for the door not wishing to hear any more of Rachael's teasing.

Rachael's laughter filled the room "When the ghosts find out who their fearless leader is, they'll probably revolt and not show up. Hey. Don't forget the letter." Her comment fell on deaf ears. Rachael, knowing this would be her only laugh of the day, leaned against the door jamb and enjoyed it. She grabbed a pillow from the couch and threw it at the departing Meg. "And don't forget you have to go to court with me tomorrow. 9:00 a.m."

"Yeah, yeah."

Chapter 3

HER HAIR LOOKED LIKE RED COBWEBS tucked under a blue baseball cap.

The hoodie jacket was inappropriate attire for such a warm summer day, but she felt she needed the anonymity. She glanced sideways at the creepy man standing next to her, hanging on to the boat railing. His constant expression of 'no worries' annoyed Stella. She tried to rationalize what the words meant, but her mind blocked all reason again. Why was he with her? She couldn't remember how they met, but she knew she didn't love him. She only loved Josh. *Oh, yeah. Dred is along to protect me. From what? No, that's not it.* The memory almost screamed through, but all too soon, it disappeared. The Catalina flyer's bow dipped into a deep ocean swell tossing Stella Davis against the man. "Sorry, hon." The boat's deck was slippery from ocean spray. She grabbed his arm.

"No worries." The man pushed her hand away and zipped up his sweatshirt, pulling his hoodie forward to hide his annoyed face. The straggly jeans, combined with the worn tennis shoes epitomized his character with all the flaws. Druggie.

Even though the lights were dim in the Newport Beach bar, he'd spotted Stella from the verbal description given to him three days ago. Early thirties, straggly red hair, overweight from the recent delivery of her baby and obnoxious. He didn't anticipate any competition. Who else would be interested in the frumpy broad? He dressed to attract her…tight t-shirt that showed off his six pack, tighter jeans frayed from age, sandals, and a dangling cigarette. Dred moved in. He planned on schmoozing her but found it unnecessary. She was all over him from the first beer, ready for sex.

"I'm going to Catalina tomorrow. Wanna go with? I'll pay." Her words left her mouth in a slurred version of English, but he caught their drift.

"Sure, baby. Anything you want." Her took her hand and pressed it against his erection. Catalina was part of the plan.

The unsuspecting Stella floated in and out of her own reality, thinking this excellent man would take care of her many needs. She liked what she was feeling. Get laid, get drugs, find Josh and happy ever after, in that order.

Dolphins frolicked in the wake of the boat temporarily mesmerizing Dred, but then his mind returned to the present assignment. What a loser. She was fat. Hadn't lost the weight from her pregnancy so her flabby belly flapped over the tight waist band of her jeans. Revolting. Supposedly she was on meds for a bipolar or schizophrenic condition, meds that she forgot or refused to take. As a result she held on to some pipedream about a blissful ending with a Catalina cop that she constantly talked about. Poor guy, he thought. This Josh person had no idea what was coming his way. Dred leaned over the side of the boat peering through the early morning haze that shrouded Catalina Island.

"Havin' fun?" Stella flashed him a toothy smile.

"God, when was the last time you brushed your teeth?" He stymied the repulsive look that was forming. He had to keep her happy for a few more days, an assignment which was proving to be a taxing job.

Stella stopped, relaxed her lips over her yellowed teeth, and pouted. Well, she thought, when we get to the Island Josh will be waiting. Maybe on a white horse? She giggled and started rocking out to an imaginary tune. Her baseball cap flew off. Her red hair tangled in the ocean spray.

Stella's aunt Sharon was standing next to the two, holding a tiny baby boy in the crook of her arm, grasping the boat rail with white knuckles, trying to steady herself. She pulled the receiving blanket over the baby's face protecting him from the sun and then quickly grabbed the rail again. She grimaced with pain from her arthritic shoulder. Months of dealing with Stella's problems and her baby had aged the woman. She tugged at the blanket again and mentally lapsed back to a happier life six months ago. At age 67, she was a widow with ample social security and a small retirement fund enough for one international trip a year with her senior citizen friends. But that was yesterday and her today reality was standing next to her. Everyone believed Sharon was the protector, but few knew of the resentment that was mounting. "Another fifteen minutes and we'll be there. Have you heard from your attorney?" Her worry lines were deepening.

"She sent me a text. Will meet us tomorrow at the courthouse. Nine o'clock." Stella turned back to her male companion, reached forward and massaged his crotch. "Can you wait a little while longer, Dred? Promise I have a few moves you haven't seen yet." The yellow teeth appeared again.

"No worries." Gross teeth or not, she was a wild beast in bed. Along with the money that he'd been promised and the outrageous sex, he could hang on a little longer. Besides, he was curious about his new employer. Connections throughout the dark web were always secretive, but something about this assignment was familiar. He looked at Stella's profile and wondered what story she held that someone would pay money to get.

"Did your parents name you Dred, or is there some story behind it?" asked Sharon. She didn't care about the answer or the man either for that matter. Small talk to fill up an embarrassing moment. She pretended not to see Stella's wandering hand.

"Picked it up in LA when I was hangin' with my bros. Right-eous, huh?" He started to reach for Stella's breast, but withdrew his hand with disgust. Wet lactation stains stretched across the front of her blouse and soaked through the hoodie.

"Oh, that it is." Sharon rearranged the baby blanket and turned her focus back to the pending court proceedings. Her concern was the deception and the looming court fight. The potential tug of war. She hadn't talked to Josh. What if he doesn't want the baby? What then? Leaving the future of the tiny baby in the hands of the courts didn't set too well with her, but raising a child was not going to mar her future. She had plans.

"Let me hold Zach for a while." Stella reached for her baby, but Sharon pulled away.

"The boat's too unstable, Stella. I'll go to the lower deck and hold him 'til we reach shore." She turned and slightly nodded to the Orange County Child Protective case worker, Jodi, who followed Sharon down the slippery stairwell.

"Hey, Stel. You know that twisted sister that's followin' Sharon?" asked Dred as he watched the two women disappear down the stairs.

She glanced toward the woman. "No." She felt him up again. "No worries." She shot a toothy smile his way as she felt his growing erection.

An observant mother further down the deck yanked her teenage girl's hand and pulled her away. "Quit your gawking," She ordered.

On the lower deck, Sharon changed Zach's diaper and then tightened the receiving blanket around him. She cradled him against her chest and turned to the case worker. "If all goes well tomorrow, Josh will have custody and he and his girlfriend, Rachael, will get married and raise him. He's got a great job, cop here on the island and she's a detective with the Bullhead Police Department. Wonderful people." She paused, feeling the necessity to push her goals on the case worker. "You are aware of Stella's medical history aren't you?"

"Yes, mental problems. Schizophrenic with suicidal tendencies, per her history. As I see it, your testimony and my recommendations are what the courts will need tomorrow. Right?" The case worker scribbled some notes on a pad and then tucked it in her purse.

"Yes. After the judge recommends that Josh have sole custody and the baby is delivered to him, I'll get Stella back to the mainland and her mother has agreed to institutionalize her. Left me power of attorney. I wonder if she'll ever be able to function." A shudder ran through her body. She felt she was betraying her niece, her own blood, but it was for the better good. And yet…

"Has Josh agreed to take Zach? It's my understanding that he wants nothing to do with this child." Jodi raised an eyebrow and stared at Sharon.

Sharon twitched. "Not in so many words." She stared down at the tiny boy. "I guess that's why you're here. If he gives up his parental rights, you'll be taking Zach." She pulled the baby tighter to her chest. More sadness. "Stella's no-good mother won't stick around, chasing after any guy that wears pants. She won't take the baby, and God knows I don't have the strength to raise a child. I can't stand the thought of foster care though. It's not right." Her voice trailed off.

"Getting Stella to agree to all of this is a huge undertaking. I've seen her when she gets agitated. Will she go willingly if the decision goes against her?"

"That's the unknown factor. And that Dred guy she's hanging out with now. Well, he could be a problem." Zach wiggled. Sharon tucked his receiving blanket a little tighter, a subconscious gesture, as if to protect him from the unknown.

"What's with that guy? Looks like a real dope head. There's something almost sinister about him." She couldn't hold back an uninhibited tremble.

"The one night we let Stella out of the hospital for an hour with her girlfriend, she hooked up with that loser in some bar. I don't think there's any real connection. He's just hanging around for the sex and freebies. Doesn't really have any stake in the game, as I see it." She decided to push the case worker again, a little harder in Josh's direction. "Stella's brother Greg is a cop on the Island. Did you know that?"

"No. So how does he figure in all of this?"

"He's Josh's partner at the Sheriff's Department. He's anxious to help raise Zach. I've been in contact with him and if all goes as planned he's supposed to help put Stella on the boat after the trial. I have a friend standing by to drive us to the hospital in Costa Mesa. At least that's the plan." More worry lines gathered.

The Flyer's engines throttled down and the women stayed seated as the masses moved toward the exit, pushing to get their full dose of island fun. Ropes were tossed over the pilings and ramps were attached to the boat. A flurry of locals hovered around the bottom of the ramp, handing out brochures promising exotic adventures and happy-hour venues.

"Well, here we go." Sharon attempted a smile as Stella and Dred approached.

"Do you see him? Is my Josh in the crowd? I can't see him." Stella pounded on Dred's chest.

Chapter 4

JOSH MEYERS CHECKED ONE LAST TIME, securing the latigo on his Appaloosa, then turned to Rachael's mare. He slid the bit into her mouth by rote. "Hold still, Charlotte." The mare swished her tail and turned to look at him. "Yeah, you heard me right. Rachael's on her way. Calm down." The mare tossed her head and gave Josh a nicker in return.

His modest home on Catalina fit him. The interior could definitely use a woman's touch, but the outside was perfect for a bachelor's lifestyle. A small barn, two horse stalls, and tack room. What more could a cowboy-cop want? Tall eucalyptus and pepper trees offered enough shade for the horses during the hot summer months but didn't restrict the sun when winter came. Deferred maintenance was noticeable, but Josh was working on it.

This specific area of Catalina, high up on Sumner Road leading to the Wrigley Memorial Gardens, was once an active tourist stop. The stables corralled thirty horses for hire and offered open country for adventurous city folks. But as time marched by, the watersports expanded, attracting the sun-seekers. Snorkeling, scuba diving, fishing, parasailing, kayaking, and canoeing collected tourist dollars leaving only a few horses as neighbors to Josh's mini ranch.

The last six months had been a healing experience for Josh and Rachael's family. Rachael stayed by his side as he recovered from a gunshot wound, another reminder of the chaos that Elliott Spenser had created in Bullhead City. Josh's position with the LA County Sheriff's Department in Catalina had been held for him during his recuperation and when he returned to work next week he would receive a promotion to detective.

Things were looking up he thought as he brushed the mare. *Now if Rachael says yes to my proposal and this baby-thing goes away, life will be perfect. Done deal.* No other scenario was acceptable, he reasoned.

During their young years Rachael had been Josh's summertime girlfriend. Grace, her mother, arranged a month's vacation on Catalina every year, just a short trip from their Yorba Linda home, but a world apart in adventure. The three sisters, Rachael, Amanda and Meg, made life-time friends with the locals. Yearly vacations continued until Rachael's senior year in high school and then the fairy-tale existence skidded to an abrupt stop. Josh dated every girl on the small island, including Stella which proved to be a major mistake. When he broke up with her, she stalked him until Greg intervened, got Stella on some strong meds and everything went back to normal. So it appeared.

Josh remembered the first time he'd scored a kiss with Rachael. Awkward didn't begin to describe it. They were at Descanso Beach at sundown. Two twelve-year-old friends. "Well, since you're heading back to the mainland tomorrow, I guess I'd better give you a kiss." He tried not to blush.

"Like heck. Have to catch me first." Rachael dove headfirst off the boat dock and swam like crazy toward shore.

She was close, her feet almost touching the sandy bottom, when he grabbed her ankle and yanked her underwater. She was no match for his strength, but with a half-hearted attempt, she pulled her knees to her chest, shoved them forward and pushed him away.

"Nice move," he blurted out as he grabbed her arm and pulled her close. He could touch the ocean bottom but she was still afloat.

"You can only kiss me if you say you love me." She knew that wouldn't happen. She splashed water in his face.

Josh cocked his head to the right and produced his smirky smile. "I didn't ask permission, so I'll take the first kiss 'cause I won it, and if you say you love me, then you can kiss me back."

She puckered. Their kiss was filled with youthful anticipation along with a futile attempt to act like adults. *Do it like in the movies* was her reference. She didn't have to remember to close her eyes, because it came naturally, but where to put her arms was something else. Rachael was overwhelmed with giddiness, an irresistible desire to try it again, but an unwelcome shyness prevented it. "Well, Mr. Smarty britches. I've seen better than that on TV."

He pushed. "Say you love me and we'll try it again."

If he hadn't smiled that wicked smile again, she might have acquiesced, but coming from a stubborn background, she pushed away again and laughed. "Maybe next year."

Josh grabbed her bikini top by the back strap and snapped it as she headed for shore. "Hey, Rach. You know this might be it for us. We may never see each other again. I do love you, always have, always will."

Rachael turned, saw a sad look in his eyes, and waded back through the water to him. "Then let's make it a good one."

Five additional summers allowed them to practice their newfound kissing skills with a smattering of fooling around, but eventually the final summer came and went. They never wrote and eventually grew apart, both ending up as cops, Josh in Catalina and Rachael in Bullhead City, Arizona. Besides Josh's misadventures, Rachael had her sporadic love affairs which drifted in and out until fate intervened and they were reunited.

The past July Josh had traveled to Bullhead City to assist Rachael and the FBI in capturing a serial killer, Elliott Spenser, who had kidnapped Meg. During the final showdown, Josh had been shot and temporarily lost his memory. After his surgery, Stella, his schizophrenic ex-girlfriend, showed up at the Arizona hospital.

"Who the hell are you," Rachael demanded.

"Stella, my name is Stella. I'm Josh's fiancé and I'm taking him back to the island." She shoved a wheelchair up to Josh's bed, threw back the sheet and pulled his legs around to touch the floor. The skimpy hospital gown fell apart and Stella stroked his manhood once before pulling up the sheet.

"Like hell you are. Josh. What's going on? Who is this nightmare?"

Josh looked and acted dazed. "Oh, yes, Stella. How are you?" His pain meds controlled his common sense.

By quick talking and moving, Stella convinced Josh that they were lovers, scooted him out of the hospital, boarded a private plane and smuggled him back to Catalina. She kept him drugged and raped him before Rachael could find him. The drugs affected his memory and even now, a year later, he couldn't recall that time frame. But Stella was pregnant and happy. She realized her paranoid dream and delivered his child nine months later. Now she was back in his life, expecting …what?

Josh found himself talking out loud to the mare. "Well, the custody trial is tomorrow. God. Stella thinks it's a child support hearing. She'll shit when she finds out." Josh had traveled to the mainland last week to see his son, Zach, without Stella's knowledge, but when he arrived he decided not to look at him or hold him. The appropriate DNA tests were performed and there was no doubt that he was the father. He returned to Catalina, despondent and vacillating over his future plans.

Sharon sent a weekly message to Josh, advising him of Stella's condition. He ignored them. Stella's psychiatrist felt the baby might be in danger if Stella was allowed to keep him since she ignored her meds. Her schizophrenic moods ran rampant without them so Sharon managed to keep the baby separated from Stella by telling her the baby required an incubator to sustain life. When Stella would arrive at the hospital, the nurses would place Zach in the nursery incubator. She never realized that it was not plugged in.

Josh finished saddling the mare, led her over to the trough, tossed the reins over the hitching post and then leaned against the barn, mentally agonizing over his new position in life…a father. *Now what? Didn't seem fair to ask Rachael to care for Zach. Shit. What if he took after his mother and turned out to be a crazy loon?* He picked up the brush again and with long strokes brushed the mare's hindquarters, trying to brush away the blues.

Standing in the shade of a pepper tree, Rachael watched Josh for a few minutes. His appeal was overwhelming. Tight butt, strong arms, just enough chest hair showing, scruffy beard and unruly brown hair. What's not to love? "Hey cowboy. Wanna ride into the sunset with your favorite cowgirl?"

He jerked. "Wow. Didn't hear ya. Sure. Ready for a ride?" He tossed the brush in a bucket and walked to meet her. He took his time, eyes wandering up and down her body. "Lookin' mighty sexy there, little girl."

"Aim to please." She kept walking, mirroring his tantalizing walk until their buckles met, then snaked her arms around his neck. "You doin' okay?"

"Fair to middlin'. Just worried what that crazy bitch will pull tomorrow. Here. I'll give you a leg up."

As Rachael settled into her saddle, Josh flipped up the stirrup and tightened the cinch. "I've been thinking about Zach."

"Haven't we all." In her mind's eye she saw the three of them living in Josh's house, raising that wonderful little boy. The happy-ever-after scenario would finally replace the entire trauma of the last two years. She would love Zach as her own, and maybe next year they could add a girl to the mix.

"I think the best thing would be for him to have a complete, happy family. Mom and Dad. You know, the whole works." He handed her the reins.

"Of course. That's the best idea." Her heart smiled. She processed his remark and felt Josh would probably want to wait until after Stella was hospitalized and then propose marriage. Rachael was captivated by the fantasy.

"So, when the judge gives me full custody tomorrow, I'm going to talk to the case worker. Tell her to put Zach in a foster home 'til someone adopts him." He turned and put a foot in the stirrup and swung a leg over. "Sound okay to you?"

Rachael was speechless, frozen by sheer surprise. "Ah, well, no."

"What do you mean no?" Confusion ripped across his face.

"Well, shit, Josh." A fatal flaw sliced through her happy canvas of life. "Have you thought this through? For God's sake. He's your son."

"Yeah, I thought it through. Hell yeah."

"Well, isn't this something we should talk about?"

"Why? Not your kid."

Rachael turned away to hide the hurt. "Still."

"No. He's a child born from a wicked, crazy woman who drugged me and raped me. I never wanted a kid with her. I don't love her. Never did. You understand, don't you?"

Rachael grabbed the saddle horn, looped the reins around, and dismounted. She stared hard at the man she loved and then walked away.

"Oh, great. Typical Pennington reaction. Walk away. Fine."

Chapter 5

BACK IN LOS ANGELES, Derek Turner sat at a FBI interrogation table, awaiting Amanda Pennington's arrival. His usual intense blue eyes were dull and a noticeable five o'clock shadow added to his appearance of despondency. The space was bland, no color, depressing, just like his mood. The only life in the room was from the predictable cameras blinking in the corner.

He had been in custody for six weeks. The FBI called it protective custody, but Derek was an attorney and he knew better. They hadn't decided what to do with him. Six weeks of waiting for a decision. Trial? Jail? Confidential Informant? Derek was instrumental in breaking the human trafficking scam that his brother, Elliott, had masterminded, a scam that included Meg as his primary victim. Thanks to Derek, Elliott had been apprehended, confined, and supposedly assassinated in his cell block at San Quentin. Little remained of his body, so forensic testing from the inferno was almost non-existent. He was smoked. One tooth was found in the smoldering ashes. The DNA matched Elliott's prison records and while the warden insisted it was Elliott, Derek and Amanda had their doubts. They expressed them to no one, especially Meg. The warden reviewed every inch of tape and concluded that there was no way Elliott could have switched with another prisoner and escaped. No matter how rich or powerful he was in the underworld, it couldn't have happened, so he said. But that was weeks ago, and here Derek sat in custody.

Initially, the FBI didn't let up on Derek's interrogation. The sweat box was his daily entertainment. He requested a visit with Meg to apologize again for her kidnap and torture, but the request was denied. He was confined to isolation. He waived his attorney rights and assured the FBI that he would be totally forthcoming with information for a price, namely that his sister, Marisa, would not be held accountable for any wrong doing. That was part of the delay. They couldn't find her. Supposedly, she had gone to Mexico and transferred all of Elliott's money into an account for her and Derek. But no word, no phone call, no message came from Marisa. Derek wondered if she was the turncoat who had alerted Elliott about the FBI? He struggled over all the unanswered questions and was increasingly annoyed with the slow progress of his unlawful incarceration.

"Either book me or set me free," he said to Amanda. "You know I'm an attorney and I definitely know that my civil rights are being mutilated."

"Don't like the cell? Seems only fair." Amanda knew the FBI was pushing their luck, but she didn't want Derek to get anywhere near holding the upper hand.

"What the hell is the problem? I said I'd tell you everything." That was two days ago and since then, nothing. Now today when his cell door opened, again he followed an agent down the vanilla halls to the all familiar interrogation room. His temper was teetering at a C-4 level.

Amanda entered. Tall, dark hair pulled up in a bun, standard dark business suit, and sensible shoes. Her appearance and demeanor differed 180 degree from her sister Meg. Spontaneous, flirty, gorgeous Meg verses this model FBI agent. How could they be sisters?

With her no-nonsense attitude, Amanda pulled out the chair, sat down across from Derek and waited.

Derek took a deep breath, and entered the game. "Amanda. You look well."

Even though Derek had been incarcerated and robbed of his own surroundings, his manly appeal was intense. Less than perfectly coiffed, Derek still appeared self-assured which annoyed Amanda. The perfect hair had grown out, and the two day stubble only acted as a magnet. At the beginning Meg had such a crush on him but his good looks had finally given way to a dark side. She pushed a file across the table.

"I'd like to know how Meg is. Was she harmed in the escape? And, by the way, I still have a hard time adjusting to the fact that you two are sisters, And Rachael too? You really had Elliott fooled, which is a hard thing to do."

"Meg is fine." Amanda wouldn't allow him to manipulate the conversation. She pushed the file toward him again.

He read through the papers, studied the pictures of murdered women and men, recognized the boats with drugs and the containers of smuggled body parts. When he looked at the pictures of Meg's tortured body, he was visibly shaken. He read through the interview analysis relating to his kidnapping and abduction of Amanda and Grace, her mother, and finally looked at the decapitated head of Beckett, and Jessie, the twin's mutilated body. This picture was taken following the explosion at the Oasis Casino. The last picture was the incinerated prison cell where the warden claimed Elliott had died. He closed the file, shoved it back and lowered his head. He couldn't make eye contact. The pictures of Meg's abuse tore through his gut. He stood and walked to the two-way mirror, knowing his every move was being analyzed by someone on the other side.

Acting? A ploy? She started. "Derek. Sit down. I have no time, nor do I care about carrying on a social conversation with you. The FBI has reason to believe that Elliott's drug business is still flourishing, in Arizona, Nevada and Catalina. What can you tell me about that?"

Derek sat and leaned back in his chair. It was time to negotiate his future. He steepled his fingers, a family habit. "Well, first of all, what are you going to do for me and Marisa if I continue to cooperate? I believe a deal's in order, since I called you and was instrumental in capturing my brother."

"Not that we're interested, but what do you have in mind?" She had already met with her superiors on many occasions and thrashed out the parameters for a 'deal.'

He studied her face wondering if she played poker. What would be her tell? "Let's discuss Marisa first. She was never involved with any of Elliott's overt actions. Merely a bookkeeper and CFO."

"As my memory serves, she also assisted you in mother's and my kidnapping in Yorba Linda." Her mind flashed back to that desert scene. Hands and feet bound, one hundred and fifteen degrees, no shade, no water and dumped three miles off-road.

"Collateral damage. I brought you there. Not Marisa. She didn't know you were going to be coyote bait, or she would have stopped me."

Amanda didn't believe him. "Well, then. What are your so-called demands for her?"

"She goes free. No charges." His attorney skills of negotiating were still sharp.

"Do you know where she is?"

Derek thought about his answer. "I will tell you after negotiations have been mutually agreed upon. In writing and signed by the D.A."

"Is that a yes?" He was starting to play games. When he didn't answer, Amanda continued.

"And then on to your demands."

"I would like two years' probation, agree to wear an ankle bracelet, and my record is expunged so I may continue practicing law."

Amanda laughed. "Fool. Why not ask for housing and support. You're a felon, Derek. What makes you think you're worth this, or anything for that matter?"

"Because I'm sitting here, your sisters are alive, and you want something else from me." He leaned back, relying on 'the first to speak, loses' maxim.

Amanda recognized the game and played along. "I'll take this to my boss, but it won't have my endorsement. You belong behind bars." She slid the photos in the folder.

Derek leaned forward and focused on her eyes. "Amanda, quit screwin' with me. I've been around the system long enough to know you have a bottom line. Give it to me. I know I can't come out unscathed, but … well, what is it you want? What's it going to take?"

Amanda knew there was probably some give in his proposal, but it wasn't that far off the FBI bottom line. She decided to go for it. "If you guarantee that Marisa was not responsible for any of Elliott's crimes that would be a start. We need to be in touch with her and will keep her in our custody until your part in our plan is complete. If we find it necessary to involve her, then she has to agree to cooperate."

"She is innocent, and she will not want to be incarcerated for something she hasn't done."

"Not incarcerate, but come to Catalina under protective custody. Has to wear a tracking devise. Like you."

"You know I haven't been in contact with her. You've had me in custody. Like I said, she was the money person. I doubt that she has any contact with the Mexican mafia, but I can't guarantee that. She has plenty of money to live on without dealing anymore, and she certainly doesn't have the guts to kill."

The room fell quiet. Derek leaned back and closed his eyes, searching through his mind to find any loopholes. "Say I'm wrong about Marisa, which I don't think I am. What if she is still involved with the drug activity and won't come on board with your plan. What then?"

"Then you would have to be instrumental in catching her. You would have to turn state's evidence against her at the trial." Amanda watched him carefully. "Can you do that?"

It was not an easy answer since Derek harbored a true sibling love for Marisa, and felt she would be cooperative. Wishful thinking? Faced with the realization that he might send her to prison, he hesitated.

"Well?" Amanda leaned forward and studied his face as he decided on an answer.

"Yes." Instant worry.

Amanda sensed the uncertainty and wondered if his answer was true. "Next. Sources say that Catalina is the halfway point for the Mafia to regroup. Previously they were only delivering to Nevada, but now their focus is on San Francisco also. You may have to infiltrate the gang, give us the information."

"Confidential informants usually get paid, don't they?" He smiled at the absurd remark.

Amanda didn't return the smile. "If they're caught, we'd go along with the probation and ankle monitor. Expunging your record is negotiable, depending on the results."

"Excellent." Derek knew dealing with his records was a long shot. "I want this in writing and signed by the director of the FBI along with the D.A."

"I'll forward our arrangements to the powers immediately."

"Now. When do we start?"

Derek seemed relieved which made Amanda more anxious. Had he played her?

Chapter 6

"WHAT IS WRONG WITH YOU WOMAN? Duke Wilson stopped Grace from rinsing out his coffee mug for the fourth time. "Sit down and talk to me before I have to leave. The Escalade will be here any minute."

Grace Pennington set the cup down on the black granite counter, leaned against the sink and glanced through the French windows. Another perfect Yorba Linda day was gathering outside. The Evergreen Pear trees were blooming, Gerbera daisies were ready to open and the grass had fully recovered from the previous year of drought. The ranch was spread across an acre of land, in a city known for its rural atmosphere. Duke had reentered her life. All was perfect, yet her heart was heavy and her mind whirling. She tried to disguise her mounting discomfort from him, her lover, friend, paramour, and father of Meg. She knew he would tell her to stop meddling, that the girls were grown up and able to take care of themselves. "Well, for starters, they haven't called."

"They?" He knew who she meant but loved to tease her.

"Brat. You know who I mean. I know that means they're in trouble, thinking about trouble, or in such shit they don't know what to do and won't call me." She turned and wiped her hands on a tea towel. "I think I'll take a little one day trip over to Catalina and see for myself." She waited for his negative response.

"Don't you have any leftover CIA friends that could use a vacation? Maybe they could go over there and snoop around instead of you pissing off your daughters?" He smiled and peeled the banana he had been waving at her. The last six months of their lives had been all that he had anticipated for twenty-three years. His love had never veered. The first time he met her he knew she was it. No need to look any further. The CIA mission in Paris brought them together. She was married with two girls, but he would wait for her. His smile lingered now as he glanced at her beautiful, yet aging face. Her face for him to love forever. "Look, honey. Don't get crazy on me like last time. I don't have time to bail you and your wild brood out of trouble again." He reached over, gave her a quick kiss and pinched her on the butt. "Let's talk this over before you disappear on some wild sortie." He checked the clock. "Running late, gotta go. I'm outta here."

"Any chance you can tell me where you're going, or for how long?"

"The how long is about a week if all goes well, but the where, can't do." He knew she was organizing a plan just by the expression on her face. "Why not call Penny and go to a movie?"

"Silly. I'm just talking out loud. You know I have my quilting class today." Now she was pushing him toward the door. "And it's time to plant some more flowers."

Duke laughed. "That'll be the day."

Grace, during her normal life, was a high school English teacher and writer while her secret life had been in the service of her country. A CIA operative. When on assignment, she would often take the girls with her. "A vacation" she would call it. Last year, during the warfare with Elliott, she finally confessed her secret identity to the siblings. The sisters had fun with the new truth, looking back on the various counties where they had traveled as their mom put on a sexy trench coat and played spy. The CIA revelation was nothing compared to the big shocker. Rachael and Amanda were pure sisters and Meg was their half-sister. Finding out that information at the age of twenty-two was painful for Meg but the real show stopper was meeting Duke, her biological father.

Duke pulled Grace into a quick embrace and then headed for the door. "Ride's here. As much as I'd love to discuss the pros and cons of your idea, I've got to get going."

When Grace left the CIA, Duke stayed with the department, steadily climbing the ladder. His latest position of Assistant Director placed him in Los Angeles which worked out perfectly for the two.

"You know how the traffic will be on the 5 Freeway if I wait any longer." He reached for his briefcase.

"Oh, don't give it another thought, sweetheart. I've already let it go. On your way, soldier."

Once Grace heard the convoy of cars leave the curb, she reached for her cell phone. "Yes. Could you give me the departure schedule for Wednesday…Yes, the Catalina Express from Newport to Catalina."

Duke made a quick call as he took a seat next to his agency buddies. "Change of plans."

Chapter 7

SOME OF MEG'S FRIEND were loitering outside the Galleon Bar when she hurried by. "Great get-up, Meg. Victorian hustler in tennis shoes." The men howled and punched each other, followed with high-fives. "Come on over here and hustle me." They knew she could handle their teasing.

She tossed her blonde hair back, gave them a smile accompanied by a finger, sprinted up Crescent Avenue and approached the crowd that was gathering in front of the casino. First day on the job nerves were showing. Talking with Rachael had made her almost late for the first ghost tour. Five minutes to start. No one seemed grumpy and actually seemed to be enjoying the light island breeze as the hot day started to cool down. A pungent aroma mixed with the sea air.

Meg used her flashlight to scan the list of paid patrons, and then placed the light under her chin, casting an eerie image. "Welcome to the Catalina Island Ghost Tour. My name is Meg and I'm your fearless leader for the excursion. If you have a smart phone, here's the name of an app that you can download, 'Ghost Crashers.' Also, please take as many pictures as you can because most times the camera will catch something that the naked eye will miss."

She tugged down on the bodice that was creeping up and walked around the crowd helping them with their phones. She handed out 'glow-in-the-dark' necklaces as she took roll. "These expensive necklaces are supposed to ward off evil spirits."

One lady refused to accept the necklace, pulling her hoodie down to cover her face. She sank back and embraced a weird looking man also wearing a hoodie, running her hands up and down his body as she snuggled closer.

"That's okay, you don't have to wear it. It really isn't guaranteed to protect you anyway." Meg shrugged at the rejection. She walked away, stopped, and then continued but felt she had met her first real ghost of the evening. A new evil one on Catalina Island.

"I'll try not to bog you down with too many stories about our resident Catalina ghosts but some are too delicious to ignore. Stories of murders and ghostly apparitions have plagued the Island starting way back in time. It's said that on this very spot, under the paved cobblestone that we're standing on, are bones of Indians, smugglers, gold miners and children. Some buried alive.

"Zane Grey has been seen over by the Bell Tower, still trying to hide from his demanding wife. All he wanted to do was smoke one of his favorite cigars, but his wife didn't like the smell and she was a tyrant." The crowd laughed and Meg knew she had them. "You've all heard stories of the millionaire William Wrigley. Well, sometimes he materializes by his grand home, chewing gum."

"Ah, come on. Now that's a bit of a stretch," an elderly man shouted.

"Maybe … maybe not. How about the ghost of Natalie Wood strolling along the beach? Is that contemporary enough for you? Okay, let's get started. Follow me." Meg continued on with the ghost stories starting with the man on the balcony of the Casino. "Even if you don't see him, take a picture of the window and check it out when you get home." She waited while everyone snapped their pictures. "One of the most famous ghosts haunts the upstairs bathroom in the Casino ballroom area, like I said. History states he was a laborer who fell to his death during the construction around 1929 and was encased in cement. He rummages around sometimes. Might want to look out for him. Still a little pissed off I hear."

The group murmured to each other and snapped a few more shots with their cell phones.

"Before we leave. See the stone bench at the end of the walkway? Well, that's another story about Zane Gray. He loves to sit there and smoke, but will disappear in the vapors if you get too close. Oh, look. Is that him?"

Twenty-four heads swiveled in unison. When they realized they'd been punked, they broke out in laughter. "Good one, Meg."

"His wife would get all ticked off when he'd meet his buddies for golf 'cause they always brought him home hammered. Fun, huh? Okay, we're walking."

They stopped in front of the Yacht Club for another photo shoot and continued down Crescent. Some of the drunks lining the bars came out and made howling noises, much to Meg's annoyance. She took her job seriously. The odd guy who wouldn't wear the necklace, hung back with the strange woman. They kept groping each other so Meg had to work doubly hard to keep the attention of the group focused on her.

"You seen any ghosts, Meg?" It was the curious old man again.

"Not so far, but I've got a lot of skeletons in my closet. Does that count?"

"Sure like to be one," he murmured.

"You and a million other guys, I'll bet," chimed in another man.

"We're near the end of the tour, but tomorrow if you take an excursion to Two Harbors, there is a hotel called the Banning House Lodge, built in 1910. One of our official ghosts dwells there, the White Lady, She floats around every now and then and there's a strange smell that permeates the hotel. Like tobacco and fish. Ugh. That's where Natalie Wood usually hangs out and also around the south end of Two Harbors. It's very close to where she drowned.

The crowd started on a whispering campaign. "The husband did it. Poor dear, she didn't have a chance. Robert Wagner was the one, wasn't he? He got away with murder."

Meg waved her arms to get their attention. "Okay, gang. This is the end of the tour. Hotel Catherine. 'Twas built on top of some of our famous burial grounds. The resident ghost is really angry 'cause the Conservancy has purchased the hotel. From what I hear, the hotel will be torn down, but for now it's still the best place in town for a cold and cheap beer. It's said the hotel got tired of refunding money to the overnight guests, so now all the people have to sign a release. Kinda like a waiver in case your sleep is disturbed. The ghost shows up at her pleasure and runs the guests out into the middle of the street so often, it looks like a parade. At the end of summer, it will close for good. Sad day for the island." A wistful look passed across her face.

A few people gathered around Meg to ask questions and compliment her on her knowledge of the island folklore. She chatted with them but was more interested in the weird couple who never joined in with the group. They seemed to be fondling each other, giggling, and licking each other's faces. As she watched them enter Hotel Catherine she grimaced. *Oh, great. I'm really looking forward to cleaning their room tomorrow.*

Chapter 8

AS OF 2012 when nine L.A. County courthouses were closed, the Catalina courthouse was scheduled to remain open only on Fridays. All litigants would travel across the twenty-six miles by ferry the night prior to the hearing. The defendant, judge, prosecuting and defending attorneys, clerks, witnesses, arresting officers and court stenographer would cluster in their own areas of the boat and disembark at the same time, each walking down the pier and heading to Hotel Catherine where they would spend the night, After an early breakfast at the hotel bar, the varied groups would gather in the foyer and walk to the courthouse quietly discussing their positions.

Anxiety held vigil over many of the days' players. Rachael and Josh had met, but their reunion was marred with their argument on horseback. Meg spent a restless night in the Catherine Hotel, visited by visions of the weird lady with the hoodie boyfriend, Stella and Dred kept Aunt Sharon awake with their moaning and bed-creaking activities all night, while Zach slept like the baby he was.

"Well Judge Perry, how did you sleep last night?" the court clerk tried to keep up with his long strides as the judge hurried down Crescent Avenue toward the courthouse.

"Bed was a little lumpy, like last time, but no ghost visitation, if that's why you asked." He mustered up a partial smile. He was known as the hanging judge and would never smile unless speaking to the court reporter. When his half smile turned to a frown, the clerk continued on in silence wondering what was so special about that cute court reporter.

The rest of the entourage scurried to the courthouse in small herds, each discussing their own agendas.

Zach was left with Rosie, Meg's friend from the Conservancy, outside the courthouse during the hearing. All interested parties, except Stella's group, entered the glass door to the courthouse when it opened at 8:00 a.m. and settled into their assigned seats.

Minutes before they entered, Aunt Sharon straightened Stella's red, wiry hair, applied some makeup and tucked the white blouse into the dress pants that she had brought from the mainland. Dred, dressed in his tattered jeans, KIIS tee-shirt and flip flops held her hand and steered her toward the front of the room, where her attorney waited.

Josh and Rachael entered the courtroom at different times, but nodded to each other. Stella straightened up in her chair, and smiled the most beguiling smile she could muster when Josh entered. There he was, the man who would be taking her home today with their beautiful baby boy. She could hardly contain herself. Her change in attitude was noted by Dred, who pulled out his iPhone and sent a quick text message. The bailiff started toward him with an annoyed look and Dred held his phone high in the air as he turned it off and tucked it into his tight jeans.

All parties stood as the judge entered. The court clerk spieled out the traditional "Hear Ye," and the room fell into quiet anticipation. Peering over his half glasses, Judge Perry took out a Kleenex, blew his nose, surveyed the room and turned to the court reporter. "Looking especially proficient this morning, Agnes."

"Thank you, judge." The young woman bowed her head to hide the blush and melted in her seat.

The clerk told the room to be seated and faded into the background.

"Well ladies and gentlemen, we are here without a jury for this morning's proceeding. It's called a Bench Trial. Do all parties understand and agree to this?" The judge looked up as the attorneys answered for all with a resounding 'yes, your honor.'

"Let's begin with opening statements from the prosecuting attorney."

Josh's attorney stood, cleared his voice, adjusted the bottom button on his suit, and began. "We are here this morning your honor, to ask that the infant, Zachary Meyers, be made ward of the court, and subsequently be placed up for adoption."

A resounding gasp filled the room.

"Wait." Stella leaped from her chair. "No. We're here for child support until Josh and I get married." She screamed the words. She grabbed her attorney by the lapels. "Tell them, you shithead. Don't just sit there." Her nails found his neck and bit into his flesh. The attorney winced and tried to break away from her terminator grip.

Aunt Sharon jumped up from the gallery. "No, your honor. This is not what we decided. Josh wanted full custody of Zach. We didn't agree to this. There's been a mistake." Her voice faded into the uproar.

The judge pounded his gavel. "I'll see the attorneys and case worker in chambers. Now. Someone settle that woman down."

The bailiff rushed to the front of the defendant's table, threatening Stella. "Settle down now. Otherwise, I'll have to cuff you. Understand?"

Aunt Sharon moved behind Stella, reached over the wooden rail and grabbed her shoulders. "Stella. Hold on. We'll take care of this. You have to be calm. Don't blow it."

Meg and Rachael were seated behind Josh. "Did you know about this, Rach?" Meg's face flushed with indignation.

"Josh told me last night. That's why I came home so early. I didn't know what to think or say." She stared at the back of Josh's head as he stood to leave the room.

"Shit. I thought you two were here to get the baby, like full custody. What gives? Is this okay with you?" Meg was livid.

"His decision." Rachael was heartbroken.

"Like hell." Meg leaned over the wooden banister and punched Josh on the shoulder. "What the hell you doing?"

Josh turned and looked at Meg and the woman he loved. Rachael couldn't meet his stare, "My business, Meg. If you don't approve, then leave. Get the hell out of here."

Meg's gaze threw daggers. "You jerk. It's not me you should be worried about. What about Rachael? Shit. She'll raise the kid if you don't want to. Even a part of you would keep her happy."

Rachael pulled Meg back to her chair. "Leave him alone, sis. His decision."

"What the hell is wrong with you people? Geez, I thought I was screwed up." Meg sat down and turned her attention to the redhead who was waving her arms around and cussing at the bailiff.

Stella's voice was getting louder as the minutes passed. She hadn't taken her meds this morning. She wanted a clear head to make plans with Josh. "Josh, honey. Tell the son-of-a-bitch judge we're getting married." She reared out of her chair again, swung a fist at the sergeant-at-arms, but this time he was ready. He drew his handcuffs, and sent a threatening gesture her way.

The chamber door opened and the judge re-entered the room with the attorneys following. "Young lady, you settle down or I'll have you removed from the courtroom."

Stella acquiesced. She dropped her head, pulling her hostility inward.

"There are far too many decisions to be made in this case. Before I render an opinion, I will meet with the attorneys and case worker one more time. It is your obligation to make sure they totally understand your position. For the present Zach Meyers is now a ward of the court until such time as a decision is made for his future. Mind you, his well-being and safety is of primary concern. Court adjourned." Bang.

Stella stood and turned to Dred, her eyes darted frantically between Dred and Josh. "What should I do? Where's my baby?" Her focus passed Josh and landed on Rachael. "You. It's you, you bitch. You're the problem." Before the bailiff could stop her, Stella pushed through the swinging gate and threw a punch at Rachael.

Meg caught her by her wiry red hair, pulling her back as Rachael exploded into action, twisting Stella's left arm behind her and slamming her face on the wooden bannister.

Stella screamed, "Let me go you home wrecker. You bitch."

Aunt Sharon was in the corner of the room talking—no yelling —at Josh, hands waving in the air. When she saw Rachael slam Stella's head she turned and sprinted to her niece's rescue. "Let her go."

"Order. Order. We'll have order in the court." Judge Perry pounded his gavel. "Bailiff. Clear the room."

Rachael dropped her hold on Stella and backed off.

Dred moved in and whispered in Stella's ear. "Don't worry. I'll take care of this for you." He started to lead the clueless woman out of the courthouse, but was stopped by Greg, Stella's brother. "Can't go yet, sport."

Chapter 9

A FBI HELICOPTER HOVERED over the Catalina Beach Heli-
port as the trial was beginning. Derek glanced down at the lush
foliage around the Holly Hill House and the surreal blue of the
Pacific as it rushed to meet the white sand in front of the line of
hotels. Coming back to the island only reinforced his commitment
to rid himself of his brother Elliott's maniacal hold on him. When
the helicopter doors opened, he grabbed his small suitcase and
joined Amanda as she headed to the office to rent a golf cart.

After rental arrangements were made Amanda snatched a copy
of the Islander News and threw it in the back seat of the cart,
tossing her purse on top. "We'll head to the rental house first, and
get you settled in. I'll pick up groceries for you later and bring them
by." They drove the short distance to the house on Eucalyptus in
silence.

While it appeared Derek was enjoying his first stretch of freedom, he was spending the quiet time analyzing Amanda. Maybe
thirty-four years old? Hair the darkest brown he had ever seen,
neatly tucked under a baseball cap. Such a contrast to Meg's hair
which resembled spun gold. Green eyes like Meg's, but beyond that,
no real discernable features that matched. Body types, similar, but

Amanda's frame was more muscular, probably from the Quantico training. Meg was tough, but willowy. He stopped the comparison there and inwardly chastised himself. Meg. His one-time chance at love that probably would elude him forever. He'd really screwed up. They pulled up in front of a small bungalow located in a cramped but well maintained neighborhood. As they entered the old house, Derek looked for the surveillance cameras that he knew would be there.

"You've done a good job of trying to hide the cameras." He spotted one hidden in the bookshelf.

"We spared no expense, Derek. Not that we don't trust you." She opened all interior doors, checked the closets and shower.

"Yeah, right." Derek tossed his suitcase on the couch and started for the kitchen.

"Each room is equipped with a motion sensor device, with the exception of the bathroom.

"It has one window with bars on the outside, so trying to escape unnoticed will be impossible. We rented the house next door where the 24-hour surveillance team will be listening and watching your every move and conversation."

"So as I understand it, I'm to act like I'm an extension of Elliott and make contact with the Mexican Mafia to establish my presence on the island and negotiate a cooperative arrangement. Drugs. Great. Is that the working scenario?" He looked around the bleak room. His life to this point had been filled with the best of everything. The Lamborghini, mansion in the Hollywood hills and every amenity life had to offer. Somehow the simplicity of his current situation seemed workable, justified and growing on him.

"We need names here, Mexican contacts, means of drug transport and schedules."

"I'll need a cell phone, computer with internet and transportation." Derek checked out the bedroom and unassuming bathroom.

Amanda opened her briefcase, took out a cell phone and handed him the key to the cart they had used earlier. "Computer and printer are already hooked up." She motioned to the tiny desk in the living room. "Understand that your phone is bugged and we'll monitor all of your internet time. Don't plan on buying a throwaway phone. We have people working at various places in town who will be watching you."

"Sounds like you have all the bases covered, which wasn't really necessary. I'm the one who called you and offered to take my brother down, not the other way around." Annoyance registered through his words. He was tired of the stalling FBI techniques and wanted to close this chapter of his life.

Amanda nodded. She'd never been totally convinced of Derek's turnaround. His history was deeply imbedded in her memory, history of seduction, attempted murder and betrayal, all revolving around her sister, Meg. "Penance doesn't suit you, Derek. We'll see." Amanda walked through the house once more then returned to find Derek picking up the newspaper. His jaw was set as he concentrated on page one.

"The paper says that there's a court hearing going on. Something about Josh Meyers and a child custody suit. Isn't he Rachael's old boyfriend?"

Amanda knew Derek eventually would be privy to this information, so she decided to fill him in. "Yes, one and the same, so here's the deal. I'm on my way to meet with Rachael, Josh and Meg right now."

Derek stopped her. "Meg's on the island?" He took a deep breath and held it before pushing it out. His nostrils flared.

"That's hands off to you. I'll tell them the situation with you and the undercover assignment. That's another set of eyes that will be on you." Amanda felt the rush of his emotions fill the room. "Listen up. I'll be working at Jack's restaurant. That's my cover. You'll have breakfast there every morning. No deviating. Every morning. That's our contact point. Understand?"

Derek mulled around the new information. "So both Rachael and Meg are on the island?" He was stuck on the last tidbit of information.

"Yes. But you're not to contact them." She fought the anxiety that was ripping through her stomach. She knew without a doubt, that Meg's presence on the island could be a game changer.

Derek fought the smile that was forming. A hint of something wonderfully fulfilling raced through his thoughts. Being careful not to allow the thought to overtake his facial expression, he proceeded, "What about Marisa? Has the FBI found her yet?"

"No. Your sister is still in the wind. That's part of your assignment. Her location and activity is keen to our investigation."

"Got it." He picked up the new cell phone. His arrogant attitude was returning and he continued, "Would you like me to call Marisa now?"

Amanda had sensed all along that Marisa was only a call away. She took the phone from Derek and dialed her FBI counterpart. "Is this phone ready to go? We might be making an international call that needs to be recorded. Start an immediate trace." She returned the phone to Derek. "Go for it."

Chapter 10

MARISA TURNER, DEREK AND ELLIOTT'S sister, was lolling poolside at the San Marcos Spa in Cabo San Lucas with only a sip of Tequila Sunrise remaining in her glass. "Uno mas, por favor," she called to the waiter. She tossed aside the magazine that held only a fraction of her interest.

Bronze from the Mexican sun, she stretched her long legs on the lounge as she had done for the past five weeks. Her normally mousey brown hair showed streaks of blonde, with a few gray strands. Time and tamales had added some pounds to her nearly perfect figure. Boredom kept her from caring. At thirty-five, she was glad to be away from the sordid life that Elliott had forced her to live. She had been so controlled by his maniacal demands that she had no foundation for a life of her own. No semblance of what a normal life should be. Without Derek at her side now, she floundered.

It seemed a lifetime had passed since she escaped the FBI net that had closed in on her, when Derek had called and told her to empty Elliott's accounts and head south. Three million dollars had been transferred into a Mexico bank and other offshore accounts, so there were no money worries. All was good, except where the hell was Derek? And Elliott?

Her job was to sit and wait. Derek knew where to find her, so she waited for her next drink, and the next. And then the call came.

"Marisa. It's your baby brother calling. How ya doing?"

Amanda frowned. "Baby brother? Really Derek, how simple of you. Give me the phone." She yanked it from his hand.

Amanda identified herself and explained the current situation with Derek's incarceration and cooperation in the FBI's sting. "I know this is a rather simplified explanation, but before you're privy to any more details, I need a commitment from you. You'll be exonerated from all issues involving Elliott once you arrive in Catalina and cooperate in this final covert operation. Any questions?"

"Tons. Has Derek agreed to this?" Marisa's voice registered frustration. "Has the FBI signed a letter clearing me?" The trust level didn't even register on her scale.

"Yes and yes. All of this will be resolved when you get to the island. We're prepared to sit down with you and answer all of your questions. Where are you staying right now?"

Marisa hesitated and Amanda handed the phone to Derek. "Do your thing. If she doesn't cooperate, the deal's off and you'll go back to jail." She said it loud enough for Marisa to hear without straining.

Derek explained the further complications of not cooperating and soon Marisa divulged that she was in Mexico a fact that Derek already knew. Amanda took the phone and gave her instructions that the FBI would meet her at the border and transport her to Catalina the next day. "Take a taxi to Tijuana and walk across the bridge to the California side. You won't have to wait in the long line or deal with a car. An FBI agent will meet you at the check point. Tomorrow morning, 11:00 a.m. Got it?" Amanda was a person-to-person profiler and hated the phone for this type of negotiating. She wanted to see faces, the change of expression, the eyes narrowing, a twitch, lips curling in, all the indications of lying that she had studied for years.

"That doesn't give me much time to pack, but okay. Got it."

Marisa grumbled some profanity as she disconnected the line, turned, ordered another drink and sent a text.

Derek stopped Amanda as she was leaving the room. "There's only one other thing I need to know."

She knew what was coming.

"Meg."

"Meg has nothing to do with any part of this negotiation."

"You going to tell her that I'm cooperating? Maybe put a band-aid on our relationship?"

"There is no relationship. If I had my way, you'd never see my sister again. But, it's a small island." Amanda could see real concern on his face. Meg had been so near loving this guy and possibly still harbored feelings. "It helped that you tried to save her, but she's leery of you like the rest of us. Be natural. But I wouldn't suggest you try to date her, she'll probably cut your balls off." She followed the threat with a hearty laugh.

"Oh, right." Derek knew there was a large portion of truth in that statement. Meg had earned her black belt in Krav Maga the previous year and certainly knew how to implement the technique.

After a few more departing do's and don'ts Amanda left and walked to the courthouse, knowing that a battle was inevitable when the family learned of the FBI's operation and Derek's presence on the island.

"Shit, this had better work," she mumbled as she rushed down the street to the courthouse.

Chapter 11

AL FILLED THE 1932 BEER STEIN with Goldfinch Ale, sliced the froth with a knife and methodically walked over to the table next to the front window of Catherine's bar. The wind was whipping around Catalina, a leftover Santa Ana condition from the mainland. Papers and leaves whirled about the wooden porch, and sandy grit obscured the view to the casino. He pulled out a chair, placed a napkin on the table and then the beer. "I know you'll be grumpy tonight. The wind and all. Enjoy, my love."

A young couple watched the demonstration and when Al came back to the bar they quizzed him. "Do you serve a beer to that empty table every day?"

"Yup."

"And always talk to the chair?"

He nodded at their ignorance, took a quarter out of his pocket, rang up the sale on the cash register, and dropped it in.

"Old fool," the young man said to his girl.

"Stupid ass," mumbled Al under his breath. He prayed Catherine would ignore their rude remarks. That plus the wind was not a good combination. "Behave, my love."

When the couple left twenty minutes later, they realized the glass was empty.

Chapter 12

THE COURTROOM WAS CHAOTIC. Attorneys yelled, Rachael and Josh were arguing, Stella was in mid-tantrum and Aunt Sharon was looking for Zach's case worker. The judge disappeared into his chambers leaving the bailiff and deputy to manage the mayhem. Jodi, assigned to the baby's care, immediately left the courtroom, met Rosie outside, and started up the street to her room at Catherine's with the baby squalling in her arms. She was nervous and almost tripped over the curb in her haste. "Why is that weird friend of Stella's following me?" she muttered as she hurried to get away from him.

Amanda shoved her way inside the noisy courtroom and, standing on tiptoe, located Rachael and Josh near the judge's bench. Fighting? "Rachael. Rachael!" She waved her arms and Rachael, hearing her name, sought out the likely source.

"Amanda. What're you doing here?"

Josh grabbed Rachael's arm. "Wait a minute. We need to talk."

Meg shoved her way in between the two. "Back off, Josh."

"Don't interfere, brat."

Amanda pushed past the last of the interference and reached for Rachael's hand. "We need to talk. All four of us. Outside."

Realizing the urgency in her sister's voice, Rachael gave a head nod to everyone and they broke their way through the crowded room.

"Over here, under the tree." The wind blew leaves in their path as they crossed the street. They bunched together, looking for shade under the one available tree.

"Good news, bad news time," Amanda started.

"First a group hug," Meg said. "Haven't seen you since you saved my life, you creep, you." Meg was always the one to pull emotions back to home base.

Rachael moved between her sisters, avoiding Josh's arms encircling her. "What's going on? Don't tell me Elliott has risen from the ashes."

The chilling thought made Meg twitch. She rubbed her left wrist where he had burned her skin with a cigarette.

"Not that I know of, but you know that Derek's situation was never resolved. He's been in L.A. locked up for the last six weeks while we decide what to do with him. The FBI is a little slow sometimes, but careful."

"Amanda," Josh broke in. "We have more important things to talk about. How about you wait your turn?"

Rachael pushed forward, interrupting his questions. "That's why we haven't heard about a trial. Is that legal?"

Amada scoffed. "FBI has their ways." She lowered her voice and filled them in on the details of her new drug bust assignment in Catalina, supplied them with Derek's address and cell number, told them she would be a waitress at Jack's and took a breath. "Any questions?"

"What do you want from us? Josh is right in the middle of a child custody battle, along with working for the Sheriff's Department," Rachael exploded. "How come everyone's life is more important than his...ours?"

"Rach, this is just a heads-up in case you meet Derek on the street. You don't have to panic. Nothing is expected of you. Live your life. Just watch your ass as usual."

This quieted Rachael but Meg was still spurting. "What if, what if. Are you sure this isn't a double-cross by Derek? We all, especially me, know his history. How can you trust him?"

"Trust isn't what we're doing. Monitoring is more like it. The FBI needs to stop this drug trafficking. This is the drop off for San Francisco and the Arizona corridor. We've never had the inside scoop. This is it."

"Are you working with the Sheriff's Department? Have you talked to my captain?" Josh asked.

"That's my next stop. Can you go with me so we cover everything at one time?"

Josh looked at Rachael. "I don't want to fight with you. I know you're disappointed in me but we'll figure this out. Come by the house tonight?"

Rachael couldn't look at him, but muttered, "Fine." As they left, she gave a high sign to Meg. "Come on, I need someone to talk to." They turned right on Crescent, but stopped to watch a commotion at the end of the pier. "Oh, God. Is that Stella? And the cops? They're putting her on the Flyer? What's going on?"

"The trial isn't even over yet. Why are they making her leave?" Meg squinted to clarify the picture. "Weird as she is, she should still have a voice." She focused on the group. "Is the baby with them?"

"Doesn't look like it. That's her brother Greg with her, and Aunt Sharon."

Meg gave her full attention to the commotion. "Is that weirdo guy with her?"

"Don't see him. He left the courthouse when Stella started yelling."

"They've got her strapped in that wheelchair." Meg was feeling a little empathy for the redhead.

"Guess she's strong when she gets agitated." Rachael flashed back on seeing Josh's rape through the window and knew Stella was tough.

"I'm surprised she didn't kill you when she had the chance." Meg shook her head in disbelief. "But, okay, what's up? Talk to me. Keep it short though 'cause I have to spend the night at the hotel again. Al has to take the night off and I'm playing bartender and closing up."

"Catherine won't like it if Al's gone, and you know what she does when she's cranky. She'll run everyone out of the hotel, including you." Rachael smiled as Meg's expression changed.

"Just because I run the ghost tour doesn't mean I believe all that shit." She punched Rachael in the arm then ducked.

"Careful, young lady. Can't go around disrespecting our resident ghost." They both laughed but Meg hoped, this time, her sister was wrong.

Since it was almost time for Meg to start bartending, Rachael decided to walk her to the hotel and check out her room which wasn't much to talk about. On the second floor facing west, over-looking the public beach, the room had few amenities.

"Sparse comes to mind," Rachael said as she examined the tiny room with the small adjoining bath. "You'll certainly know if any ghost comes in and breathes your air."

"Hey, don't be putting down the hotel. We're talking built in 1911. Was a real swanky place then." Meg changed out of her knee-knockers, yanked up her tight jeans and reached for her favorite t-shirt. "I know what you want to talk about. It's really not my decision but you know I'll definitely have an opinion, and you're asking for it. Go ahead."

Rachael walked away from the dingy, curtain less window. "Josh and the baby, of course. When he told me what his plans were last night, well, this mental picture I had of him—and us— totally blew up. He doesn't want his kid. What's that all about?"

"Okay, sis. I don't have a lot of time, but try this on. One, he loves you. Two, he was actually raped by a schizophrenic, bipolar, wild animal. Three, reverse the role. Say it was me and Elliott's kid. Would I jump with glee at the prospects of raising it?" Meg brushed her blonde hair, grabbed a rubber band, made a pony tail, and waited for Rachael to see the logic in her analysis.

"I know you're right, but I expected more of Josh. He's like… well, Superman to me. Dumb, huh?"

"More than dumb. Be careful or I'll call Grace to come over and council you, and you know what that means."

"Enough. Don't threaten me with the ultimate micromanager." She shifted her train of thought. "But I'll tell you one thing. If mom gets wind that Derek is here on the island with you, both she and Duke will be here in a heartbeat. CIA plus gun-toting mom. Scary."

"For Pete's sake. Don't tell her. I had to deal with her all summer. Please, please." The sentence was more than a request. A fair amount of pleading poured forth.

"Not to worry. None of us need mom right now. I've got a date with Josh tonight. Be safe, so catch you later. Don't do anything to aggravate Catherine."

Moments later when they entered the bar, people were lined up two deep waiting for drinks. Al ceremoniously took off his apron and headed for the door.

"It's all yours. Good luck, Meg."

"Crap. I can't do this by myself." She reached in her pocket, found her cell phone and dialed. "Rosie. Help. I need you to be my backup bartender tonight at Hotel Catherine."

As the evening wore on, Rosie nudged Meg's arm, "What's with the weird guy, sitting by the front door. Spooky-like."

"I saw him on the ghost tour the other night. I'm sure he was with Stella. Had a weird name. Dead? No Dred. Who names their kid that?"

"Hey, Meg." The mustached customer at the bar yelled to her. "Better not let Al know that you didn't save Catherine's table for her."

Meg looked toward the corner and realized there were people sitting and drinking at Catherine's table. She groaned. "Geez. I forgot to put out the reserved sign. Catherine's really going to be pissed tonight." She glanced up toward the corner of the room. That damn blood was already appearing, and it wasn't time. "Oh, I'm really in deep shit now." Her expression morphed into worry lines.

Chapter 13

BY ELEVEN ALL GUESTS HAD HEADED FOR THEIR ROOMS, Meg was humming as she took the cash from the bar register and started for the lobby. Earlier she had locked the back exit door, turned off all extraneous lights and secured the front lobby door. She reached for the desk light as the phone rang. "Front desk."

"Oh, thank goodness you're there."

"How may I help you?" Her voice disguised her irritation. It'd been a long day.

"This is Jodi Walker in room 321. My air conditioner went out. It's stifling in here and the baby only sleeps with the white noise. Can you call someone to fix it?"

"Miss Walker, I'm afraid I won't be able to get anyone out at this time of night." She thought for a minute. "Look, I have the room next to yours. Haven't unpacked. Give me five minutes and we'll swap rooms. I'll be right there." Meg counted the day's receipt, put a rubber band around the bills and tucked them away in the safe. She twirled the dial around then headed for Jodi's room.

"No need to pack. We'll move the baby's crib and you can manage the rest of the stuff in the morning. Okay with you?"

"Great. I can't thank you enough." Jodi helped Meg roll the baby's bed through the doorway and into the adjoining room.

Meg started down the stairs to change the guest registration log, but was stopped by the obnoxious Texas lady climbing the stairs. Beads of sweat were emerging on her upper lip.

"Oh, Miss Meg. I see you changed rooms with the baby. You probably can't tell by my looks, but I'm 76 years old and the stairs are very difficult for me. Might we have the baby's room and you take ours on the third floor? We haven't unpacked yet."

Meg sighed from fatigue, but murmured an, "Okay, but there's no air conditioning in the room."

"We don't use the air anyway."

Meg proceeded to change keys with the lady. "My stuff is sitting right inside the door. I'll grab it right now. No problem."

"Sleep well." Meg climbed the second set of stairs, unlocked room 323, made sure the air conditioning was working, tore off her clothes and fell naked across the bed.

It was 2:00 a.m. before the first happening. Lights in room 223 clicked on and the middle-aged couple grabbed their suitcases, threw in their belongings, left their personal items in the bathroom, and went screaming down the hall and outside to the street. "She was in our room. She screamed and threatened us to leave or get murdered. She had a long knife." The lady's screams resounded off the vacant walls. The woman continued her tirade through the empty halls running for the exit. Quickly drained of all energy, she was near collapsing. The hotel lit up like a Christmas tree.

Greg, deputy with the Sheriff's department, was on duty and ripped down Crescent in the mini patrol car when he got the call. Through the years he had heard stories about the female ghost in Catherine's, but always scoffed at the written reports. Now it was his turn. He met the victims in the middle of the street. "Okay, ma'am. Just settle down and tell me what you saw."

The frightened lady reiterated her story of how the ghost appeared in the room. "The door never opened and this thing started moaning. Woke us up. I sat up in bed and George pulled the covers over his head." She shot a disgusted look his way. "Then this 'thing' called to us and said to get out or get murdered. It was dressed in white. Floating white. Then we saw the knife."

Her husband stuttered, "No sweetheart, it was dressed in black. I think you got it wrong."

"The ghost had a knife?" Greg smirked. "Did you lock the door when you went to bed?"

"Of course. We always do."

"Was the door still locked when you ran out?"

She hesitated. Blinked. "Ahh. Yes. I think was. It just appeared out of thin air, I tell you."

Greg realized that nothing else would be forthcoming from further interrogation, so he told the nervous couple to wait in the hall while he checked out their room. He pushed his way through the growing crowd and entered the foyer. Nothing. Flipping on the lights, he scanned the restaurant, found nothing out of order so headed for the bar. Just as he was ready to leave, he noticed a pair of shoes protruding from behind the bar. Al was propped up, unconscious.

"What the hell you doing, Al? Sleepin' on the job?" Greg nudged him with his foot, and Al slumped over, his eyes were fixed and glassy, a syringe stuck in his arm. "Shit." He felt for a pulse. "Thank God."

Pulling his gun, Greg stood, called for backup and then searched the room. "Boss, we've got a mess here at Catherine's. Al's out cold. Looks like an overdose. Al's been off the shit for years but... Better send the medic and crime scene guys over here. Catherine was here and scared some people. Shit. Send backup." Residents were headed for the front door but Greg stopped them in the lobby. "Sorry, folks. Go back to your rooms for now. Everything's fine." Some residents complained, but eventually all complied.

The frightened couple returned and sat on the floral couch in the lobby, still unnerved by the experience.

"Did you eat dinner here last night?" Greg made notes and gave a nod to a fellow cop as he entered.

"We did. We were the last ones in the bar. That cute little gal, Meg, took our credit card and then we went directly to our room."

"Meg? So Al wasn't tending bar?"

"We don't know Al. Meg was working."

Greg had heard that Meg was a temporary hire, cleaning the rooms and bartending when Al was busy. He checked the registration log and saw that Meg had taken room 223 room for the night. Ten rooms were occupied. He checked the names and realized that most of the visitors were associated with the court proceedings. "What's your room number?"

"Two twenty-three. We traded with Meg."

"Where did she move to?" Greg was tiring of the woman's hysterical answers.

"Our old room," she sobbed "room 323."

"Fine." He motioned to a fellow officer. "This officer will wait with you. If you need anything just ask." He started for the stairs and decided to pick up Meg first. Her room was right above the room where Catherine had appeared, so she might have heard something. People were wandering around the hall, gossiping, as Greg walked up the three flights to Meg's room. Pounding on the door he yelled, "Meg, you in there? It's Greg."

Meg had slept through the chaos. "Yeah, I'm here. Where else would I be?" She rolled out of bed and looked through the peephole. "What's going on?" She unlatched the night chain and peeked around the opening in the door, being careful to hide her nakedness.

It took only seconds for Greg to supply the details.

"What do ya mean, is Al dead?"

"No. Medics are with him now."

"No way. Hang on." Meg closed the door, sleep still holding part of her attention, and stepped into her bathroom to pull on her jeans and t-shirt. "What the hell is going on around here?" she yelled at she opened the door for Greg.

"Looks like an overdose. A syringe stuck in his arm. Happened sometime last night. I found him just now."

Meg plopped down on the bed and shook her head as she pulled on her sneakers. "You crazy fool. He didn't use drugs. I've known him for years." Meg was dumbfounded. "You found him?"

"Yeah. I wanted to interview him about the ghost that appeared and…"

"Ghost?"

Greg was getting frustrated and knew that time was precious. "Later on that, but when I went into the bar, I found him. I'm on my way to room 223 to check out the ghost story and figured you might have heard something." Greg realized that Meg had nothing to offer and said, "Gotta go."

"Not without me." One blink and she was on his heels. "You're so wrong on this. Syringe? It's attempted murder, not an overdose." She grabbed her cell phone and raced after Greg down the stairs to room 223. "Also, Catherine can't be involved. She loved Al." The initial assessment was unremarkable. Other than two drawers being opened and the bed messed up, everything was in place. As they were about to leave, the door to the adjoining room squeaked open a crack.

"That's weird," said Meg as she walked toward the door. It stopped moving when she talked. She remained silent and it moved again. Meg turned back to Greg, who was watching, and shrugged. "I'm going in."

Her neck was slit. Blood spatter slid down the wall creating a crimson Picasso design. She was fully clothed as any good case worker should be. Jodi was dead and Zach was missing.

Chapter 14

MARISA PACKED HER FEW BELONGINGS and made contact with Gilbert, the pilot Elliott used for years to transport illegals and drugs. "Chart a flight to Two Harbors on the back side of Catalina. Pick up a new cell phone for me." The midday Mexican sun burned her fair skin as she waited for a taxi outside the Cabo hotel. She scanned the most recent text message she'd received. It was short and succinct. "Come now. Catalina." She thought it was strange. Derek was never redundant. She opened the back of the phone pulled out the SIM card and crushed it under the heel of her sandal.

The FBI expected her to cross the Tijuana Bridge by noon, so she had little time to stay ahead of them. There was no way she would surrender, but she did have to help Derek. Elliott had certain people, his followers, who were still working with her, so she made a mental note to email explicit instructions and establish a meet up time with the helper on Catalina when she was airborne.

Within an hour, her taxi pulled into Popotla, an Americanized community south of Rosarito Beach. Marisa ordered one, then a second tequila shot, and sipped the magic. The bar was filling up with tanned faces who smiled at her and men who flirted by tipping their baseball caps her way. Marisa enjoyed the simplicity of the moment. She loved hearing English again and watched the collage of personalities. People with no cares? How did that happen? Choices, of course. She thought about all of her choices that had gone so tragically wrong. But had they really been her choices, or Elliott's dictates? Her eyes moved to the glass wall and gazed across the endless Pacific. Tranquil. Enjoy the tranquility, she thought, because it will be short lived. She settled the bill, slowly lifted her purse as if to forestall the inevitable chaos facing her and headed for the waiting taxi. Within minutes it was speeding down the dirt road to the fishing village, aiming straight toward the next adventure.

The sea plane landed and taxied toward the sand. Village children, hoping for a tip, eagerly swam out and helped to beach the plane. Gilbert threw a handful of coins their way and watched as they dove for the shiny money. Marisa, eager to get out of the country, chucked her sandals and waded out into the warm ocean, followed by the children carrying her luggage on their heads.

"*Señor, Mas dinero, por favor,*" the children yelled, begging for more coins.

"Gilbert, thanks for being on time. Elliott always trusted you. Did you get a new phone for me?" Marisa was out of breath as she struggled to settle into the copilot's seat.

"*Si, señorita.* It ees fix for you." Gilbert gingerly held the phone out to her.

She eyed him suspiciously. "Are you nervous? What's going on?" Marisa felt uncomfortable, a slight touch of panic. She checked her surroundings. Betrayal was always a possibility.

"I fear your brother, so I fear you."

Marisa could relate to his answer. She had seen Elliott punish betrayal with threats of torture, murder and total annihilation of a whole family if they stepped out of line.

Marisa elected to let the comment die realizing that a little fear made it easier to control the employees. "Let's go." She fumbled with the seat belt and then gestured to take off. As the plane taxied across the gentle swells, Marisa glanced over at the next cove where the Titanic had been rebuilt for the movie. Local fishermen stopped mending their nets and watched as the plane took wind and headed north. Soon Rosarito was left behind, giving way to the San Diego coastline and ahead, a blip on the horizon, was Catalina.

Marisa fiddled with the new phone and finally made contact. "What's the status?" was the last call she made leaving Mexico.

Chapter 15

"SHE TOOK OFF WITH GILBERT from the fishing village next to Popotla."

"When?" the gruff voice asked.

"Five minutes ago. She said they're heading toward the back side of Catalina Island. Two Harbors. Wants to meet up with me. Go over some plans."

The person at the other end of the phone didn't speak for a minute. "Interesting," and then another period of silence. "You fucked up at the hotel last night. Wrong mark."

Dred sucked in a deep breath. He knew he would have to answer for the screw up. "I know, but she traded rooms in the middle of the night. There was no way for me to know."

More silence. "I don't pay for your mistakes." Silence. "Has the Catalina contest been set up for tomorrow?" When a 'yes' answer came back, the man continued. "Make sure the boat is rigged properly. I will not communicate with the contest winner, but I will drive the boat."

"Is that wise?" The minute the words were out of his mouth, he froze.

The silence was deafening and the unspoken answer was obvious. You never questioned the boss.

"That's all for now. Money will appear in your account for your services. You know the drill. Destroy your phone and buy another. I will be in contact if I need you."

The line disconnected and the man punched the 'hang-up' button on his burner phone. He never was able to overcome the undeniable threat that this man projected.

When he contacted the dark web for an assignment last week he'd had no idea who would respond, but once he heard the resonant voice he knew the identity although he never acknowledged it. *I'm more a man than he'll ever be,* he thought, but still a pervasive uneasiness prevailed. The man always paid top dollar for his jobs, but he should. Most of the time murder was involved. Life always felt precarious when he worked for him and today was no exception. Well, maybe one. *Guess this makes me a double agent.* He liked the idea.

Chapter 16

"WHAT THE HELL? Excuse me." Grace turned ready to punch whoever was pinching her butt. She had been waiting in line to board the Flyer for five minutes. "How dare yo…"

"Calm down, sweetheart. Just trying to get your attention." He gave her a kiss. "Thought you'd sneak out of town without telling me? We have satellites to take care of those oversights." Duke started laughing as Grace lightly punched him in the stomach.

"I was going to call but the Uber arrived early and…"

"Yeah, right. Don't add to your criminal intent. I'm all over it."

They followed the crowd up the gang plank, headed toward the bar inside the boat, ordered two Bloody Mary's and found an empty booth to talk. It was Wednesday, light traffic traveling to Catalina, so no one joined them. The boat's horn honked a fond farewell to Balboa and pulled away from the dock. Duke and Grace watched the million dollar homes slip by and soon they were past the break-water, heading out to sea.

"So, what gives? Why the abrupt trip? And don't bother with cover-up, the truth works fine with me."

"Well, I couldn't find any of the girls. Amanda was supposed to be in LA, Meg and Rachael were supposed to be in Bullhead, but my gut was telling me different, so I called Rosie at the Conservancy and she was holding a baby when she answered. I could hear it. Josh's baby. Well, it took a bit of persuading, but she confessed all. Guess who's on Catalina?"

"Who?" Duke went along with the soliloquy.

"Amanda, Josh, Rachael, Aunt Sharon, Stella and the baby, Zach."

"They probably forgot to tell you. Just a quick trip regarding child disposition." He inwardly smiled, knowing she wouldn't fall for that lame excuse.

"Yeah, well, the clincher is that Meg is also there."

"Same ole, same ole. No biggie. Just sisters being sisters."

"Oh, I forgot one other person."

"Who?"

"Derek…"

Duke tensed. No more questions. Fraternal instinct took charge. Game on.

Chapter 17

MEG SEIZED THE FIRST free minute to call Rachael on her cell phone. "Rach. You've got to get over here now."

Rachael rolled over in bed and glanced at the clock. "Do you know what time it is? What's going on?" She flipped on the lamp and took a second look at the clock.

"There's been a murder at Catherine's and Zach's missing. Get your ass over here now." Meg was pacing back and forth behind the bar. Guests milled around in the halls, too anxious to sleep.

"Let me check out. You can't keep us here," screamed an angry woman. An officer explained the situation again as her husband pushed his way toward the door.

The coroner was still with the body and the forensics team was standing by, waiting to start their investigation. The team consisted of two men, not really trained for the job since murder was a rare occasion on the island, but they knew enough not to contaminate the crime scene until someone arrived from state-side.

"Have you called Josh?" Rachael wrestled the sheets out of the way and reached for her jeans. Cradling the phone on her shoulder, she sorted through the clothes on the floor, found her bra and fumbled with the straps. "Does he know?"

"Greg called him. Rach, it's a bloody mess. And the baby. Who would take the baby?"

"I'm on my way. Don't touch anything. Call Amanda. The FBI will need to get involved."

Rachael finished dressing, strapped on her gun and quickly added an ankle gun. Catherine's was only six blocks away so she sprinted the distance and met up with Josh as he screeched to a stop in the patrol car.

"Josh. Wait up. Meg just called. Wait."

Josh leaped from the car, left the keys in it and raced to the hotel's front door. "Hurry up, Rach." He ducked under the yellow crime tape and headed up the stairs, three steps at a time.

Greg met him at the top of the second stairwell, grabbed his arm, and yelled, "Whoa, buddy. Hold up. Let me fill you in on the scene before you go in."

"Where's the baby?" He pulled away from Greg, turned and met him eye to eye. "Where's Zach?"

Rachael was only a few steps behind and rounded the corner of the hallway in time to see fear register on Josh's face. Fear that only a father would feel.

Booties were quickly pulled on and they entered the bloody room. The social worker's corpse was clothed in a cotton night-gown, her body lying prone lengthwise on the bed. Her face was twisted into a grotesque mask reflecting surprise, fear, horror, pain and the frozen image of death. The five-inch slice across her throat had parted multiple layers of tissue, muscle and finally the jugular. Massive amounts of blood had soaked through the mattress and seeped onto the floor.

"He must've killed the woman first then turned to the baby. There's blood on the baby's bed. Just smears. Must've worn gloves." Greg turned to Josh. "Sorry, pal. Can't tell if the baby was hurt. Forensics will have to figure out whose blood that is."

"We've got Zach's DNA on file for the court shit. That should help." Josh looked at Rachael as she came in the door and froze. Bewildered. He didn't move. Logic was gone, emotion ruled. "Who would have done this? What kind of a sick fuck would hurt a baby?"

"Any security cameras in the hallway or by the registration desk?" Rachael hit her detective stride.

Greg was quick to answer. "No, place's too old. Gonna be torn down this year."

"There's a back door to the hotel. Anyone check for prints there?" Rachael checked the window and door sills.

"Working on it," Greg responded.

"I'll go check the registration log at the front desk. We'll match it against the remaining guests. If anyone has disappeared we can start there." She grabbed Josh's arm. "Get it together," she warned, then bolted from the room.

Meg overheard the conversation as she entered. "You know, that weird friend of Stella's spent the night with her two nights ago and hasn't checked out yet. I saw him this morning. I'd start with him."

"Is Stella still here? She's the logical one to snatch the kid." Josh said.

"Didn't Stella leave on the ferry yesterday? I saw a struggle on the pier," Meg chimed in.

Greg nodded. "We had to give her a tranquilizer and tie her to the wheelchair. She was totally out of it. Sharon stayed with her and as far as I know. Stella should be hospitalized by now. I'll make a call. What weird guy are you talking about?"

"You know. You grabbed him after the trial." Meg started to enter the room to check the pooling blood and blood spatter on the walls, but Greg stopped her. "They went on the ghost tour two nights ago. Weird as hell. Stella kept calling him Dred. She's the only one that signed for the room. I checked 'cause he was so strange and I was going to be stuck with him under the same roof all night."

"Oh, yeah. At the trial. I tried to grab him after the hearing but he slipped away," Greg said as he checked under the bed.

Amanda entered. Now all three Pennington women were involved. "Sorry, Josh. We'll do everything we can to find your son. The FBI's been alerted. Finishing up with an Amber alert."

The words, 'your son,' gave Josh a start. He walked over to the baby crib and looked again for evidence. "What would anyone want with a kid?" His third denial of fatherhood.

"It may not be about you or Zach," Rachael said as she returned to the room. "It may be about me and my family." She leaned against the door jamb and dropped her head.

"What are you talking about?" Josh stared at Rachael's somber face.

"The last time I visited Elliott in prison he was ranting. Seems he had lost all sense of being, but was rational enough to threaten me."

"Are you saying Elliott is alive? For sure?" Meg words, filled with fright, shot across the room. She paled. "That explains a lot. This was my room. He killed the wrong person."

"No, don't go there. I'm not sure but as far as I'm concerned, we have nothing definitive except his tooth to verify his death. Not enough for me. And then, there's his threat…"

"What?" Everyone anticipated the answer when she mentioned Elliott, but she said it anyway.

"He plans on killing the whole family and anyone else we love."

Chapter 18

AT 7:00 A.M. AMANDA CHECKED IN with the surveillance team located next door to Derek's house. "Any activity?" She glanced at the monitors and saw Derek dressing in the bedroom. "Not very modest, is he?" He slowly pulled cargo pants up over colorful boxer shorts taking a good five seconds to button each button. Next the wife beater was pulled over his head and slid down his six pack on its own. "All he had to do was go into the bathroom for privacy. Sick bastard."

The female agent gave her a grin. "My last assignment was so gross. The guy was 90 years old, flatulent and wrinkly. This guy's a far cry from that." She returned her gaze to the monitor.

"You're sure he didn't sneak out last night? There was a murder at Catherine's Hotel. Baby kidnapped." She watched the monitor and felt Derek was enjoying the moment. Entertaining the agents fed his ego. He knew they were watching.

"No, he was in last night. Watched TV and went to bed." She questioned Amanda. "Is this Derek guy involved in anything other than the drug case? Did I miss something?"

"Not that I know of. But Derek's whole family is so nefarious. Slitting throats is child's play for the usual torture they spread around. Just being a little paranoid I guess." Amanda knew this case would cross over to a personal condition, but tried to separate the two. She pulled a chair over to the second monitor and reviewed the tape from the previous night, scrutinizing each frame until satisfied that Derek hadn't snuck out. "Nothing to write home about." With that she headed next door.

"Morning, boss." Derek was his handsome self, freshly shaved, smelling like a sultry jungle morning, and self-assured. Relaxed. His perfect clothes, stature and smile irritated her. *No wonder Meg ogled him.* Amanda l whisked past him and checked out the rooms.

"So, what's on the agenda for today?" He finished off the cold coffee and rinsed his cup in the small sink.

Every time Amanda was in Derek's presence, she sensed an inexplicable twist yank her stomach into a knot. Today was no exception. *Listen to your instincts.* "I have a FBI GPS and wire for you to wear so when you leave the house we can track you and monitor your conversations. Take off your shirt." She unwrapped the electronic devices and spread them out on the dining room table.

"Best offer I've had all day." He reached behind his neck, grabbed the shirt and pulled it over his head, flexing his muscles as he complied with her request. As he walked over to face Amanda, a wry smile crossed his face.

Amanda glared. "You're having too much fun with this, Derek. If it were up to me, I'd throw your ass in jail. Turn around." Amanda taped the equipment on his back and walked around in front of him to tape the receiver. "This will do for today. I'm getting a smaller and more efficient setup delivered this afternoon." She ran a test of the equipment with the agents next door. All systems were go. "Put your shirt on. Let me see if it's noticeable."

Derek did as directed and performed an elaborate 360-degree turn in front of Amanda. "Well?"

"Okay, it's fine. Won't be noticed unless someone hugs you and that's not in the plans. Listen up. It's time for you to do your thing. Call all of Elliott's contacts and let's get this started. From now on I won't come to the house in case someone from the cartel identifies you and decides to follow you."

"I was never privy to the dealer's phone numbers. That was mostly Elliott or Marisa. There may be a few I recognize. I'll look. I could use some help with dialogue. How will I get in touch with you? Remember, you took yesterday's phone away."

Amanda reached into her briefcase and pulled out a phone. "This phone is to be used making contact with your dealers. We've copied all of your old contacts and are tracing them as I speak. It's your original cell number. Use it to make ordinary daily calls, post office, cable TV and things like that. The cartel will probably put a tap on it."

Derek took the phone and thumbed through the contact list.

"There is an FBI pager hidden in the watch. We'll know your every move, but if something happens, use the pager and punch in 911. We'll be there within minutes to help you."

He examined the nickel-plated watch and strapped it on. "Got it. Any word on Elliott's death? Did the DNA sample match up?"

"Do you have reason to think it wasn't Elliott who was incinerated?" She didn't want to tell him too much.

"No, just curious."

"I'll let you know if I hear anything." *Like hell I will.*

"You've erased some of my contact numbers. These are Elliott's not mine." He thumbed through the list. Derek checked the message and phone apps on his old phone. "I didn't memorize any of that stuff. What do you expect of me?"

Amanda handed him a photocopy of the information he needed.

Glancing over the list he commented, "You've been busy. More contacts redacted than remain."

"We're not stupid, Derek."

He finished with the typed phone list. "Good. You have Gilbert's number. He was Elliott's last pilot, one of the few people Elliott almost trusted. He'll still have our seaplane and the number for our Tijuana contacts." Derek worked quickly to transfer the numbers.

Amanda watched as he finished reviewing the list.

"I'll start there." He pointed to Gilbert's number.

"Did he ever use boats for transferring the drugs?"

"No, he didn't trade through this route. The trips were from Mexico to Arizona and then on to Nevada, dealing with a small independent branch of the Tijuana cartel. The Sinaloa Cartel runs everything now. There's no way Elliott would be stupid enough to try and channel anything through Catalina. It's protected territory. At least it was."

"Maybe you can work a deal. You cut them in on your Arizona accounts in exchange for a small portion of their San Francisco business, working through the island."

"I'll think that one through." He fell into a trance-like state. "It'll take a few days to set up a meeting, and it's dangerous. First of all, they don't know me, and they're not stupid. I'll have to earn their trust. Not an overnight fix."

"We're here to protect you." Amanda started for the door.

"Lady. You don't know who you're dealing with. Their organization is a well-oiled machine. They have structure and policies, finance and HR departments, safe houses, weapon and drug warehouses. They own the government and they rule by threats, intimidation and murder." He walked Amanda to the door and sighed. "Let me get started. You'll know everything I'm doing. Don't hold your breath for any quick fix."

"Don't forget. I'm working at Jack's Diner. Come there for breakfast every morning and pick up on me. That'll serve as an excuse if anyone sees us together outside the restaurant."

"Fringe benefits. I like that. I hope Meg doesn't get jealous."

His fetching smile irritated Amanda. "You smart ass. This isn't a game. Meg's been practicing her Krav just waiting for the right moment to thank you for her screwed-up life."

"I plan on marrying her and having three kids." Derek sat and opened the laptop, waiting for a barrage of words or a punch in the back of his head from his outrageous statement. He wasn't disappointed.

"That's never going to happen. Never." Amanda lost it for a second then pulled back. The thought of a union between the two sent chills to her very core. Meg had been so close to suicide after her abduction that Amanda vowed nothing like that would ever happen again.

Derek watched her as she left his house. When someone answered at the other end of the line, he grinned and said, "*Hola.*" And now it began.

Chapter 19

"HEY, ROSIE," Meg yelled through the phone. "I won."

Rosie was struggling to pull up her jeans when she answered. "What? What did you win?" She changed her iPhone to speaker.

"The contest that both of us entered. Remember? That new parasailing company that's opening on the island. Their promo contest. Winner gets a free ride. They'll have photographers there today, a hundred dollars cash and the winner's picture in the paper. Remember? We signed up for it on the pier the other day."

"Oh, yeah. And you won? Super. When do you have to pose and stuff?"

"Now. Right now. Can you come down to the beach and support me?"

"Damn. I have to go to work. I'll call Jenny and see if she'll cover for me. Chances are no. Short notice and all."

Meg was disappointed but understood. "Okay, well. I'm off to the pier. I've got my new string bikini. Would that be too skimpy?"

"No, perfect. Have fun."

Meg pulled on the two ounce suit, covered it with a long t-shirt, grabbed her flip flops and headed out the door. It took five minute to get to the pier at her jet speed pace. A crowd gathered around the new parasailing business and the local reporter was searching the group for Meg. They had been friends for years.

"Meg, Meg. Over here." Bob waved his camera in the air.

The crowd parted and Meg blushed with all the compliments being hurled her way. She shook hands with the company promotor, took off her t-shirt to the smiles of all the men and checked out the thirty-one foot commercial Watersports parasailing boat, equipped to the max. Meg knew her boats and was psyched to see such a beautiful craft.

"Yippee. It's red." Meg called. "What're you running under the hood? Looks like a 496 Mag."

"Plenty of power to get your skinny butt up on the air," the promoter yelled and the onlookers roared.

The engine started and Meg wasted no time jumping on board. Only the driver and one crew person. "Don't you need another observer?" Meg's excitement momentarily paused. She wasn't new to the sport and knew the rules.

"Nope. This is how we always go. Hold on. Here we go."

The crowd waved their goodbyes as the boat cruised through the moored sailboats toward open water. It was a perfect Catalina day. No haze and only a slight amount of air moving around. When the boat idled down Meg squeezed between the seats and stepped up onto the platform. As they helped her into her life vest and harness, she handed over her cell phone. "Take a picture would you? Now and when I'm up there." She turned sideways, chest high, tummy in and posed. She reached for her phone. "Change of plans. I'll take the pics from up there."

"Silly, you can't take the phone with you. I know you think you'll land in the boat with all your expertise, but what if? I'll keep it safe for you."

"Well, at least take a video of my take off and also if you dip me so my toes touch the water, get that too." She handed over the phone.

"Sure 'nuf." He tucked the phone in his jacket and glanced at the boat driver who was nodding. End of discussion.

Meg stood at the edge of the platform. A radiant smile passed over her face as the speed of the boat increased and the pull of the unwinding parachute took over. Within seconds she was airborne as the boat headed at thirty-five miles per hour toward the south end of the island.

Meg was enjoying every free moment of the experience. While she had gone parasailing off Malibu, Balboa and the Colorado River, Catalina Island with its surreal blue ocean was a new experience for her. The driver slowed the boat and Meg's chute responded to the diminished rush of air. Her toes dipped in the water for a few feet and then up she rose again. She watched as the Casino and Wrigley mansion faded into the distance and wondered why they were taking her so far out in the ocean. And toward the South end of the island? *They should be turning back by now. Strange. The trips were usually only 1000 feet or so off the shoreline. She'd been up here forever. Looked to be ten miles back to shore.*

She leaned forward and focused on the boat 800 feet below. The boat was slowing and then it stopped. The taut lines attached to her chute went limp. A sudden gust of wind whipped her chute upward and then instantly she dropped five feet.

Below, the boat driver smiled at the success of his plan.

What the hell's going on? She gasped as the boat took off again. The tether lines had been cut. She was on her own careening through the sky and within seconds she knew she would be plummeting down to the endless ocean when her chute collapsed. Alone and vulnerable as the towboat headed back to the California coast, she struggled to detach the chute. The tangled lines slipped through her fingers and the nylon drifted down, covering her head.

Don't panic.

The impact was hard. Meg managed to keep her head above water as the chute pulled her across the flat ocean surface. She untangled most of the cords, but struggled with the harness hook. The colorful chute covered her and she fought to stay above water. Instead of keeping her afloat, the life vest was pulling her down. She submerged, detached the life vest first and when that problem was conquered she slipped out of the chute harness. Air. Beautiful air.

She filled her lungs and started to untangle the mess of lines while treading water.

I've got to keep the chute above water. No one can find me otherwise. Moments were filled with trying to capture some air in the nylon to no avail. The chute disappeared into the deep and the useless life vest drifted close by but would not support her weight. She turned on her back and floated for a few minute to rest. *There's still six hours of daylight thank goodness.* She rolled over and started the first of countless strokes aimed at the south end of Catalina

Chapter 20

"OH, LOOK, DUKE," Grace pointed to the south end of Catalina as the Flyer glided into its slip. Engines reversed. She bumped back into Duke's chest and grabbed for the railing. She pointed to the small, colorful parachute at the south end of the island. "Really heading far out to sea for a rental." The thought quickly disappeared as the couple made their way to pick up the key for their prearranged cart rental.

"I feel like we're on some covert CIA operation. Is that wig really necessary?" Duke smiled at his lover.

Grace dropped the handle of her small suitcase and touched her brown wig. "I really don't want the girls to know I'm on the island. They all object to my help, say I'm micromanaging their lives." She threw her luggage into the cart and sat in the passenger side.

"You think?" The devilish smile on Duke's face didn't go unnoticed. He received a sharp slug on the shoulder for the comment. That action was one of Grace's more endearing characteristics, he felt, along with her wit, glowing personality and infinite love for her girls.

"Let's drive to the pier and check out the locals first. That's where all the gossip will be. You're lucky no one on the island knows you, otherwise you'd be sporting a wig too."

"Not hardly."

"If Meg's running amuck, the town will be talking about it."

"Oh, come on, honey. Let's get to our hotel, unpack and then go snooping around."

Grace glanced around, eyeing the end of the pier. Her nails slightly bit into his arm. She looked skyward. "No. Duke, there's something wrong."

———

"Rachael? This here's Al at Catherine's."

Rachael was surprised by the call. "Yes, Al. Is there something wrong?"

"Yup. Meg's not here yet. Her shift started an hour ago. Look. I don't mind coverin' fer her, but I got me a doctor appointment. Ya know where she be?"

"She won the paragliding contest and went to the pier early this morning. Should have lasted an hour or so. Look, close the bar if you have to, but I'll check this out. How are you feeling?"

"Not that great. Might have to go back to the hospital."

"Sorry to hear that. But look, I'll get back to you soon."

"Thank ya, ma'am. She's been a mighty big help, but shit-howdy. Catherine won't like it if I have to close 'er down."

"I understand, Al. I'll let you know as soon as I find her. Thanks for the call." Rachael tried not to overreact, but given the butchery of the last twenty-four hours, she went on high alert. Calls to Rosie, the newspaper photographer, the bartender at El Galleon and Eric's restaurant on the pier all ended with a negative answer about Meg's whereabouts. Always in the back of her mind was Elliott's threat, so Rachael headed to the pier for a first hand interview with the locals.

"Sure, there were a bunch of us here watchin' Meg. She looked great, smiling and all. Great swim suit, what there was of it. Took off about three hours ago."

Rachael looked up and down the pier for the speed boat. "Did the boat come back? Did anyone see it?"

"Gosh, as a matter of fact, no," answered a local. "Any of you guy see Meg come back from that parasailing ride?"

"No, but it was kind of weird. They took off south and didn't turn around. We were going to wait for her and eat some burgers here on the pier, but they didn't come back. Figured they picked her up and went to the back side of the island or something for more pictures."

Grace was sitting on a stool at Eric's, back turned to the ongoing conversation, listening to Rachael's interrogation of the group, intent on the answers.

When everyone else answered in the negative, Rachael called the Coast Guard facility located at the south end of the island, and informed Amanda at the FBI office. The Coast Guard immediately responded and sent a cutter and a Dolphin helicopter scurrying from the base. They plotted a search grid with the FBI utilizing their chopper also. The hunt was on.

Chapter 21

MARISA SIGNALED TO GILBERT as they approached the south end of Catalina. "Circle around this area. Looks like some Coast Guard commotion is going on down there. That can't be good for business."

A year had passed since Marisa had been to Catalina, a year of gathering information on cartel air and water drug drops. Through the binoculars she could see that no panga boats were involved in the off-shore activity. "Must be a lifesaving operation...another dummy lost at sea." Content that the Coast Guard was not threatening one of her boats, she leaned back and signaled for Gilbert to continue toward their destination. Whatever was going on below was none of her concern. Let the poor bastard drown.

Five minutes later the seaplane throttled back, banked to the left, straightened out and made an almost perfect landing on the ocean swells, two miles south of Catalina. Marisa watched as the sleek red and white mini day cruiser crashed through the waves, pulled alongside and lassoed the uprights attached to the plane's pontoons. A cleaned-up version of Dred yelled at Marisa as he jumped onto the seaplane's pontoons.

"Have a good flight?" He leaned forward and grabbed her small overnight bag and handed it to the boat driver.

"Short and sweet." Next came the computer equipment and finally Marisa took his hand and slid out of the cockpit onto the pontoon.

Dred waited until she was steady and then helped her onto the boat's deck. "Watch it. A little slippery here." He didn't release her hand, but instead pulled her close and brushed the wind tossed hair away from her face. "Almost forgot how beautiful you are."

Even though she had business on her mind, she relaxed into the kiss and pressed against his body. "It's been awhile. Been sitting around waiting for me?"

"Not exactly. Got a job through the web. Hanging out with a psycho redhead."

His answer amused Marisa. They had shared 'moments' when he worked for Elliott in Bullhead. "Sure you want to drop the redhead and work for me?"

"My God, if I ever take another assignment like that, I'll—"

"You'll what? Quit?"

"No." He thought. "No. I'll make you watch how a schizophrenic makes love. Her name's Stella. What a trip."

As they held onto the windshield and teetered along the narrow freeboard, Marisa glanced back at Dred's handsome face. "Glad you found your razor. That text selfie you sent me was horrible. I can't believe how ugly you were as a druggie. That dirty stringy hair, and beard. I was surprised even a psycho had the hots for you."

They settled into the backseats of the boat and Marisa directed the driver to head for Paradise Cove.

"Oh, once I grabbed her and pressed her against Big John, she was hooked. I could've been a scaly lizard and she still would've wanted it. She's one crazy bitch. But, why are we going to Paradise Cove? Only one mooring there."

"Exactly. No company to watch what we're doing." She relaxed into the crook of his arm and inhaled the pure ocean air, realizing these moments were rare and would disappear within the next hour. Crazy with the anticipation of setting up the new business and yet feeling the wonder of a human's touch mashed up in her brain.

When they reached the cove, the driver slowed the boat, idled onto the sandy shore, and jumped out, pulling the craft forward. Marisa and Dred hopped onto the sand and headed for the waiting jeep. She took his hand, actually happy to touch him, but careful not to get pulled into a romantic maelstrom again. Her life had been void of intimacy until Dred was recruited by her brother. Now, with Elliott dead, and Derek incarcerated, Marisa was in charge of the family business. Isolated from any family contact for the last year had been difficult but the isolation put everything in perspective. Sex, not love, was the key to her momentary needs. Mexico didn't quiet the demand for companionship. The cabana boys were young and virile, but didn't fulfill her emotional needs. But here he was. Dred, to be used and misused by her as desired.

Dred looked for the rental house through the windshield. He knew time was up. He had to prepare her for the surprise. "There's something I need to tell you." Explaining away the baby needed to happen before Marisa saw the screaming brat. He quickly brushed over his other assignment, the botched one, and got to the bottom line. "So we have an extra house guest for the time being, the redhead's kid. I'll take care of stashing him out. Figure we could use him for a bargaining chip or sell him on the black market. Anyway. It is what it is."

"A baby? What the hell were you thinking? Oh, shit. Anything else?"

"No, but I need to know what's going on. Is the cartel going to work with us? Are we getting out of the pot business?" Dred tried pushing for some answers, but knew that only minimal information would be offered up, if any. He probably knew more than she did but he also knew how to play the innocent game.

Marisa had no intention of telling him the truth, the plans. She only needed to drop enough information to keep him compliant and cooperative. Sex would handle much of that so she resigned herself to outwardly show interest in him. She needed to check with her international contacts now that she was in the States and make sure they would work with her. Elliott's death may have closed that door. "It's pretty involved. We'll talk about it later."

Dred inwardly scoffed, but didn't display his annoyance. "Just before Derek was arrested, Elliott said his real goal was to kill all of Meg's family. Possibly kill her last, so the suffering hurt more. Are you committed to his obsession?"

"Not in the least. But back to this baby thing. How did you get involved? Not your usual type of assignment."

"I hadn't heard from you in forever and money was running short. I took a job I found on the dark web. This Stella-bitch was involved. Everything went as planned until the last minute. I zorked the wrong chick. Grabbed the kid on the way out of the hotel. Collateral damage. I can always toss him in the ocean when he's no longer valuable."

Marisa seemed satisfied with his explanation, but not happy. "Elliott was emotion-driven before he died. Not thinking clearly. Crazy. Obsessed over Meg's rejection. Betrayal. Ha. She never cared about him, as far as I could tell. He was making irrational decisions at the end." She had a perplexed look on her face and mumbled, "Revenge murder is not in my plans."

"Well, Elliott's gone, so why are we dancing to his beat? Screw Meg and her family. I don't have a beef with them. Let's get our drug trade established and leave the island."

Marisa was trying to be patient. "What about the brat? Where is he?"

"Here for tonight only, but I found a temporary babysitter on the back side of the island. No questions asked, but we need to move him."

"Gilbert's wife is on the seaplane. She can manage the brat so we don't have to mess with him. We don't need strangers nosing around our business." She was glad to see that Dred didn't have an opinion. "Did you have any other problems last night with that assignment that'll come back to haunt us?"

"No, just had to time everything perfect. Took care of the bartender first, knocked him out when he came rummaging around downstairs, then went to where the room where the mark was sleeping, but she woke up. Wrong broad. Had to slice the lady. Clamped my hand on her mouth so no one heard anything. But her blood went squirtin' all over hell. The kid started squalling so I grabbed him and hit the bricks. First time I've had to do a double hit in an hour. Might ask for more money next time."

"You could try, not my concern. All things are negotiable, and if I were your client we could discuss fringe benefits." She reached under her blouse, unhooked her bra, and slid it out through the sleeve. She watched him as his eyes followed her every movement. The porch was dark. He took advantage of the presented offer and slid his hand under her blouse, realizing she was using sex to change the conversation, but he wasn't about to complain.

She moaned and kissed him.

Dred was no idiot. He was an expert at timing. He decided to forgo any further questions at the moment. He knew Marisa shared the same DNA as Elliott and that was reason enough to tread lightly. The sexual intermission ended all further discussion. It was one of their silent and bumpy encounters in the backseat.

The driver continued along the deserted dirt road on the back-side of Catalina, dodging a few wild buffalo that inhabited the location. The isolated cabin came into view as the jeep's lights reflected off the rise in the road.

"Have the driver bring in the bags," demanded Marisa, "and turn on your flashlight. It's darker than shit." She had returned to her bitchy self. She spotted the wooden hand rail and started up the steps, feeling her way along. Sparsely decorated, but ample in supplies, the cabin had been equipped per Marisa's demands. No luxuries compared to her year's stay in Mexico. She grunted, but accepted the bleak surroundings, knowing it was only temporary.

"First thing, we have to find a way to contact Derek. The FBI should be looking for me by now since I skipped out on the Tijuana meet. We need to get you set up in town. Maybe work at Jack's or else Catherine's. Both will give us access to gossip. But first," she took his hand and headed for the bedroom. It was time to finish the business they'd started in the back seat.

Chapter 22

GIVEN THE GENERAL DIRECTION of the boat pulling the parachute, the Coast Guard and FBI set up a grid pattern of fifteen miles southeast of Catalina. With such a small target, a lone figure, they were limited in the elevation they could fly. Rachael knew Meg was an excellent swimmer and felt she would be heading back to the island. Within an hour of sunset, she was spotted.

"There, there. Three o'clock, north. Is that her?"

Four sets of binoculars switched focus.

Amanda's blood pressure spiked. "Well, it's a swimmer for damn sure. Take her down," yelled Amanda. She reached for the loud speaker and blurted out, "Need a ride, sis?"

Meg had spotted the helicopter before they saw her. Instant relief passed through her body that was sorely tired of swimming. She talked to herself, wondering when the point of giving up would have arrived. Always, in the back of her mind, she knew Amanda would be there to pull her out. Relief and tears came instantly. She rolled over onto her back and floated.

The helicopter hovered, the basket lowered and all watched as Meg waved in appreciation. Although athletic, she struggled with the erratic movement of the basket and the rotor whirlpool of water.

Putting all modesty aside, she threw a leg over the basket and hoisted herself inside. Clumsy, but effective.

Once inside the chopper, Meg was wrapped in a Coast Guard blanket then Amanda hugged the hell out of her. "You okay, hurt?"

Meg, shaking from the cold and exertion, stammered, "Fine. Thanks, sis." An appreciative tear tumbled down. "Just a little scared 'cause it was turning dark and the island wasn't getting any closer."

Amanda waited as the basket was hauled back into the chopper and the door closed before starting her interrogation. "What the hell happened?"

"Elliott."

Chapter 23

GRACE AND DUKE PUSHED the cart to full speed and arrived at the Coast Guard helicopter pad. They waited in the shade of a metal shed. Darkness soon surrounded them as they listened for the sound of the chopper's rotors.

"How you holding up?" Duke put his arm around Grace and pulled her close. "You know she'll be fine. She's a survivor like her mom."

"God, that girl is going to be the death of me. How many times has Amanda or Rachael had to pull her out of harm's way?" She chewed on her upper lip and, hearing the helicopter, straightened to a stalwart position. "They're back." She slid from the cart's seat and peered around the building, observing Amanda helping Meg from the chopper cockpit. They exchanged some talk with the pilot and one other man.

"Perfect. I'm sure Amanda will take Meg home. Great, now we'll know where the girls live. Save us some time. Wait a bit to start up and then don't follow too closely."

"Yes, ma'am." Duke's grin came through in his humble reply. *Sometimes I think she forgets that I used to be her boss in the CIA.* Cute, he thought. That was one of the more endearing qualities that he admired about Grace, along with her overwhelming maternal instinct.

Grace responded to the edgy reply with a "sorry."

"Grace. I don't think we need to do this cloak and dagger shit. Let's talk to the girls, find out what's going on, and then help them, if needed. Or, is this going to be like a CIA op? Am I going to move satellites around for you? Do you have a plan?"

Grace enjoyed Duke's pseudo teasing. Under ordinary circumstances his plan of watch and wait would be acceptable, but her gut told her there was something truly amiss.

"Is it a gut thing?" Duke asked.

"Yup."

"Well, who am I to fight that?" They waited , giving Amanda a head start then followed Amanda home.

———

After the Coast Guard helicopter landed, Meg and Amanda headed back to the house. Amanda called ahead and told Rachael to come home. They sat impatiently outside the bathroom door waiting for Meg to finish her shower. When she appeared, wrapped in a towel, they handed her a cup of hot coffee with a healthy shot of Jack Daniel's. Meg took a long gulp, put on her underwear and sat on the couch.

"Better?" Rachael asked as she helped Meg dry her dripping hair. Amanda clicked on the hair dryer and helped the process.

"Quit hovering, you guys. I'm fine Just need to defrost from the cold water douse." She didn't want to mention the sore muscles and painful shoulder. They'd make her see a doctor.

Amanda took charge. "What the hell happened?"

Meg turned off the dryer and rolled her head around, slowly raised her shoulders, trying to loosen the tight muscles. "Who the hell knows? I won a contest, took a boat ride and someone decided to dump my ass in the drink." She waited.

Rachael jumped in. "When the Coast Guard picked you up, you were trembling and mumbling, 'Elliott.' What's with that?" She waited for Meg's reply but had already come to her own conclusion.

Meg tossed the towel on the floor, tucked her legs under her and started. "Who else would go to all the trouble? A bogus company, contest, a boat probably with the wrong numbers painted on it, and chute lines intentionally cut? This was an intricate plan that almost got me killed. There's only one person who loves convoluted plans, who dwells on elaborate tactics that include my demise. Someone who has threatened to kill me and our family. That's Elliott."

Rachael resisted. "Meg, you don't know that. There's no proof that he's still alive, that he escaped from prison."

"Wait," Amanda offered as she read an incoming text. "The Coast Guard checked with the mainland's boat rental shops. A paragliding boat fitting the description of the one that was used today was stolen last night, sometime between midnight and dawn. If someone stole the boat, showed up here for the well-advertised contest which was apparently rigged for Meg to win, pulled her out in the middle of the ocean and dumped her...well, that all fits." She moved over to sit by Meg. "Sorry, sis. Looks like you might be right. But... forewarned is forearmed as they say."

Rachael groaned. She didn't want to give in to the horrific idea. "Will the boat shop have a surveillance tape to examine?"

"It's already been sent over. Meg and I can look at it later."

"Why bother? Elliott's had months to change his appearance. He was always an expert on disguises." Meg remembered that in Bullhead he had a perfect disguise of an old hump-backed man and also showed up as an FBI agent. Disguise was his middle name.

"The FBI's already opened a case on this. In the meantime, let's get back to our daily routine. We're still dealing with Zach's disappearance, Marisa's whereabouts and Derek's position in all of this."

Meg stood and started for the bedroom. "I'm good with that, but tired as hell. Gotta hit the sack." She smiled at the concerned faces looking at her. "Thanks for saving my butt again, and thanks for loving me. I know I'm a pain in the ass sometimes." She disappeared into the bedroom. When the door closed, she slid down the wall and sat on the floor. A quiet moment, alone, to let the tears flow.

Sleep didn't come easy. She tried all of her customary methods of dozing off like counting numbers backward, concentrating on the warm summer days at Black Meadow Landing, water skiing in Bullhead, with no success. Between each scene, Elliott always appeared, chasing her.

Chapter 24

"WHERE IS SHE? Damn it, Derek. Where's your damn sister?" Amanda slammed the door of the interview room and stomped in, ready for battle.

Derek, waiting in the small room, looked around and decided that all interrogation rooms were designed by the same person. Boring, simple, lack of imagination. He could have been in the Los Angeles FBI office instead of the Catalina Police Department. "How the hell am I supposed to know? You heard our only conversation. Beats the hell out of me." He anticipated her tantrum.

"You planned this. How could I have been so stupid?" She was close to growling. "There's been a report of another drug drop on the island and I'll bet your sister's behind it." Amanda picked up the wooden chair and slammed it down.

"No. Don't think so. We never used Catalina. She hasn't had enough time to set it up. You're wrong." He stared at Amanda straight on, enjoying her ruffled feathers. He was comfortable since he had nothing to hide.

"She was supposed to meet our agent in Tijuana. Never showed. Now, that phone number you used to contact her two days ago is no longer in service."

"Can't help it. You should never underestimate Marisa. She's both intelligent and street smart. Probably felt something was amiss. But, what does that have to do with our arrangement? I still have contacts. Let's do the deal without her, or is this personal?"

Amanda was livid. She quit pacing the well-worn floor and settled into the chair opposite Derek, watching him. The FBI was putting pressure on her to resolve the issue. "You'll throw your sister under the bus that easily?"

"Apparently she's done the same to me. Survival of the fittest comes to mind." His expression changed and he focused on the table top.

Amanda watched his eyes. There was something there. A faint sadness? Betraying an allegiance to his sister? "What do you know about the murder at Hotel Catherine's and the kidnapping?"

"Absolutely nothing. Who's dead and who's missing?" Surprise registered on his face. Surprise that Amanda considered sincere.

Amanda knew Derek had not been privy to the TV or newspaper accounting of the incident, but watched his face for any tell. It was public information, so withholding the information was pointless. He could Google it. "Case worker was killed and Zachary, Josh's baby, has been kidnapped."

Derek shifted in his seat and his head jerked to the left, eyes immediately rolled upward searching for any information that might be connected to the crime.

Amanda waited.

"No link that I can see." He paused, dropped his head forward and focused into space. "Elliott did say he would kill all of Meg's family at one point. That would include the extended family, I assume. She was going to be last." He paused, digging deeper into his memory bank. "But I believed it was the ravings of a lunatic when he said that. He was really out of it by then."

Amanda saw no reason to withhold Meg's recent scrape with death from him. "An attempt was made on Meg's life yesterday."

Derek shot out of his chair. "What? Is she all right? What happened?"

She relayed the details of the near boating disaster, but

cautioned him. "We are telling the reporters it was just a fluke. Don't want to raise any more pandemonium in town. Need to keep the public calm if possible. Do you know anything about this?"

"No. But it sounds like something Elliott would do. He always liked elaborate plans. Like the explosions in the Oasis Casino. Will the FBI be guarding her and the family?"

"Not for now, but we all have heads up." Amanda decided to press a little harder. "Rachael was the one who captured Elliott in Bullhead. He had it in for her, Rachael loves Josh, Zach is Josh's son. It fits. But if Elliott is dead, who would be carrying out his legacy? Did he have a following?"

Derek didn't have to think about that. In the last year, before Meg's kidnapping, Elliott had insisted Derek learn all of his trade secrets. "There were a lot of mercenaries that worked for him, and maybe some made that jump, but he's dead. Can't imagine they would carry on without him. They called him El Jefe, but with no praise from the master and no monetary incentive…" His voice trailed off as he thought through the cult-like relationship. "There was one guy that might still be a follower. Don't remember his name, Weird dude. I guess I don't know."

Amanda wanted to question his comment "he's dead" but pushed ahead. That discussion would have to wait. "Well, with the betrayal by your sister, there's that."

Derek shifted again, leaned his head back, and closed his eyes. The betrayal was becoming clear. "Yes, there's that."

Chapter 25

"OKAY, I'LL KEEP MY EYES and ears open. Gotta go and open the bar, the owner just called me. Looks like this is going to be a full time job. Okay, okay, Amanda. I'll be careful." Meg disconnected the phone. After her parasailing adventure, her sisters had fussed over her, trying to reassure her that Eliott was not the problem, but eye contact between Amanda and Rachael fully disclosed their concern over the possibility that he had masterminded the attempt on Meg's life.

Meg pulled on her white knee knockers and Catherine's t-shirt and headed down to the bar. It was 10:00. Standing on the sidewalk in front of the Hotel, Meg performed the yoga sun salutation exercise to loosen up all the muscles and get some deep breathing in before the solid work day started. She masked the pain of yesterday's fall from the heavens. The sun reflected across the quiet ocean and she could see the massive Carnival Cruise ship anchored off shore with the swift tenders scooting toward the Island to drop off passengers.

Inside, Meg did a quick wipe down of the bar, started the air circulating through the system, opened the shades, completed a hasty sweep job of the outside patio, put on her bartending apron, and finished washing the few glasses from the night before. She stood at the window, watching the tourists pour down the street, stopping first at the souvenir shop next door.

"Yay, a bar."

"Hooray."

"Let's start the day out right."

Fifteen eager travelers flooded into the bar and Meg started serving. Dred took advantage and walked in anonymously amid the party group, settling on the last bar stool. His transformation was remarkable. Clean shaven, hair styled, tasteful summer clothing and a pleasant attitude prefaced his entrance.

"Come on, lady. We ain't got all day. Geez, how long does it take to get a beer around here?" His girlfriend poked the mouthy patron in the ribs.

"Hey, buddy. Give her a break," Dred yelled back, and Meg managed a smile toward him, mouthing a 'thanks.'

"What's it too ya? If you're so hot to save the barmaid, why don't you go help her?" The man was feeling the effects of early morning Bloody Mary he'd downed on shipboard.

Dred shot off his stool immediately. He didn't even have to implement a plan to meet Meg, the jerk did it for him. "No worries." He went behind the bar, smiled at Meg and said, "Hi, I'm Dave. Been a bartender in San Diego for years. Looks like you could use some help."

"Thanks. I've only been doing this for three days. You're right. Could use the help." She liked his smile, and the perfect physique didn't go unnoticed. "What's your name again?"

"Dre…Dave. Move over, I'll handle the mixed drinks. You cover the beer."

She stopped mixing the Bloody Mary and looked at him again. "Have we met before?"

"Don't think so. Just arrived this morning. Here's the Mary for the jerk on the end."

"Wow, you're fast." She momentarily let his answer go, but

something kept nagging at her. "Any chance you can work till 6:00? I'll have to make a few phone calls to find someone to take over."

"No worries. And, by the way, I'm looking for a job."

"I'll keep that in mind." Meg sent a dazzling smile his way. *Holy cow. A handsome hunk just fell into my lap. That hasn't happened since… Derek. Oh, dear.*

Chapter 26

MARISA STARED AT THE MIRROR, examining her reflection. *Blonde with blue contact lenses? Both Meg and Amanda saw me, but only for a few minutes and I had black hair then. This will have to do in case we cross paths on the island.* The tan that she'd acquired in Mexico would help her disguise, along with the sunglasses and baseball cap. It was early and the warm Catalina sun was taking its time arriving. A lazy sea-haze lingered off shore. She left her bedroom and headed toward the small kitchen, passing the room where Zach had been crying all night.

"God. Who would ever want kids? That brat squalled all night."

"And good morning to you, too." Dred tried to hug her to offset the hostile air she brought to the kitchen. "Coffee's ready."

Marisa poured a cup, added some Bailey's and rummaged in the refrigerator, looking for some fruit. Living in Mexico had spoiled her. There, her breakfast was prepared to her exact specifications, then the masseuse would show up at 10:30, followed by a stylist to fix her hair. She paid the pool man a bonus for taking care of her sexual needs which seem to be increasing with the lack of intrigue from handling the daily drug trade. That was her yesterday. Today's world was a shabby rental house deep in the backside of Catalina with only a tired cantaloupe.

"The FBI should be out looking for you today," Dred mentioned casually as he leaned over to tie his Nikes. "Will Derek get the message that you didn't show up for the meet?"

Marisa had been pondering that question all night. "I'm sure they'll tell him, but what he does with the information will be the interesting part."

"What? He'll figure you're here to break him out, won't he?" He put some butter on the toast and slid a piece her way.

"Sure. Unless." She hated the crust. *Why can't he remember that?*

"Unless what?" He knew the answer but pressed anyway.

"Unless he's really decided to go straight. Either I have to betray him or he has to lead them to me." She shoved the toast away. "We have to be ready for either scenario. But now how about you? Did you make a move on Meg last night?"

"Happened yesterday morning. She was still freaked out about some parasailing accident. Old timers were asking her about it, but she just laughed it off. She was definitely on edge though, spilling drinks, a mess. I dropped by the bar as some jerks were getting off the cruise ship."

"And?"

"And I helped the poor maiden in distress. Putty in my hands. I could be in her pants in a week, if that's the plan. She's a hottie, by the way."

"What accident? Tell me."

Dred filled in the details as he knew them. "She's paranoid as hell about Elliott. She mentioned him while we were serving drinks. He must have scared the shit out of her."

"She mentioned him by name?"

"No. Just said things like some maniac had tried to kill her in four or five different ways last year, but now he was supposedly dead." He reached over and picked up her toast.

Marisa's mind drifted back to two years ago when Elliott kidnapped Meg. Derek had told her of the abuse Meg suffered at his hands, and since Marisa also had been at the receiving end of

Elliott's unbridled wrath, she understood. She almost admired Meg's fortitude to come through the maelstrom still alive. "Look, don't get too amorous. She's not dumb. Will spot a con if you move too fast, at least that's what Derek said."

Dred took a sip of coffee and decided to ask the question that had been bothering him. "Is there any friggin' chance that Elliott's still alive?" Dred never believed Elliott died in prison. He had too much money and too many contacts.

"No," answered Marisa without hesitation.

"Well, excuse me for asking, but with Elliott dead, what do you want with Meg?"

Marisa glared. "Not any of your business." *Revenge for hurting my family, you stupid jerk,* she thought. She mentally questioned his new push to be in on the planning of their operation. Forgetting his 'hired-hand' position? Being a partner would never happen. "First, we need to make contact with Derek. Both of Meg's sisters will know his location, so figure out a way to get his address. He'll be wearing a wire, or some kind of FBI monitor, besides his house will have a ton of surveillance too." She thought for a minute. "If you can get close, you can slip him a note or better yet, a cell phone. Yes. That'll work. A phone with my number programmed in."

"I can handle that. You supply the phone?"

"Of course." She mentally dismissed Dred. He was only good for two things...a little muscle when needed and impromptu sex, which she had to admit was exceptional.

Dred was getting antsy. "Glad we don't have to work out of this shack. That kid hollering every night would drive me nuts." Dred rinsed out his coffee cup in the sink and glared at the bedroom door. "Shut up, you little brat." His fist hit the drywall with a solid blow.

"That was your mistake, so deal with it. Bargaining chip you decided. I'm still not sure it was such a great idea, but here we are." Marisa had gone along with the idea, but looking back tried to reassess Dred's reasoning.

Dred glanced her way. *Bitch.* Marisa's damn superior attitude pissed him. He did all of the heavy work for the gang, the killing, the kidnapping, dealing with the mafia, and she sat around playing with the books, making the big bucks and then telling him when to take off his pants. *Maybe after this deal I'll take over,* he thought, *especially if the FBI keeps Derek. Why not?* The remarkable thought gave Dred a new outlook and he smiled.

"What's that all about?" Marisa questioned.

"What?"

"The smile."

"Just thinking how great you look this morning. Will we have time for a swim before we head to Avalon?"

"No."

It wasn't even a pleasant 'no.' Just 'no.' Dred started collecting these condescending remarks, amassing a pool of insults to further his new resolve.

A driver loaded Dred's luggage and computer into the jeep. Marisa joined him and they started across the rugged terrain driving up the steep slopes of unmarked trails on the backside of the island until they met up with the dirt road named Lone Tree. From the 1600 foot elevation they could see Avalon and the California coastline peeking through the early morning clouds.

"When I drop you off, Miguel and I have to hurry to mark the drop-off site."

"What time and where?" Dred asked.

Marisa usually wouldn't discuss business in front of anyone, but Miguel had been with her for years. "Two hours. We'll drive cross country over to Coffee Pot Canyon then on to Bullrush Canyon Trail. We'll use gypsum to mark the 'x' on the south facing slope."

"You using the Cessna?"

"Yeah, had it painted sky blue and changed the call letters. Ninety percent cocaine this time. Should bring a pretty penny."

"Coke? You know you're courtin' trouble. The cartel doesn't like competition." Dred wanted no part of crossing the big guys.

Marisa shot him a 'how stupid' look. "Who's to tell? One simple trial drop. Next shipment'll be mostly weed so we'll use the panga boats. Got a stack of them lined up at the fishing village by Popotla."

"That's safe enough, but the coke...dealing with the cartel's a whole different world. You don't have enough information to start a war. Bolivia's very protective of their cocoa." He shook his head and mumbled something obscene under his breath.

Marisa didn't like any of her employees overthinking her decisions. She grabbed his knee and squeezed. "Probably should drop it." Her facial expression underscored her words.

Dred got the message. "Looks like you've got it covered." He added another item to his ever growing list, thinking when I'm in charge I'll go back to Elliott's system. Bullhead City and Vegas. Smaller scores, but longer life. "Now, what's next?"

"Build a relationship with Meg, stay clear of Derek."

"That's pretty lame. Let me contact our supplies or something."

Marisa was growing tired of placating him, but decided to stay with the conversation one more time. "Not now. Look, the only unknown is Derek and his intentions. I'm not worried about the aerial drops 'cause he doesn't know about them. That's my project. But when we deal by boat…Well, he knows the system."

"So if he turns on you, do I kill him?" He watched for Marisa's reaction.

Marisa's body twitched. She couldn't hide it. She hadn't come to terms with that reality. She had never loved anyone in her life except her brother, but his decision to possibly cooperate with the Feds would be his own, not something they decide on together. "We'll see."

Chapter 27

RACHAEL WANDERED THROUGH the small house picking up misplaced items and moving them around, hoping the activity would help organize her thoughts. Mindless activity to keep from going stir crazy. The last few conversations with Josh had been deliberate and yet aloof. Neither had said what they were thinking, only addressing the murder of the social worker and the disappearance of Zach. Now Meg's disaster at sea added another dimension to her worry list. She cleaned the coffee pot for the third time and then grabbed her purse and headed for Jack's Restaurant.

Amanda was working the tables at Jack's and gave Rachael a head nod when she entered. Rachael picked the table in the corner. With her back to the wall there was an unrestricted view of the entire restaurant, a technique pounded into all good cops until it became automatic. The plastic-covered menu and a paper napkin set-up were given to her as she sat down.

Amanda poured a cup of steaming coffee, set the pot down, and whipped out her order pad. "What'll it be?"

"And good morning to you, too."

"Oh, excuse me, miss. We're just really busy this morning. Do you need a little more time to order?" She tossed a weak smile at her sister, one that Rachael recognized as meaning, 'you're enjoying this too much.'

"Surprise me." Rachael wanted to talk to Amanda, but realized the timing was off. She dropped her voice and continued, "Any chance of talking later? I need some advice."

Rachael glanced up and saw Amanda's expression change. "Oh, fiancé material walking through the door. Okay to direct him to your table?" She didn't wait for an answer. "Too bad, I'm doing it anyway. You guys need to work this out. I'm not very good at running defense." She dodged around the tables, smiling at the patrons she bumped into, and got Josh's attention. "Excuse me."

He was standing tall in his sheriff's uniform, handsome and self-assured. Josh saw Amanda out of the corner of his eye and then Rachael. He immediately turned back toward the door, not wanting a confrontation over breakfast. When Amanda grabbed his arm he pulled away. "It looks like the restaurant is full. I'll come back later."

"No way. She's waiting for you." She shot him a pissed look. "Why don't you grow a set and man up? You two are acting like teenagers. Now go sit down. I'll bring coffee." Josh had been a family friend for years, so addressing him as a petulant teenager was totally in character for Amanda.

As directed, he sat. "Mind if I look at the menu?" He reached across the table and brushed Rachael's arm in the process.

"Won't do any good."

"I beg your pardon?"

"The bitchy waitress will order what she wants you to eat."

Josh leaned back and laughed. It felt good. "You Pennington women never change. You know what's best for me and damn it, that's what I'll get."

Rachael, giving out a belly laugh, grabbed her napkin and wiped tears from the corners of her eyes. "God, that feels good." She reached across the table and took his hand. "You jackass. I sure love you."

Josh returned her smile, stood, and pulled Rachael from her chair. The kiss was warm and long overdue. "You are one stubborn woman, Miss Pennington. Now kiss me back."

She did.

The gossip about the courthouse encounter between the two lovers had made the Catalina circuit and the hometown diners surreptitiously watched the discourse between the two. After the kiss, applause started at the breakfast counter by three locals and then spread throughout the room. Josh, embarrassed by the paparazzi exchange, helped Rachael to her chair with a gentle-manly flair, raised his coffee cup and announced, "Coffee's on me."

When Amanda's choice of breakfast arrived and the room settled back into their own private conversations, the two attacked the problems at hand. "Any new leads on Zach?"

"No. We dusted the room for prints but, hell, it's a hotel room. Also checked the video leads from the store next door. Whoever did it must have known about the camera. The one image around 3:30 a.m. shows a figure around six-foot two, medium build, might have a beard, hooded jacket, and looks like he is carrying a package. Probably Zach. Film is grainy."

"Has the FBI done any profiling yet? Motive?" She paused. "Wait a minute, you know what you described sounds like that weird guy who was with Stella at the hearing. Have they checked him out?"

"He's disappeared too. Long gone. No trace." He took a bite of hash browns and washed it down with coffee.

"Was he with Stella on the Catalina Express when they finally got her on board to go home?"

"No. That's another unexplained detail. Doesn't look like he checked into any hotels for the night, unless he changed his appear-ance which wouldn't be too hard to do. Shave, glasses, new clothes…new guy." He poured more syrup on his pancakes and took a bite.

"Any reason to believe Stella's behind this? Like…hired someone to steal Zach since the court decision didn't go her way?" Rachael looked at the scrambled eggs and decided against them.

"We checked with Aunt Sharon. She feels sure Stella is oblivious. I go along with that. Stella's been too wacked out on meds, and confined to the institution. No way could she have organized this."

"Well, what about her brother, Greg? Would he help?"

"No. Definitely, no. Greg knows everything about Stella's medical history. He wouldn't help her."

"Then, if not Greg, how about this hoodie guy? Stella called him Dred. He involved?"

Josh had no answer.

"Who's pissed off at you? What reason would someone have to hurt you? If someone was at the hearing when you suggested Zach be put up for adoption, then the reason to hurt you is out the window. Dred was there, remember?"

"Yes. The court cameras caught a good picture of him. FBI is running their facial recognition program as we speak. Should get results today."

Rachael dropped her fork onto the plate and grabbed Josh's hand, spilling coffee from the cup he was holding. "Look who just walked in."

Derek had barely released the door knob when he spotted them and immediately turned toward an open table at the other end of the restaurant.

"Could he be a part of this?" Rachael's fingernails punctured Josh's wrist.

In the far corner of the diner sat a middle-aged man, leaning against the window, steepling his fingers, observing the Pennington women. Derek's appearance added another level of interest to his people watching.

Chapter 28

BY THE END OF THE FIRST DAY on the Island, Grace caught up with all the news. Local newspapers were strewn across the living room floor of the modern flat she had rented. Five years ago the two-story house on East Whittley had been a neglected blight in the neighborhood. An imaginative contractor purchased it, did a total renovation which included adding a third story with separate entrances to each flat, incorporated many of the island treasures and transported a ton of upgrades by boat. Now, the Sullivan mansion was acknowledged as an island icon. Every inch had been rehabbed and the result was a multimillion dollar residence with a view that stretched across the Pacific.

"Was the Island News reporter helpful?" Duke lay stretched out on the balcony lounge and sipped his coffee with a touch of Bailey's added. While he was hoping for a real vacation, he settled for assisting Grace with her mission. He knew better than to get in the way of momma and her cubs, so he relegated his role to assistant snoop.

Grace walked outside to join her man. "Well. The girls have been busy. Meg's got two jobs, one at Catherine's and one as the ghost tour guide. There's been a murder and Josh's baby is missing, which brought in the FBI, hence, Amanda. There was an attack on Meg's life via the parasailing. Josh is trying to give his baby away, so that explains the rift between the lovers. Stella has been escorted off the island and locked up in some mental institution. Interesting huh?"

"Just a typical week for the Pennington girls. So what's your plan?"

"Well, on the surface it looks like everything is going okay for the girls. Just busy. I'm figuring out how to get into Jack's restaurant for breakfast and lunch. That's where the gossip spreads."

"Has it ever dawned on you that your daughters might resent your interference in their lives? Why not call and ask them out for dinner. Tell 'em we're here for a short trip. I love a simple plan."

"Not this time. They know me too well. The truth will come out in seconds." She thought for a minute. "Meg would be the only one who might see through your disguise."

"What disguise?"

"Hold on a second, it's all coming together."

Duke groaned. He was recalling all of the disguises Grace had invented in Spain when they were working undercover together.

"I'll make a few calls and we can do it tomorrow." She went into the house and dialed Information.

Chapter 29

AS PLANNED, THE FOLLOWING DAY Derek flirted with Amanda at Jack's Diner and within hearing distance of the diners she said she would meet him after dinner for a drink. The white haired old timer at the end of the counter made a swift remark her way. "Well, fellas, looks like both of the Pennington girls got lucky. Rachael scored a kiss yesterday and Amanda's picked up a hottie today." Amanda bunched up a tea towel and threw it his way, much to the delight of the retired group.

"Morning, folks." Amanda poured coffee in the elderly couple's cups. Realizing that the woman was blind, she placed the cup at two o'clock on the right side of the dinner plate. The male companion smiled her way at the extra consideration. "My friend and I would both like the early bird special, crisp bacon, eggs over easy and an English muffin, please."

Amanda had to listen carefully since the man had a heavy German accent plus a lisp. No rings on their wrinkly hands so she assumed he was a paid attendant. "Coming right up."

The grey-haired woman adjusted her black eyeglasses to the left and asked her partner to add some creamer to her coffee.

After Grace took her first sip, she leaned into the man and whispered, "Oh, shit. Change of plans. That's Derek Turner. What the hell is he doing here? My intel missed that, said he had left the island. Something is truly amiss."

———

They met for happy hour at El Galleon, downed a couple of drinks, maintaining the flirtation and then drove Amanda's cart to the turnout by the Holly Hill House. She pulled out a folded map of Catalina and laid it on the flat part of the cart. An ocean breeze caught the corner and flipped the map against Derek's chest.

"Damn it." Amanda picked up four small rocks and anchored the map. "Yesterday, around four o'clock, our undercover agent working at the airport saw a small plane circle this area and head back toward the backside of Avalon." She turned on a flashlight and pointed to a spot on the map. "Our contact at Wrigley Memorial observed the same plane circle around in the area of Bullrush Canyon." She moved the light to a small dot on the paper. "The plane dipped out of sight, came back up and took off for the mainland. What's your take on that?"

Derek studied the chart, his soft brown eyes scrutinizing the map. Finally he commented. "Sounds like an aerial drop to me."

"And?"

"Initially, Elliott only transported drugs via Mexico and the Arizona corridor. His Catalina plan did not include aerial trafficking. Was going to use panga boats, speed boats, or submersibles, leaving from Ensenada or Rosarito and either beaching on the back side of the island or throwing the bags over with a floating marker that a pick-up boat would come by and snag. Boats were equipped to fish the drugs out. If the plan changed it was after Elliott's death and my incarceration."

"So, that leaves Marisa. She's implementing his plan." It wasn't a question.

Derek seemed dismayed by that conclusion. "You don't know if it's an aerial drop, but if it is, they've probably upped the marijuana game to include cocaine, and that's scary. I don't think Marisa would attempt anything like that on her own. It might be a cartel drop. That was their favorite way of moving the drugs last time I was involved."

"But, if she thought you'd be here to help her, why not?"

"Why not, indeed." The thought bothered Derek more than he wanted to admit.

The two stood there as the rest of the day slipped into the Pacific, stretching their imaginations, hoping to come up with some 'ah-ha' moment. Amanda, feeling the subject was exhausted, moved on. "Now, to the missing baby. Elliott's last caper before he was caught was human trafficking. The bathing beauties were being sold to foreign investors."

"That proved to be his downfall. I don't believe Marisa, if indeed she is involved, would be dumb enough to try to continue that. Not her thing. But what are you suggesting? Baby trafficking?"

"Crossed my mind. First, she'd be splitting the FBI effort to find her by handling both the drugs and the baby at the same time. Second, if she couldn't break into the cartel's business here on the island, she could fall back on baby trafficking until she moves on to another enterprise. Make any sense?"

Derek knew it made perfect sense and the light finally dawned. Marisa was here for him, to help him escape from the FBI like any good sister would do. She never had any intention of joining forces with the FBI and had only taken that phone call in Mexico to find out where he was being detained. He had underestimated her cunning and now realized that most of what Elliott had accomplished was by her careful planning. She had been the brains all along. Elliott was the brawn. He mentally ripped through the last five years of his life and saw the total picture. She was the mastermind, not Elliott. *Oh my God. Could that really be? Now what?*

Amanda waited for an answer. She felt he was vacillating, teetering on the brink of making a fatal mistake. To cooperate or to flee? She instinctively knew and yet was willing to give him enough rope. Her FBI chief had discussed this exact scenario, almost line by line, and she knew this moment was pivotal. Would his loyalty to Meg influence his decision? She remained silent.

He turned away from the cart and walked to the precipice over-looking Avalon. Lights from the city shimmered across the flat, endless ocean, but his mind's eye was searching to see the future. "To answer your question, yes. It does make sense." His emotional pain was obvious. "I'm having a hard time visualizing Marisa harming a child or dealing in cocaine, but, it's not inconceivable." He turned to Amanda and his expression read 'help.'

"Look, Derek, this is what needs to happen. First, if you still want immunity from your previous crimes, we will rewrite the agreement, excluding Marisa. Give me a yes or no on that right now, or we're finished."

He didn't hesitate. "Yes."

"Good. I'll have that ready this evening. Now, I don't believe Marisa could be doing this by herself. She needs a confidant. Search your memory bank and find any likely suspect that would meet that criteria. Also, she'll have to contact you soon. I want you to meet her, convince her that you're in, willing to continue with the operation, and find out as much as you can."

"Won't she be suspicious if she sees us together?"

"No, she believes we've turned you. It would be suspicious if we tried to hide it. This dual allegiance will be difficult to keep straight. You'll be acting as a double agent. Are you up to it?"

Derek was involved in mental gymnastics when Amanda posed the next question. He actually liked this new position. It held out all kinds of possibilities. His simple answer again was "Yes."

"Good. One other thing. Gossip at Jack's this morning included the scary mishap with Meg and the paragliding. She insists that Elliott was behind this. Anything to that? Has he or any of his henchmen contacted you?"

"Absolutely no. If they do, you'll be the first to know. Meg is my number one person to protect in this world. I love her."

Amanda could only shake her head at this pronouncement. *What in the world was he smoking?*

Chapter 30

DRED WAS HANGING OUT at El Galleon waiting for Meg to get off work. They had a date. He marveled at how easy it was, she being so trusting and fun. A far cry from the raging Marisa. She seemed comfortable in his presence and thankful for his assistance, helping her at the bar. She was running late so Dred waited in a dark corner of the bar observing all of the patrons. Now was the time to gain her trust he decided, but when he spotted Amanda and Derek his plans for the evening changed. He followed them when they left, watched as they parked by the Holly House to talk, and trailed them to Derek's house. He called Meg and broke their date, saying he had an interview at Steve's Steakhouse for a bartending job. He parked his cart down the street and started his surveillance of Derek's house. Since the FBI was on the case he knew the house would be monitored and he didn't dare attempt to contact Derek there. He dialed Derek's old cell phone number on the throwaway phone Marisa had provided. When Derek answered, Dred asked for 'Margie,' one of Elliott's old code words for 'meet me.' Derek said 'wrong number' and hung up. Dred waited.

Derek left the small house an hour later and headed for Vons, grateful that the FBI ankle bracelet was not attached yet. Dred anticipated his move and was waiting a block south of the store. The dimly lit street was a perfect spot for the two to meet. Dred located some hefty rocks and his expert aim extinguished two parking lot florescent lights to further accommodate the rendezvous. He grabbed Derek's arm as he turned the corner.

Before Dred had a chance to speak, Derek covered his mouth and opened his shirt, revealing the FBI wire. His focus changed directions, looking for Amanda. He relaxed a little when it was obvious no one was following.

Dred nodded. He reached into his pocket and pulled out a pad of paper, writing a quick cryptic note. 'I'm Dred, Elliott's old side-kick. Working with Marisa. When do you want to split?'

"Is she okay?" Derek's hands shook as he wrote. His stomach did a flip-flop.

"Fine. What's your plan?"

Derek thought he saw someone in the shadows and moved deeper into the foliage. "Too dangerous to talk. House wired." He grabbed Dred's collar and pulled close to his ear, whispering. He knew Marisa would be suspicious of any actions he made, so he was careful with his words. "Get me a throwaway phone. Leave it inside a newspaper on the bench by Macrae's, 6:00 a.m. tomorrow. Okay?"

Dred shook his head. "Marisa…"

Derek grabbed his arm and squeezed it hard. Stop, he motioned, and then demanded an answer, scribbling a quick note. "Did Marisa snatch the kid?"

"What kid?"

Derek questioned the quick response. Dred was a polished liar. Initially Dred had been head security officer for Elliott when their only crime was laundering cartel money through the Laughlin Casinos to Las Vegas. Later, Elliott expanded his criminal career to smuggling body parts from Mexico to Las Vegas and some drug activity. Elliott found Dred to be loyal, strong and void of any moral compass. He eventually ended up as Elliott's number one man, efficient in killing and torture. When Elliott managed to get away from the Bullhead police, Dred was by his side in setting up the human trafficking in Catalina He escaped before the business was shut down by the FBI.

Derek slid out of the dark and resumed his walk to Vons. *Liar. Liar.* It was obvious to Derek by Dred's expression that he knew about Zach, but what was not obvious was whether he had been told not to share any information with him. *Well, little sister, what are you up to?*

Chapter 31

STELLA FAITHFULLY TOOK her medication, presenting herself as a model patient. Compliant and complacent. By the third day the four point hard restraints had been removed, she was dressing herself and the counseling sessions with the psychiatrist were showing marked improvement. Violent temper swings were now history, and she interrelated with the other patients in a civil, friendly manner. She was moved from the twenty-four hour suicide watch cell and placed in a ward with two other women. The nurses at Seaside General Psychiatric Hospital in Costa Mesa helped with her unruly red hair, and teased her about her history of pole dancing, not knowing if that was part of her twisted memory or the truth.

Aunt Sharon walked into the room and sat beside Stella's bed. Her breathing was slow and regular so Sharon took advantage of the timing and accepted a call from Stella's brother, Greg. "What?" she whispered into her cell phone. "Kidnapped?" Sharon caught herself half-way through the second word. "Za...?" She shot a glance Stella's way to make sure she was still sleeping.

Stella steeled herself, trying to catch the rest of the muffled conversation. Her baby missing? The only other words Stella could understand were 'Two Harbors.' After Sharon finished the call, Stella waited a few minutes before mumbling and rolling over. "Oh, Aunt Sharon, I didn't hear you come in. So nice of you to visit." *You lying old bitch.*

The two women exchanged pleasantries for ten minutes and then Sharon excused herself saying she had a hair appointment. "I'll give Greg a call this afternoon. He worries so much about you."

"Thank you . Is there any word from the courts about my case? Has the judge granted me sole custody of Zach yet?" *See what you have to say now, bitch.*

Sharon leaned over the bed to kiss Stella goodbye, wondering if she had heard any part of the phone conversation. There would be hell to pay if Stella knew Zach was missing. "No word yet. Greg is keeping a close eye on everything, visits Zach each day. Says he's really growing fast." Sharon hated to lie but accepted the necessity of it. She patted Stella's hand and smiled. "Gotta go. I'll be back tomorrow, honey."

Lying is what your wrinkly old mouth does. I've got to get out of here. Find my baby. Why hasn't Josh called me? Stella's mind was erupting. Frantic images floated through the haze.

"Time for your meds, Stella." The ample nurse checked the label and handed the paper cup containing antipsychotics to Stella.

Stella smiled and held out her hand. She remembered to smile her most beguiling smile.

The nurse handed her a water chaser, and Stella promptly popped the pill in her mouth. "Okay, open up." Her mouth was checked to make sure she had swallowed the medication. "Good girl."

After the nurse left the room, Stella turned and popped the pill out of her mouth. *That's three doses missed. Feeling like my old self again. I'll make my move tonight.*

Midnight. Lights had been out for two hours and the nurse had made her rounds. Stella stared straight up to the ceiling, willing herself to stay awake. One o'clock. Time for another bed check.

Light from the open door spilled across the room. Stella concentrated on her breathing, not moving a muscle. The light disappeared and a soft screech from the nurse's rubber soled shoes filled the quiet void. The hospital was short staffed so the nurse was saddled with checking two floors. She scurried toward the elevator.

Stella rolled out of bed, stuffed pillows under the blankets, slipped out of her hospital pajamas and raided the closet. Sharon had brought a pair of jeans from home. She pulled them on but couldn't get them buttoned. She found her bra. Maternity size. Her breasts had finally dried up and were now mere whispers of their former glory. She layered three blouses and slipped into the hall. The nurse's station was empty. She pulled open all the drawers and found a purse and cellphone. Her foggy common sense said to cover her ass, so she left the nurse's station as she found it. Only one set of stairs. She knew the hospital set up and when she opened the ground floor door she was not surprised.

The night guard was dozing as usual, sitting in front of the hospital monitors. Stella slid into the hallway and walked brusquely toward the door to freedom. Five feet, four feet, three feet, two feet.

"Hello there young lady. May I help you?" The sleeping giant had awakened.

Shit. "I didn't want to bother you, but is there any way you could call me a cab?" She smiled and pulled the nurses' purse close to her side.

The guard stood and pushed a book toward her. "Sure thing, but you know the rules. Need to sign out." He smiled.

"Of course. So sorry." Stella turned the book around, glanced down at some of the registered names and picked one with a scribbly handwriting. She copied it and turned as the guard called for a cab. "Thanks." Out the door she walked and kept on walking, then trotting, then running toward the closest bar.

She locked the ladies restroom door and spread out the contents of the purse. Seventy dollars, a Visa card and an ATM card caught her eye. She searched through the checkbook and found a password. *Stupid woman. Making this too easy for me.* The bar's ATM machine spit out three hundred dollars, Stella called for a cab and gave directions to the Nautical Inn Bar in Newport, an old hangout.

Finding a grisly old sea captain that would take her to Catalina for a hundred dollars only took an hour and soon she was stepping on board his fishing vessel, heading home to Catalina, Josh and her baby.

Chapter 32

MEG WAS MIFFED when Dred, aka, David, aka Dave, cancelled their date. She'd found him both handsome and smart and decided to go all out to impress him. Now she ended up with no plans for the evening and an irritated attitude. She'd never been stood up before. Meg knew her own moods. It was either go home and pout or go out with a friend and have some fun. The second alternative sounded healthier so when the replacement bartender arrived Meg took off her apron and called her buddy, Rosie. "Just got stood up. You got plans for this evening?"

"Nah. Same ole, same ole."

"Let's meet at the pier and go see a movie. How 'bout that?"

"Sounds good. I can make it in twenty minutes. That work for you?"

"Yeah. I'll swing by Vons and pick up some junk food. Dinner sounds boring."

Rosie opened her desk drawer and dumped all of her files in. "Just cleaned off my desk, so see ya." She pulled her purse off the shelf and headed for the door, happy to now have plans. Meg always supplied an evening with surprises.

Meg and Rosie had been summer friends for years. Originally

from Orange County, Meg and her family would spend two weeks on Catalina and the rest of the summer at Bullhead City, Arizona. Rosie hadn't been around when Meg was abducted by Elliott, or when she had fallen for Derek, but last year when Elliott had his human trafficking scheme working on Catalina, Rosie had been caught up in the chaos. Both she and Meg were kidnapped, but survived, so they had history and loyalty all swirled up together. Best friends. As Meg turned the corner on Crescent, she bumped into Mr. Draper, a writer for the local paper. "Oh, so sorry."

"Always in a hurry, you little whipper-snapper. Say, missy. Got an update for an old newspaper dog? Anything going on with the baby kidnapping?"

Even though Meg was in a hurry, she took time for the old-timer. "Nothing that I know of, but I'll call you if I hear anything." She tried to leave.

"Any comments on your dip in the ocean yesterday?"

"Yeah, it was wet." She tried to push by him.

"Seen any ghosts at Catherine's lately? That's always copy."

"A couple said they saw her the other night, but that's the same night as the murder, so I guess she only deserves page two. I really got to get going." She finally dumped him and started toward Vons again. Rounding the corner, she caught a glimpse of the guy who stood her up. *What?* She stopped and then ducked back into the shadows of the corner building. *David? You asshole. Doesn't look like you're on an interview to me.*

Meg, being Meg, bristled. *What was he up to?* Instead of confronting him and dishing out a slice of verbal castration which would be her usual move, she decided to watch. There was another man talking to him, hiding in the bushes. She waited, listening intently, trying to pick up on any of the conversation. No sounds, just gestures. What? Getting stood up by another woman was maddening, but by a 'guy' was pretty disgusting, she thought. Their exchange was short and when the two men split up David headed up the street while the other man crossed the street to Vons. She watched. Under the street light his features were distinguishable. *Derek?*

After he entered the store, Meg headed back to Crescent Avenue and ducked into El Galleon to make a call. She waved off the bartender and settled in the back booth to call Amanda. "Hey, sis. Guess who I just saw."

"Meg, I really don't have a lot of time. Spill it." Amanda was at FBI headquarters pouring over aerial maps of the island.

"Derek."

"So? You knew he was here. Look, Meg, I don't have time to chit-chat, and if you're thinking of taking up with that guy again, forget it."

"He was meeting someone…surreptitiously, I might add." She waited, knowing her sister would pounce on that morsel.

"Spill it. Don't be a brat." Amanda dropped the map and sat, totally focusing on her sister's news.

Meg filled in the details and when she finished Amanda asked, "So the other guy is the new guy in your life? God. When will you learn?"

"Or catch a break?"

"Yeah, that too. This other guy, David. Describe him." Before Meg could start, Amanda had an idea of what she was going to hear.

"Six two or so, good build, brown hair, almost handsome. Nothing gross about him. No tats that I could see."

"Hey, you saw that snarky looking guy in court with Stella two days ago didn't you? Well, cleaned up, could they be one and the same?"

"The doper?" Meg grimaced a little, and imagined the weird guy without a beard. "Well, he and Stella went on the ghost tour the other night, I'm almost sure. They were both hooded up and freaky. Also saw him when she checked into Catherine's." She thought for a minute. "Yeah, could be." Meg felt perplexed as she realized she had tried to hook up with yet, another loser.

"Okay. Listen. We've been looking for him. He might be involved with Derek's sister, Marisa, and also with the kidnapping of Zach. Are you up for some intrigue?" Amanda knew the answer before asking. Intrigue was Meg's middle name.

"Lay it on me."

"Right. Honey up to this David guy. I'm sure he's one and the same as Dred. Let him take you to his house and look around. You know what to do. He's probably playing you too. But you're sure it was Derek he met?"

"Right down to the bulge in his pants that I remember."

"You are so gross." Amanda laughed. "Be safe and stay in touch. I'll let the department know what's going on. Love ya."

"Love ya, too." Meg disconnected, grabbed her purse and headed out of the bar, excited to be involved in another adventure with her sisters. She rushed through the bar door and bumped into an old lady with a white cane. "Sorry." She kept on going, heading for the pier, wondering what this turn of events said about her. *Another loser? Crap.*

Chapter 33

AT 6:00 A.M., Derek paused at the bench in front of McCrea's Hotel and picked up the covert newspaper with the burner cell phone hidden inside. He continued on his morning run with the phone snuggled tightly in his sweat pants. Later, when Derek's pocket started vibrating, he headed for the bathroom of his tiny house, the only room the FBI wasn't monitoring. He stripped down, took off the wire and turned on the shower.

"Hello?" There was no display on the phone so he answered with caution. "Who's there?"

"It's me, silly," Marisa said. "How the hell are you?"

Derek drew in deep breath. "Better now that I hear your voice. Shit. When you drop out of sight you do a good job of it."

"Had to. When they took you into custody I rented a car, drove to the border, walked over the bridge to Tijuana and disappeared."

Derek nodded. She'd stuck to their age-old plan.

"Ended up in Cabo after a short stint in Ensenada. I miss you, baby brother." So far, the truth.

"Me too." Derek realized he really did miss her. They had been so close in their young years, a study in survival where they reacted as one when attacked by their maniacal mother. He'd always felt

Elliott was the only recipient of their mother's crazy DNA, but now with the changes in Marisa's actions he had reason to pause. "Glad you had a fun time while I was rotting in jail."

"Now, now. Don't sulk. I'm here and ready to move ahead. We need to meet in person and get everything set up. You'll have to fill me in on what plans the FBI have for us."

"That's going to be difficult. I'm wearing an ankle monitor 24/7 and there's total in-house surveillance, someone usually follows me when I go out."

"Not to worry. Here's what we're going to do. You met Dred. By the way, his Catalina name is David. The fact that he could pass for you is no mistake. He'll need to get a different haircut but the rest is easy."

"Are you planning an escape? God, sis, that'll never work."

"You need to listen."

Her tone changed from light-hearted to menacing in one breath making Derek tightened his grip on the phone. She sounded like Elliott when he was pissed or ready to launch a lethal attack. *Why hadn't he seen this before? Was it possible Marisa was a reincarnated Elliott? What did that mean for him if he moved forward on a clean life?* "Go ahead, I'm listening."

"Dred rented the house behind yours. Used a fictitious name. When the time is right, he'll crawl through your bathroom window, switch out the ankle monitor, take a shower… You know, all that stuff. We'll do it after dark. You let him know where the cameras are located in the house and he'll keep his head down."

"The FBI guys are sharp. I'm not sure it'll work. And, there are bars on the bathroom window."

"Not any more. Dred loosened all of the screws. It'll only take seconds to remove and replace it. Took care of it last night."

"How did you know where I live?"

"He followed you home the other night after you met at Vons."

"Still…" The crossroad was here for Derek. Which way to go? Stalling for time, and not wanting to raise questions in Marisa's mind, Derek acquiesced. "Okay, but what if…"

"If something goes wrong, then Dred's our fall guy and you and

I will take off. Just have to change a few plans. We still have Gilbert and the seaplane if all else fails."

"What kind of plans? Hey, I need to know what's going on."

"Later. Don't be so negative. It'll work."

The phone went silent. Marisa strained, waiting for his approval, but could only hear Derek's deep breathing.

"You're on board with this, aren't you? You aren't cooperating with the Feds are you?"

"God, no. You know better than that." Derek wasn't sure if his voice was convincing or not.

"Good. I'll be in touch." Marisa disconnected the line and leaned back in her chair, steepling her fingers until she realized that Elliott used to do that. "I wonder, little brother," she uttered out loud, "I wonder."

"Oh, shit," was all Derek could say.

Chapter 34

THE FISHING BOAT maneuvered a soft landing, dug a v-shaped gouge in the wet sand and cautiously slid into shore. The captain shut down the engines and tilted them up before they got stuck in the sand. "Hold on, gal. No need to jump yet. Too deep."

Stella tied the laces of her tennis shoes together, draped them around her neck and jumped into the shallow water as the boat came to an abrupt stop. She ignored the old man's comments and threw a hundred dollar bill his way. Her mind was whirling. Being on the island brought her closer to Josh and Zach. First stop would be the general store for supplies and then find her baby. She walked the half mile with a newfound energy and purpose, humming all the way. The morning sun broke through the clouds and painted a light blush on her cheeks.

"Do you have any receiving blankets, oh, and bottles? Diapers?" Stella was having a hard time focusing on the needed supplies. She would stop and stare at anyone walking in the store, confusion mounting. Where was she again? Where was Josh?

"Stella?" Sally, an old friend, was surprised to see her. They had history, kindergarten through high school. Everyone in town had noticed as Stella's mental problems grew to gargantuan proportions, but knew that her brother was watching out for her. People would cross the street rather than make eye contact with her.

Sally peered at her. "Didn't know you were back on the island. Another court appearance?"

Stella glared and wiggled a finger her way. "None of your damn business. Now do your job and help me get some of this baby shit." Stella walked down the 'on sale' aisle, among leftover items from the Christmas season, and stopped. "What the hell you think you're doing?" She snatched up a life size infant doll, wrapped in plastic. She pressed a button on its hand by accident. The toy cried out, "*mama*." Stella ripped the plastic away from the cardboard box and yanked the baby doll from the package. She cuddled the toy and screamed. "My God, you could have killed my baby. What were you thinking." She nestled the toy close to her breast. "There, there, sweet cakes. Everything's going to be fine now that I've found you."

Sally was speechless. She moved toward the counter, hoping to make a call to Greg or the police.

Stella grabbed a baby bottle, a can of formula, diapers, a receiving blanket and threw them in a wheelbarrow displayed by the front door. "I'll take this baseball cap, too." She rolled the wheelbarrow to the counter and pulled out her wallet.

When presented with the nurses' credit card, Sally stopped short of challenging Stella. Another outburst could end up with a physical altercation. Everyone knew when Stella got upset, someone would suffer. "Twenty-nine dollars and thirty-four cents," Sally offered up.

Stella inserted the card, typed in the password and waited as Sally bagged the small items. "It really sucks that this is the only store on this side of the island. It's shitty." She grabbed the credit card and bagged items, threw them back in the wheelbarrow and picked up her 'baby' she'd gently placed on the counter. She screamed at Sally, "Order some better baby shit. I'll be back tomorrow." She raised the handles on the wheelbarrow, pushed through the door and started down the street. She headed toward Lobster Bay, the most beautiful beach on Catalina where she and Josh had made love years ago.

Sally tried to notify Greg, but got voice mail. "Greg. This is Sally at Two Harbors. You need to get your ass over here. Stella's back in town and really crazy. Call me."

Chapter 35

THE AERIAL DROP went off as planned. Marisa and Miguel sat in the jeep watching the plane circle, change altitude and drop the packages eight feet from the gypsum mark. "Great, Miguel, hurry. Start the Jeep. Let's grab the stuff." She signaled to the truck behind to follow. "We never know who else might be watching." It was her first attempt at aerial transportation, and Marisa was unexpectedly nervous. It was daylight and although they had selected an area that the cartel didn't use, it was chancy. She touched the AK47 nestled at her feet, pulled her sunglasses down and peered through the road dust as they approached the site. "I'll cover you while you load the truck. Apurte." She stood at guard next to the truck, rifle ready to fire at any infraction.

Three men jumped out of the covered truck and scurried toward the cargo. The packages were separated by weight and tightly bound in forty-two separate packages. Its mid-grade street value was around $1400-$2000 a pound. A minimal amount of cocaine was included in this drop since the suppliers were not sure if they wanted to cross the cartel to do business with Marisa. That was another reason they didn't ship their hydro high grade marijuana. She was disappointed with the small amount of coke, understood their hesitancy, but didn't like it. She consoled herself by calculating the profit for the day.

When the shipment was secured, Marisa climbed back in the passenger seat and felt a sense of relief. "Okay, now head back to the cabin at Palisades." She tucked the rifle between her knees and continued scanning the surroundings for any nameless eyes. This was all new to her. Her confidence grew as she got closer to the house, feeling that Derek would be pleased with her first run. Not only was she the CFO of Elliott's old business, but now she was the CEO of her own.

Dred was waiting for the crew when they arrived and opened Marisa's Jeep door. Hoping for some expression of affection he reached for her hand. She pulled away.

"Have you got the help lined up?" She looked around then spotted a small group of men milling around the garage. The Catalina job had presented itself so prematurely that Marisa didn't have time to import Elliott's old crew. "Are they trustworthy?" She knew the temptation would be gigantic for betrayal. She didn't possess Elliott's clout yet.

Elliott had been feared by everyone. They knew his penchant for torture. "Waterboarding is kindergarten stuff to El Jefe," one helper had been heard to say. Stripping a body of its skin was one of his favorite means of keeping his men in line, a sharp pencil piercing the ear drum, along with cutting out eyeballs, sticking them down his victim's throat and then letting the sharks take care of the rest. Fear was a great motivator and Elliott was an expert in the field.

Marisa eyed the men. "Where did you find them?"

"No worries. I checked around and hooked up with them on the mainland before I came over. It took a couple of calls. They're good. I worked with them in Newport. They flew over this morning. How did the drop go?"

"Sweet. Let's get a move on. We need to get these packages separated and ready for the Catalina Express and the boat heading north." She tossed her rifle to Miguel and headed for the truck.

Four hours later the drugs were re-packaged, placed in roll-around suitcases, and circulation notes placed on each bag. Marissa carefully inspected the haul, and watched as Dred took over.

"Hey. Those cases go into my Jeep. Assholes, can't you read?" Finally satisfied, Dred started for the Jeep filled with the drugs designated for Orange County. Time was getting short for the scheduled meet-up with the college kids at Hermit Gulch Campground. Fifteen pre-selected college-aged students had been hired to meet him there, pick up their stash and head back on the Express at four in the afternoon. Some of the drugs were held back to be taken to the airport and loaded onto a private plane headed for Arizona. The rest would go by boat to Santa Barbara.

Dred was exhausted from the labor-intensive afternoon. The orange sun had been tossing rays around their camp for an hour and he knew he had to hit the road or chance missing all of his connections. "You're spreading my talent a little thin, Marisa. I've got to meet up with the distributor within the next hour and a half."

"Quit being such a baby." She had no time for his 'poor-me' attitude. "Be sure and collect the money from our contacts before you hand out any drugs. Should be a good day's work. When you finish, get cleaned up and go hustle Meg again. Her feathers are probably ruffled about being stood up. I guess you can handle that? Put on your charming self?" She gave him a sideward glance.

"Never had any complaints 'til I met you." He didn't smile.

Dred hadn't seen any money in a month, other than collecting it for Marisa and handing it over. "Need some cash to take her out. This is pissing me off. It's like I'm on an allowance. Getting tired of it." His cocksure attitude had reappeared, and he leaned against the jeep with a stubborn expression.

Marisa had seen this coming and was prepared. "Here's six hundred, nothing over a twenty. Make it last for a while, and watch your drinking. Can't be too careful around Meg. She's smart."

"Yeah, right. You keep saying that." He shoved the cash in his jeans' pocket and headed for the truck. "What time do I meet Derek?"

"He'll open the bathroom window after midnight, 1:15 or so. Be careful, and for God's sake be quiet. We can't afford to get caught."

"You worried about my ass or yours?" He knew she wouldn't answer that question, would probably throw some sex-thing at him instead.

Shit, time to placate the bastard again, Marisa cautioned, reading his body language. She hooked her left arm around Dred's neck and maneuvered her hand down the front of his pants. Only two strokes and he responded, unwillingly. "Come on, honey. We're so close to having this work, let's not get pissy. Only a few more days of hard work and Derek will be free, and our new drug route will be set up."

"Then what? Who rides off into the sunset?"

"The three of us, of course. Maybe Europe for a few weeks? Whatever you want."

His erection was throbbing by now and totally constricted by his tight jeans. He pulled her hand out, bent her backward and kissed her hard. "Don't play me, Marisa, or you'll wish you hadn't. Elliott practically raised me and I know how you've been trained. Don't let my hard-on fool you. I'm not as dumb as you think."

"I know all that. I care about you." She nuzzled his neck and ran her tongue around his ear.

"We'll see. As far as I'm concerned you only care about Derek and money, and maybe not in that order." He pushed her back, and crawled into the Jeep. "I'll call you when I unload all of this shit and before I meet with Meg." He didn't look at her. He knew she didn't care.

Chapter 36

ON ONE SIDE OF DEREK'S rental house was the FBI surveillance team capturing all of his activities and on the other side of his house was another furnished rental. The new tenant had paid cash up front for the full month, and brought in only one piece of luggage, some hand tools and an action-activated closed circuit camera setup. It was battery operated so installation took only a short time. Instead of hooking up the device to monitor the action in front of the house, it was mounted on an extension platform to the weather-vane atop the garage, focusing over the top of Derek's fence, into his backyard. This was the tricky part of the installation since it had to be completed at night, when the neighbors' inquisitive eyes wouldn't see. All images were transmitted to a laptop inside the house.

His interest was piqued about the squalling brat, who was now in the care of Gilbert's wife. As prearranged, she had transmitted videos to his laptop. He watched as she changed his diaper. *Good. He looks like a healthy specimen. If I don't have to use him as leverage to annihilate Meg and her family, I'll sell him on the black market.* Satisfied with this part of his plan he moved on to the other ongoing plan.

Yesterday's boating scenario involving Meg had not gone as

intended. A temporary setback in his overall design. He studied Meg's image on the screen as his hand crawled into his sweat pants. Her tight butt, tiny waist, ample breasts and that beguiling smile exemplifying her joy of life. He closed his eyes and hit his mental recall button taking him back to Bullhead City last year when she was his. On the train. Languishing in her nakedness he watched as she drifted in and out of the drugs. The twilight drug. True bliss with no memory to content with. So unaware, so cooperative. The perverted sex, the torture, the smell of her flesh burning. Finally he returned to the present, watched her soar through the clouds as his hand finished the job. He smiled and breathlessly leaned back in the chair. "Nice." The psychopath was pleased with his handiwork.

Chapter 37

AMANDA CALLED A JOINT MEETING of the FBI and Catalina Division of the LA County Sheriff's Department and waited patiently for the last agent to arrive. She noticed how the two departments' physical appearances differed. The Catalina cops were deeply tanned from the daily challenges of the island while the FBI men and women, although dressed in island attire, where sparkling white. "We may need to run you guys through a tanning booth," she joked. That got a round of laughter from the crew. "You're going to have a hard time mixing with the locals with your lily-white skin." Both Josh and Greg were present along with Rachael but when Meg entered the room they showed signs of confusion and annoyance. They knew what a pest she could be, and other than owning a PI license she had no business in their business.

"What're you doing here, punky?" Josh moved over and put an arm around her shoulders.

"I invited her. She has some intel to share. Go ahead, Meg." Amanda moved to the back of the room.

Meg, who was never shy about the spotlight, walked to the podium, immediately taking charge of the room. "There's a new guy in town and he's spending some time trying to pick me up." She paused for the laugh that she knew would come.

"Like every other guy on the island? What's new about that?" Greg grinned and everyone in the room knew that he fit squarely in the middle of that category. The room relaxed.

"Down Romeo. Anyway, the first time I saw him he was in disguise, like a druggie. He was with Stella on the ghost tour, in the courthouse on the day of Zach's trial, and then again with Stella when checking into Catherine's on the night before the murder and kidnap. The next time I saw him, he was clean shaven, hair styled, nice clothes and came to my rescue at the bar when I was getting behind serving beer. I didn't put the two guys together until later."

"So, what's the big deal," chipped in an officer. "He starts with a wacko red head—sorry, I know she's your sister, Greg—then cleans up and tries to pick you up. So what?"

"Let her finish." Amanda was tired of the interruptions and showed it.

"We had a date the other evening, but he cancelled, saying he had an interview for a bartending job. I decided to go out anyway, but on the way I saw him, by Vons, talking to someone that was intent on hiding in the bushes. I hid too. When David left, oh, that's what he said his name was, but Stella called him Dred, anyway, I stayed back and watched the other guy. It was Derek Turner."

"Whoa." Josh spoke up. "I thought he was under surveillance. What gives?" He flashed a quizzical look Amanda's way.

"He is now. Didn't connect the monitor until the second day on the island."

"Could you hear any of their conversation? Did they pass anything off to each other?" Josh continued.

"A real short conversation, and I wasn't close enough to hear anything. Actually, I don't think they spoke. Wrote some stuff down. But it did look like Dred handed him something small. Not sure."

"Okay, Meg, thanks for coming in. We appreciate your take on this guy. We'll be in touch." Amanda was trying to get her out of the room so she could continue her briefing.

"What? That's it? Since when do I get cut out of the loop?"

"This is an ongoing FBI investigation. If we need you, we'll call." Amanda's stern face emphasized her resolve.

"Bullshit. Either I stay now, or I'm through helping. Don't forget, Dred is trying to play me and if you let me, I can meet with Derek and find out what he's really up to. We were very close in Bullhead… and he's still on the guilt trip for the shit that Elliott put me through." She waited, not ready to be denied her right to stay.

"Rachael, Josh, Meg, Greg and Agent Shaw, let's talk for a minute in the hall. The rest of you memorize the pictures of Derek, Dred and Marisa." Amanda handed a stack of papers to the Sergeant. "This just came in. Background check on this Dred guy. Read it over. Meg took a picture of him. We ran it through the photo analysis and came up with his rap sheet." She waved the paper in the air. "Interesting reading. Review your copy and we'll check it out in a minute. Come on you guys." The group left the room.

Amanda immediately took over. "Look Meg, there's no way I'm putting you in danger again. You've been through too much already."

"Should be my decision, if the FBI will allow it. I don't want to carry a gun or kill anybody, but at least I can be your eyes and ears."

"Rachael. Any input?"

"You know mom will be pissed, but I think Meg can handle this. As long as she's only reporting to you or me and doesn't go ballistic on us." She looked at her younger sister. "How much revenge is still kicking around? You still thinking of getting even with Derek?"

"He did help me escape from the sub, and did take a bullet for me. I can let the rest go."

Amanda was hesitant, but decided to move forward. "Any other thoughts?" There was some mumbling and 'what ifs' that floated around the group, but all eventually agreed to include Meg. Once back with the full team, Amanda explained how the process of including Meg would work and then moved on. "Agent Shaw, fill us in on Dred's background."

"Dred, aka David, has other aliases, but his legal name is David Allen Jennings." Shaw rattled through the statistics. "Born in Los

Angeles, December 10, 1982, professional parents, went to boarding school, college, dropped out, joined the fast LA/Hollywood group, drugs, violence has followed him. Never convicted of anything, but brought in for gang rape, forgery, burglary and murder."

Amanda had been following along with the oral report, but straightened with a start and asked, "What was the year and circumstances of the gang rape?"

"2001. He was at UCLA. He and some guys were accused of gang raping a USC student. No conviction."

Rachael and Meg simultaneously straightened in their chairs and both shot a startled look to Amanda. She shook her head slightly and they let it drop. That was the year Amanda had been thrown into a van after a USC/UCLA basketball game, brutally gang raped, and tossed out of the van like a piece of garbage in front of the sorority house. The police had never caught the rapists. Amanda took another hard look at Dred's mug shot. There was something familiar about his eyes. She let out a quick breath, noticed by her sisters only, and decided to move on for now.

"Nice guy you'll be hanging with Meg." Josh gave her a stern look. "What's the circumstances on the murder?"

"Thought he might have been involved with kidnap and murder of three women in Santa Rosa, but was cleared." Agent Shaw started to continue but was interrupted by Rachael.

"Wait. Does it give a year or time frame? No. Let me guess. Began ten years ago and ended seven years ago. Then nothing?"

Agent Shaw shuffled through the papers. "Yeah, how did ya know?"

This time all three sisters straightened and locked eyes. They turned to Josh and then Rachael dropped her voice and with a guttural sound, spoke. "The serial killer disappeared and reappeared in Bullhead. Dred must have been Elliott's right-hand man."

Meg stifled her initial alarm and decided to disarm everyone before they had a chance to try and pull her out of the team again. "Okay. We've got a clear picture of this Dred guy now. It makes me more determined to get this guy. Dred must be a follower and is probably working with Marisa."

"Who's Marisa?" A new member of the task force asked.

"Derek's sister. Elliott's sister and confident," replied Meg. "That's her picture."

Amanda was writing notes, names, dates and arrows on the white board. She wrote Marisa's name in huge capital letters, dead center of the board. "She's the key. Catch Marisa and we fold their tent." Her hand pushed the marker across the flat surface of the board. The black line drew a circle around Marisa and shot off to the picture of Zach and then to the narcotics case. "Marisa is the key. Get her and we close all of the cases."

Rachael could wait no longer. She had hoped that Josh would broach the subject, but when he didn't she went for it. "Well, now that we have direction on that, what about Zach? Do you have any leads on the baby?"

Amanda looked apologetic. "Sorry. The Bureau is actively working the case. This is their reasoning. Since there has been no contact from the kidnappers asking for ransom or other considerations, we had to look at other motives. If Zach is still alive, and we have no reason to believe he isn't, then the motive must be revenge or leverage. Also, since this Dred character was staying at the hotel the night of the abduction and affiliated with Stella, there might be another motive. Did she hire him to snatch the baby? These are all possibilities. Stella is confined to a mental institution now, so she didn't have access to the baby. We're watching Dred on both cases. Looks like they might merge. Any other questions?"

"Is there any way to pinpoint all new babies on the Island? Maybe get some help from the hospital or Title Company?" asked Greg.

"We have someone checking on that now."

Rachael looked for some reaction from Josh. Nothing. "Guess that's it. If there's anything I can do, let me know. I realize I don't have any jurisdiction on the Island which might come in handy. I can kick a door down without a warrant." She smiled as the room applauded.

Chapter 38

FOLLOWING THE MEETING, Amanda drove her cart to Derek's house. *A meeting with Dred? His decision to tell me about the meeting will either cement our relationship or I'll know for certain that he never had any plans of cooperating with the FBI.* She gripped the steering wheel a little tighter.

The meeting with Marisa was scheduled for 1:00 a.m. and Derek needed that amount of time to weigh his options. He didn't know what Marisa's plans were, where the FBI stood at this point, or if he wanted to flip or flop. The sun poured through the front door as Amanda entered. How much of a roll did Meg play in his decision? How long would it be before she would forgive him? If ever.

"Morning. Another perfect day in paradise. What's up, Amanda? I didn't know we had a meeting planned so early, if fact, I thought you said you wouldn't darken my door again."

Amanda went for direct. "I need to update the team and wondered if anything new has transpired. Has Marisa tried to make contact with you?"

Derek expected the question, but acted a little surprised. He had pulled the battery out of the cell phone that Dred had given him, and erased the one call he had made to Marisa. He knew the FBI would be following him. "As a matter of fact, when I was walking to Vons last night, this strange guy approached me. Was wearing a hoodie that I thought was weird cause it was 85 degrees."

"And?"

"He bumped into me, pushed me back in the bushes, and handed me a cell phone."

"Did he say anything?"

"Mumbled with a lot of sign language. Said, 'call your sister,' and then walked away. Weird dude."

"Did you recognize him?"

"No."

Liar.

"Never saw the creep before. Rather rough around the edges." Amanda had always maintained a poker face with Derek, but he thought he saw a glimmer of gratification going on there some- where behind her eyes.

"Did you call her?"

"I didn't 'cause I wanted to ask you what to say. Shall we call her now?"

"Give me the phone." Amanda checked the phone, pulled up the number he was supposed to call and called her IT man on her own phone. "We're going to be calling this number in a minute. Put a trace on it."

Amanda handed the phone to Derek. "Go ahead and call her. We need information about any attempt to break you out and what's going on with the drug business. Has she made any contact directly with South America or is she handling only stuff from Mexico?"

"Okay." Derek dialed the phone and when it connected he immediately started talking. "Hey sis, that you? I was surprised that you located me so quickly."

Marisa was sharp and went along with the ruse. "I've had my feelers out for a while, but a source said you ended up on Catalina. Are you alone?"

"Of course."

"Why didn't you call me last night when you got the phone? Made me nervous."

"FBI showed up at Vons when I was leaving, walked me home and came in. They've got monitors all over the house. I stepped outside the back door so I could talk. So, what's the deal? Where are you?"

"Close enough. The deal depends on you. The last time we talked we were both tired of our lifestyle. On the boat when Elliott was running that human trafficking scheme, remember? You decided to go straight. Got all heroic. Helped Meg in the submarine and Elliott shot you in the leg. Seems like an eternity ago. I haven't talked to you since then except for that brief hello in Mexico."

Amanda shot a stern look his way.

"Well, I've made a deal with the FBI that was supposed to take care of the two of us, but you didn't show for the meeting, so they've pulled back on the deal. It's up in the air now. If you cooperate and turn yourself in, then I get a damn good deal with them. They're hell bent on stamping out the drug trafficking. Want to catch the Mexican Mafia and stop the drugs from moving north." He hesitated to push any further.

"Why do they want me? That was Elliott's gig all the way. Can you trust them?"

Derek dropped his chin down and his eyes drifted from left to right. "Trust? Well I'm sure they trust me as much as I trust them. The difference is that they have me under lock and key. So, do you have a plan?"

Amanda was looking for a commitment she could live with. Almost not breathing.

Marisa knew the FBI was listening. "I was going to meet up like I said, I flew up from Mexico, but at the last minute, I was afraid if they had both of us they would retract their offer and we'd both be in jail. Not sure what to do, bro. It wouldn't be that difficult to break you out, but we don't want to live our lives looking over our shoulders for Elliott's crimes. We've suffered enough from his perversion." She waited.

Derek was proud of the way his sister was playing her part and could hardly wait to see her in person. His loyalty got a big boost. A leap with Marisa. To freedom? "I know. Let's sleep on it and I'll call you tomorrow with my thoughts. So the choices are?"

Marisa took a minute to organize her thoughts. "One, I break you out, we disappear and live on Elliott's money as wanted people, or two we go along with the FBI, entrap the Mexican Mafia and identify all of Elliott's gang which could stretch as far as the Columbia cartel. That would probably entail witness protection, otherwise we'd be fair game. Neither is great, but I'll think it through tonight." Marisa knew Derek cared for Meg and wondered how she would play in his final decision. She decided to jump that hurdle now. Why wait? It would be like waiting for the second shoe to drop. "Given any thought to Meg? How your decision, our decisions, would affect your relationship? Is there a relationship?"

Amanda tipped her head and gave Derek an unblinking look.

"The jury's out on that. I love her but afraid it's not reciprocal. I need some time with her to be able to answer that."

"Can't see her too excited about running from the law." She waited. "Think about that while making your decision."

"I will. Look, before you go. The FBI keeps bugging me about a baby kidnapping. Do you know anything about that?"

Marisa faltered. "Baby? Nope. I don't even like kids, but I'll keep my ear to the ground. Details?"

"It's a cop's kid, infant. Was snatched from the hotel the other night. FBI keeps pushing me on it. Any ideas?"

"Nope. Who the hell would want a kid? Not my cup of tea. Look, gotta go."

"Me too, love you, sis."

"Love you too, bro. Miss you like crazy." The connection ended.

Amanda felt in her bones it was almost a scripted conversation, but gave Derek one more shot at being totally forthcoming. She reasoned that he did come up with a good excuse for not calling Marisa sooner which was a positive point on his part, but with the intel on Dred, he must have recognized him and lied about that. One foot in the grave, one out. "She wasn't too convincing about the baby." When Derek didn't respond, she continued. "Okay, I'll come over tomorrow and we'll make the next and final call. She'll have to decide by then." She picked up her purse and started for the door. "By the way. Meg is here on the island and bartending at Catherine's. For some unknown reason, she has forgiven you and really wants to see you. It's her life, and I told her that as far as I was concerned you're a felon and should be in jail. But since you saved her life…well, she is much more forgiving than I would ever be. And nicer, too."

Derek wondered, true or false? "I'd like to see her and talk. I'll stop by the bar this afternoon. Thanks." He felt a slight tug at his heart strings.

"Well, be careful and tread lightly. You know Meg well enough to know that she has a powerful punch if she gets pissed."

He recalled the time she had slugged him on the yacht, a punch that had doubled him over. He'd deserved it. "Yeah. I remember."

Amanda held out her hand. "I'll be taking the phone with me."

"What if she calls? How am I going to explain it?"

"It'll go to voice mail and you can make an excuse for it later. You're talented that way."

He handed over the phone and she left. Once outside she used her personal phone and called Meg getting only voice mail. "Derek has been set up to meet with you. Lemme know how it goes."

Chapter 39

MEG PICKED UP AMANDA'S MESSAGE during her first break and absentmindedly served drinks for the next two hours. It was lunch time when Dred showed up at the bar to relieve Meg. "Hey, thanks for helping. Guess I can't be mad at you for standing me up the other night when you're nice enough to relieve me for lunch."

"No problem. I've got another interview tonight. Maybe I can land a job, otherwise I've got to get back to the mainland. Money's running out." He walked behind the bar and tied on an apron.

Meg watched closely as Derek entered Catherine's bar to see if there was any sign of recognition between the two men. Nothing. "Hey, Derek. Over here." Seeing him unnerved her, but she was strong enough to not let it show. "I'm just finishing up my shift. Oh, this is David, he's my relief. Also looking for a job if you know of one."

The two men shook hands. Nothing. "Sorry, old man. I could probably help you out in L.A., but this really isn't my turf." Derek turned, dismissing David. "I've got my cart out front. We can stop at Jack's and pick up some food if you feel like lunch."

"Not hungry. A ride home will be fine."

"Shall we go?" He held the bar door open for her and touched her back as she walked by.

Meg smiled, remembering his good manners. That was one of the things that attracted Meg to Derek in the first place, good manners, along with good looks, sense of humor, intelligence, education, and on and on. She never could figure out why their budding relationship had come to an abrupt halt after the kissing, feeling, and nakedness on the beach. After that, then nothing. She knew he had feelings for her. But something had happened and, of course, now she knew it was demands from his demented brother, Elliott. While Derek didn't set her up for the kidnap and rape, he should have known it was coming. They were brothers. He betrayed her and now he was back in her life.

"Let's drive up Wrigley Terrace Road. We'll get a gorgeous view of Avalon and a breeze should be coming up about now." Meg was playing it almost friendly, but guarded. She had an assignment.

They drove in silence, both a little uncomfortable with the pending conversation. When they came to a secluded outlet, he parked the cart "Come on." He took her hand and helped her step out of the cart. "Let's take a walk. Catch a view of Avalon."

Disabling the cart was a simple task. It was an uncomplicated machine. All the man had to do was cut the brake fluid line. Gravity would take care of the rest. After starting the cart the unsuspecting driver would release the parking brake and apply the brakes when starting downhill. Fluid gone, brakes gone. Crash. Perfect scenario. Once the line was cut, the man put a squirt of Gorilla glue on the passenger seat and moved away into the bushes, appearing and disappearing with stealth-like precision.

"Come on. I've got things to do." Meg was impatient to go. She wasn't comfortable in Derek's presence yet and was beginning to feel pressure from his closeness. She leaned against the nearest rock and crossed her arms.

He stopped her. "I've always cared for you, Meg. If things were different, I think we had a chance of a life together. You're exactly what I've always wished for in a partner, beautiful, smart, sexy, funny. Is there's any chance of that happening?" So much was riding on her answer. "I want there to be no mistake about my intentions. We've pussy-footed around this too long." He held her by the shoulders. "Can you let the past go?" He released his grip when she tensed.

Oh, dear. He's said everything I wanted to hear. Can't forget my mission. He's already lied today by not recognizing Dred. She didn't back away and maintained eye contact. Her gaze bore a hole in Derek's confession. "Wow. You know how to turn a lady's head. However, not mine, since I'm no lady. Too much, too late, Derek." She had rehearsed this scene many times. "Two things. One: There was a time that a picket fence and rug rats with you at my side was an appealing thought. Not anymore. Two: It will be a cold day in hell before I ever trust you again." The first half was true. The second, not so much.

Derek anticipated her reaction and smiled. "Well, I didn't think you'd grab and kiss me, although I hoped you would. But I don't consider that a final 'no,' so excuse me if I keep trying. I'm ready to slay any dragon that gets in my way."

Meg broke out in laughter. "You are so stupid sometimes." Mixed emotions didn't allow her to talk any more. She had a raging urge to kiss him, hard and long. *Damn.* Sensing the futility of their conversation, Meg walked forward and got in the cart. "Let's go."

Derek started the cart, released the brake and pushed on the accelerator. The first challenge presented itself immediately as they headed downhill to Lower Wrigley Terrace Road.

"Slow down. You're going way too fast. You'll tip us over." Meg shot him a worried glance. She had been driving the carts for years and knew their limitations.

"No brakes." He pumped frantically. "Jump," he yelled as the cart gained speed, recklessly fishtailing down the steep road, heading toward an 'S' curve.

Meg grabbed the upright with her left hand and tried to leap, but she was stuck to the seat. "Can't, I'm stuck." She wrestled with her shorts, trying to tear them off.

Derek held the steering wheel with his left hand and tried to push Meg but she didn't budge. "Hold on," he yelled as he whipped the wheel to the left. "Tree."

The errant golf cart crashed into a stubborn Eucalyptus tree. The electric piece of metal bounced back and rolled over toward the passenger side and died. Derek was pinned behind the steering wheel and Meg was jammed forward, head smashed against the dash.

"Meg, Meg. You okay?" Derek unsnapped his seat belt and rolled to the right, trying to steady himself before falling into Meg. The cart shifted left. Meg moaned.

"Shit." He rotated in the small seat and kicked the half-door open. The cart started to slip downhill. Gathering all his strength he grabbed the roll bar, pushed his way through the opening, and hurried around to help Meg.

Blood was dripping down her face, into her eyes, but Meg was conscious. "Geez, Derek What happened?" She struggled with her seat belt. "I need some help."

Rock solid, strong, bold Meg asking for help was an earth-shattering moment. Derek leaned across her body and unhooked the belt. "Put your arms around my neck."

"My pants are stuck to the seat. That's why I didn't jump. Can you take them off?"

Even though he knew the timing was off, Derek couldn't resist. It was the old, crooked, devilish smile that crept across his face. "I've been waiting over a year to undress you, and wow, here we are. My pleasure."

They both openly laughed as he leaned across her, unbuttoned her cutoffs and tried to pull her out of the shorts. "That's not going to work." Derek stood back scrutinizing the situation.

"Well, come on, hero. It's not brain surgery. Jump in the back seat and pull me up. My legs don't bend sideways." Meg was enjoying Derek's inability to solve the problem.

He hopped in the back seat. She raised her arms so he could lift her.

"Wiggle."

"I am," yelled Meg. She was laughing so hard the tears collected.

More minutes passed as they both wrestled with the absurd, and finally Meg slipped out of her shorts and stood there in her purple thong underwear. "Really glad I didn't go commando," she muttered.

"You sure you're okay?"

Meg rolled her head around, lifted her shoulders, shook her hips and answered, "Yup. All parts are still moving."

Derek snapped a quick picture on his cell phone.

"Don't you dare post that on Facebook, you creep. You pervert."

"Don't worry. This will only be added to my private Meg album. Hope to show our kids someday."

"Oh, give it a break, Derek." The words were admonishing, but the heart was smiling. She found her cell phone on the floor of the cart and dialed. "Rach. Geez. You'll never believe what happened."

Chapter 40

STELLA SPENT THE AFTERNOON gathering firewood in the cove and apologizing to her pseudo baby. "Sorry momma doesn't have any milk for you." She looked down at her flat breasts and wept. She pulled the pacifier from the toy's mouth and pushed in a bottle. "That will have to do for now. When Josh arrives, we'll pack up and go home. Your daddy is wonderful. He will love you just like I do." She sat on a rock, digging her toes into the warm sand, rocking the doll back and forth, humming as the last rays of the sun went to bed. She paused. "Did you hear that?"

The moon's first light rays were floating across the silent ocean, presenting a beguiling dance for Stella's world. She heard soft music. The three Sirens were singing their woeful song to the wayward sailors.

"Oh, Zach. Josh is here. Do you hear him? He's waiting for us." She bundled up the plastic doll and waded into the inviting Pacific. "Wait, Josh, we're coming."

Chapter 41

JOSH PULLED THE EARLY SHIFT and managed three arrests before noon. Rowdy vacationers trying to bend the rules. Since Avalon was a resort designation, the police were encouraged to work with the offenders especially the drunk and disorderly. It was nearing seven by the time he changed and reached Rachael's house. "I'm coming in." He opened the screen door and entered without knocking.

Rachael was in the kitchen sweating over a pot of boiling water, watching the spaghetti boil, hoping for the point of al dente. "I'm in the kitchen." She took the hand towel and cleared the tiny beads of sweat collecting above her eyebrows. "Cookin' for my main man." She shot a dazzling smile at him as he rounded the corner.

Her baggy T-shirt displayed a quote 'annoy me at your own risk' and her short shorts revealed enough butt to generate Josh's famous crooked smile. "Umm. Nice."

"So you got the hots for spaghetti?"

"I got the hots for the cook." He walked around the cooking island and stood behind her, both hands reaching under the T-shirt, heading north.

"Apparently you didn't read the T-shirt."

"Am I annoying you?" He started kissing her neck and nuzzling through her pony tail.

She turned off the stove and wiggled around to face him. "Screw the noodles."

"That's my girl." He pulled the T-shirt up and she raised her arms to facilitate the process. "Oh, what a bad girl. No bra?"

"I have evil intentions. It's been a long time."

"Not to worry. I fully intent to take care of your intentions." With that he picked her up, not the romantic way, but tossed her over his shoulder, and marched down the hall. "Like I always say, screw the noodles."

―――――

What followed was passionate and unpretentious. They delighted in the small imperfections that were results of their lifestyle. Their first lovemaking session had been a series of revelations: *Who knifed you here? Was that wound from a .38 special? You must've been restrained to get that burn on your inner wrist.* Each had been cops for eight years and carried the battle scars to prove it. Rachael rested her head in the crook of Josh's arm and ran her fingers through his chest hair.

"I've missed us." She nuzzled closer. "Guess we need to do some talking." She gave him a quick kiss, sat up and straddled him.

"I'm not going to do much talking if you're sitting naked on top of me." He pulled her forward and kissed her. She grabbed him around the neck and rolled right, pulling him on top of her.

"This better?"

"You are a bad girl. I'm through messin' with you. I came over for Italian food and all I've had so far is a little English sex." He tossed her off and smacked her on the butt. "Now get your lazy ass out of bed and feed your man."

She threw a pillow that missed, and tumbled out of bed to search for her T-shirt and shorts. "Get some clothes on, mister. What kind of restaurant do you think this is?"

The noodles were overcooked and the sauce slightly burned, but no one complained.

Shaking the last remnants of parmesan from the can, Josh switched to the problem at hand. "We're no further ahead on Zach's disappearance. Our department's so shorthanded we can't spare the man power to go door to door. Has Amanda come up with anything yet?"

"Not really. I told you about Derek, Marisa and this Dred guy, but their drug business has never included kidnapping a kid. I keep thinking that they might be holding him in case we get too close. Maybe a bargaining chip?"

"We've got the word out in town. Neighbors are all pulling together, listening for any baby cries, you know, where they don't belong. Had two calls but didn't prove to be anything. If this Dred guy is so dirty, I'm thinking we should grab him and shake him down?"

"Amanda has surveillance on him and Meg is working with the FBI to get intel on both Derek and Dred."

Josh shook his head. "Sometimes I think everyone's forgotten how long it took Meg to bounce back last year. You guys weren't with her the night she hit bottom. I was. I thought we'd lost her mentally forever. And now this? I was at that meeting, but geez, Meg is just a kid. You're putting her in the bullpen with a vicious monster again. She's had more trauma in her life that anyone I know. I can't believe you and Amanda would go for that."

"You know her. She'd be doing it on her own if we'd told her no. This way, she's being protected. But enough of that. We could go for years debating Meg's penchant for interfering." She raised her eyebrows and changed the subject. "Did your investigation turn up any other babies that have disappeared?"

"One in San Diego three days ago. Don't know if it's connected. I figure if Zach is still on the island, they have to be holding him on the back side of Avalon, maybe the Two Harbor area. The Conservancy's pitching in, checking the rural parts of their territory along with my department checking around Cottonwood area. I don't know how much the FBI is really doing. Think they're concentrating on the drug scene more."

"Amanda insists they're committed. She thinks maybe Zach's disappearance might be a new business, like a terrorist thing."

"What?" Josh pushed away from the table and sat motionless. "Why would any terrorist group want an American baby?"

"Possibly raise him and instill Muslim theology, and return this Americanized kid to the U.S, as a terrorist who would fit right in. DNA would be totally American."

"That's really stretching. I think this Dred asshole has him stashed away. A bargaining chip, like I said."

Rachael didn't want the conversation to end as it did in the courthouse, but took a chance on the closeness of the day to try again. "How does that make you feel? After all, Zach is your son."

Leaning back, two chair legs off the floor, Josh stared at her. "You sure you want to go there?" He crossed his arms and changed the direction of his gaze to the mantel where a picture of Zach was displayed.

Rachael remained silent.

"When I find him I want to hold him for the first time." His eyes travelled back to Rachael. "I'll know when the time comes."

She knew she should leave it alone, but didn't. "I hope you understand the depth of my love for you. I'll never be happy with another man. You're it. And, just in case you didn't know, I would be a really happy camper to raise Zach as our own. I'd be his real mother and your real wife if you'd ask. How's that for sayin' it like it is?"

She waited for a reply, prayed for a reply.

Josh stood, took his plate and glass to the sink and headed for the door. "I don't want to be a dick, but I guess I am. The marrying part of that equation is something I want but... Well, we'll see on the other. Love you." With that he walked out the door.

"Oh, great." Rachael threw the tea-towel into the sink and groaned.

Chapter 42

WHEN TWILIGHT ARRIVED, Dred loosened the grape stake fencing separating the two houses and at exactly 9:00 p.m. he slid through the fence, taking long strides across the grassy area, and approached Derek's bathroom window. The iron bars, installed for protection were on a hinge. No problem to remove. He opened the mini-stepstool, slid the window up, propped it open with a piece of rebar and crawled through. The room was dark and small. He used his night goggles to keep from running into anything. Derek was talking on the phone in the living room. Dred tried to eavesdrop on the conversation as he stripped down to his underwear and stepped into the shower.

Cameras on both sides of the rental were blinking, one focused on the front yard, one focused on the rear.

Derek switched on the light as he entered the bathroom, locked the door and undressed down to his boxers. He turned on the water in the sink to masque their conversation. "You sure this ankle monitor won't go off when I leave my backyard?" he whispered. He pulled on Dred's tee shirt and sweat pants.

"Positive. I measured the distance from your front door to the mail box two doors away. You've been picking up the mail daily and no alarm. You're safe. Hurry up and get out the window. One hour, that's all. Less would be better."

Derek didn't waste time putting on shoes, he scurried out the window, across the lawn and entered the small frame house.

Marisa was an emotional wreck waiting for him and when he entered she threw her arms around him and hugged him like it was their last day on earth. "My God, I've missed you." Her grip didn't weaken.

Derek freed himself and held her arms down to her side. "Wow, a blonde and glasses. Saucy look, sis." They sat at the kitchen table and Derek smiled as she poured two glasses of Jameson whiskey. "Okay, I've been waiting months for you to contact me or show up. So why now, and what's your plan?"

"First, are you okay? You look thin and not as buff. What's with that?" She squeezed his hand.

"There's an easy answer for that. Captivity comes to mind. Food's improved since we came to Catalina, but I'm on a tight leash. No chance to work out. I'm fine." He walked to the other side of the kitchen and snuck a peek out the window. Emotions were tripping around the room.

Marisa hesitated. "You know the saying about the apple not falling far from the tree." She walked to the window and put her hands on his shoulders.

"What?" While acting surprised, Derek knew what was coming. He turned.

"Are you wearing a wire? I'm sorry to ask, but I guess a lot of Elliott's suspicion mind has transferred to me. Mind if I take a look?"

"Look to your heart's content. I'm not wired. We're in this together." He backed up, pulled off his T-shirt and turned around slowly for inspection. "Satisfied?"

Marisa flashed a weak smile, and watched him settle in a chair across from her. "You're too skinny," she murmured. She glanced away as he pulled his T-shirt back on. "We don't have much time, so

I'll hurry. I've analyzed the set-up and this is the best solution to the problem. As soon as the drug route has been finalized and tested, we'll pack up and fly away to wherever we feel like. Will probably take two weeks. I'll need maybe three more air drops and then test out the water route. We'll need to go along with the FBI for now. Two weeks, max three. Is that a problem?"

Derek leaned back, crossed his arms behind his head and stared at his sister. He wasn't sure where to start. "So, when I got hold of you in Mexico and you agreed to give yourself up, that was all a show? You had no intentions of going straight?"

"Give up? Of course not. Those assholes would turn against us in a flash if they knew everything that Elliott and I did. There's no way I'd go free. We have millions in the bank, why bother?" She hid the deep disappointment she felt.

Derek sighed. "The last time we were together, on the yacht— the night Elliott turned you out like a common whore to the Frenchman—we talked about a new life. Was that a lie?"

"Not then, but keep in mind I'd just been brutalized by that guy. I was ready to say anything to get out of there."

Derek's mind was calculating and recalculating the information. "You say we have millions? How'd that happen? You only had access to Elliott's slush account, not his personal wealth."

"I hired an IT guy in Mexico and he cracked the password. Geneva, Cayman Islands, Baltics. I have it all." She smiled broadly at her accomplishments, but when she turned back to Derek, her smile vanished. "Don't tell me you're really considering coming clean and cooperating with the FBI." A combination of worry and anger crossed her face.

Derek was at the crossroads and he knew it, but now was not the time to play his hand. "Had ya going, didn't I? Of course I'm sticking with you. I figured you'd come up with a great plan to spring me from the FBI's clutches. So go ahead, hurry-up and fill me in on the details. I've only got forty-five minutes before I have to slip back to the house."

On the other side of the fence, Dred put on Derek's clothes, flushed the toilet, ran some water, flipped off the bathroom light and went into the dimly lit living room. The TV was playing a rerun of *Criminal Minds* so he went to the refrigerator, grabbed a Coors, kept his head down to avoid the cameras, and settled into the recliner to watch the show. While he looked relaxed, he was praying no one would drop by to visit. He'd have to kill them.

Marisa carefully outlined the newly developed drug exchange process. "One thing I may have to reconsider is the demand for pot. Some new laws are coming down the pike. Might just have to concentrate on opiates. Anyway, the first drop was successful. I was disappointed with the small amount of coke, but I think it was a test for us. Now we need to incorporate the airport and panga boats."

"How did you manage that so fast? You've only been here a few days."

"The planning was done on the beach in Mexico. I had to get here and make a few calls. I've bought two thirty-foot panga boats and Gilbert is scouting around for a crew."

"Three engines? We may have to outrun the Coast Guard."

"Yes. New ones. It's going to take two weeks to iron out the wrinkles and coordinate everyone's shipments. We need to get the Coast Guard and also U.S. Border Patrol schedules. Can you handle waiting that long? Otherwise, you can escape now and hide 'til I'm finished."

"No, it'll be better if it looks like I'm still cooperating, less pressure on you. We'll have more intel that way. I can keep feeding them info, just enough to keep them convinced I'm on their side."

"You, Dred and Meg will be hanging out together. Is that going to be a problem?"

"Nah. I'll play jealous and try to get rid of him. Meg's a push over." Everything seemed to be going okay with Marisa so he hesitated to bring up a problem, but it had to be mentioned. "I do have one question."

"Shoot."

"The baby. Josh's kid, Zach. That was Dred or you, right? But, why?"

Marisa's guard went up. "Yeah, was Dred. He was fulfilling a contract but missed the mark. Grabbed the kid for collateral. Stupid."

"I'll say."

"I've decided to keep the brat in case we need a bargaining chip. I have a contact overseas that's checking to see if there's a market for American male babies, so we have another source to get rid of him. I don't want to fool around with ransom, so when we leave if I haven't sold him, we'll leave him someplace."

"Leave him? Like we did Amanda and Grace, tied up in the middle of the Mohave Desert to die?" Derek tried not to show too much emotion, but it was a stretch.

"No. That's too far away. Maybe some dingy in Avalon Bay. Don't worry. I'll take care of it." No sign of emotion registered on her face.

Derek's heart dropped. He finally saw the big picture. Marisa had completed the transition, morphed into Elliott, a person capable of murder with no compassion, a money-driven and treacherous narcissist. Whatever desire to run was being considered, vanished with the last comment from Marisa. He decided to play the game right now and sort out the repercussions at another time. "Okay, you know me, I'm fine without all the details. So you'll be doing your thing while I cooperate with the FBI, and Dred will tell me when it's time to leave. That's it?"

"For now. We won't meet again. It's too dangerous. You'll have to call me later so the FBI can monitor and listen to your answers."

Derek's mind was rushing ahead, trying to dodge any major roadblocks.

"I'll just string you along. Do they know I'm on the island?" Marisa looked for Derek's tell.

"They suspect it, but it's not confirmed. I'll have to ask you next time they monitor our calls. So be ready with an answer."

"Right." Marisa stood and walked around the table and sat on Derek's lap. "You are so damn good-looking. I wish we had different fathers so I could do you." She smiled and nosed his neck. "Oh, what the hell. Incest is one vice I haven't tried yet. How about it?"

Derek wasn't sure if she meant it or not, but turned it into a joke. "Oh, sure, right after we escape from the island with our zillions of dollars. Sure, right." He stood so fast she almost fell on the floor. "Gotta go. I'll be in touch on the FBI phone."

"One thing before you go." Marisa's serious tone filled the room.

"What?"

"Are you convinced that Elliott died in the prison fire?"

Derek froze. "Shit. Do you have reason to doubt it? Have you heard from him?"

"No, but I'd be more comfortable if we knew for sure. Nothing more from the FBI? Nothing from Rachael?"

"No. How close was he to Dred? Could he be a fly in the ointment?" Derek's stomach knotted. "For God's sake, Marisa, you know he'll kill all of Meg's family and us too if he thinks we've betrayed him. Holy shit. Don't scare me like that."

"Okay, just askin'." She mustered up a weak smile as he left the room. "Be safe."

Derek heard the parting words and they were far more noteworthy than when he had arrived. He left the kitchen, sprinted across the yard and reentered the bath. He lightly tapped on the bathroom door. Dred responded, put his empty beer bottle on the sink and headed for the bathroom. After the exchange of clothing was complete and Dred had crawled through the window, Derek left the bathroom in his pajamas and headed for bed. Sleep was a luxury that was not going to present itself tonight.

When Dred walked through the door, Marisa grabbed him around the neck and kissed him. "I'm horny. Let's do it here on the kitchen table." She thought of Derek. "Now, for God's sake. What's taking you so long?"

He was pissed at being bossed around and punished her with vicious sex. He rammed her hard against the wood table, sending them into the wall where the pictures and mirror crashed to the floor.

Her depraved thoughts hurled her into a tumultuous orgasm.

Later, when the heat had evaporated, and the calm of clean sheets encompassed them, Marisa cuddled. "You'll have to watch

Derek closely. I was getting mixed signals from him tonight. Sometimes he was great, and then something happened. I don't know if it was the pitch in his voice, or a hand movement. But I could feel him vacillating."

"Whatever." Dred untangled himself from her and rolled over. *I'll be watching you too, you crazy bitch.*

Chapter 43

JOSH AND GREG SAT in the Department's specially equipped ATV. Their vantage point from Grand Canyon Road included the southern-most tip of the island by Binnacle Rock, encompassed the Palisades and ended at China Point. This was not their regular assignment. The Sheriff's department had received an anonymous call that a drug shipment was imminent, but no time or location was given. The early morning haze lingered, so spotting a panga boat skimming across the ocean swells would be difficult. The FBI had strategically placed their agents at different locations on the island. Amanda was assigned to the Shark Harbor area.

"Needle in a haystack shit, as far as I'm concerned," Greg said. "With only eight lookouts and fifty-four miles of coastline to cover, we'll never spot the SOBs." He stood to shake out his cramped muscles. His cell phone vibrated. "Shit. Forgot I had it on mute." He pushed a few buttons and retrieved the message from Sally. "Damn."

"What?" Josh asked as he continued scanning the ocean through his binoculars.

Instead of answering, Greg replayed the message on speaker. "Of all times. Sounds like Stella's been off her meds for a long time if she's wondering through those crazy fantasies of hers. God, she's back on the island without Aunt Sharon to corral her. Geez. What should I do?"

"Sorry, partner. I'll try to handle this by myself if you wanna leave. I'll call for backup."

"Hell, they won't get here for an hour. I'll check with dispatch and see if anyone is working Two Harbors now. Make sure Stella's okay."

Josh watched Greg's expressions change from annoyance to pain. "I know how tough this has to be on you. Hey, man, whatever I can do to help with Stella's problems, I will. Count on me."

Greg made two quick calls and then settled down to the mission at hand. "Sally's brother is available. He'll go look for her."

"Tell him to take his fishing boat over to Lobster Bay. That's Stella's favorite hiding spot." He twisted in the seat and focus on another stretch of ocean.

"Will do. Stella's had a hard life. No one in the family understood her disease. We'd put up with her, placate her, but we didn't do right by her. You were the only one in school that had any compassion. Guess that's why she always loved you."

"Man. I thought I was helping her by taking her to the prom and dating her a few times. It was more out of pity than anything else. Sorry."

"You were helping her. Don't get me wrong. I appreciated that."

"Yeah. Well, it didn't end up that great. Came back to bite me in the ass in the long run. No good deeds go unpunished shit."

"It's cool."

Josh rested his binoculars on the narrow dashboard and stretched, tiring of the boring game of watching. He reached around in the backseat and grabbed a box. "Donut?" He snatched the chocolate sprinkled one first and handed the box to his partner. "Have you had any updates lately on Stella's health since she went back to the hospital?"

"Yeah. Aunt Sharon says she was medicated all the time at first. Was on suicide watch, but then she turned all of that around." He paused. "If she escaped, she probably heard that Zach was missing."

Greg knew this wasn't the perfect time to talk to Josh about the baby, but decided to go for it. "This whole Stella thing has been tough on you."

"On you, too. How such a great guy as you can have a psycho sister like Stella is beyond me." He winced at the sound of those words, but couldn't retract them, so he shut up.

"Well, at the court hearing the other day, when I heard you were going to put Zach up for adoption, I kind of lost it. I was pissed at you for a while, and then... Well, I talked to Aunt Sharon and... I'd like to adopt Zach when you get him back. He'll be the only family I have left. I don't think my sis is ever going to clean up her act." He lowered the binoculars and looked at Josh.

"Interesting."

"That's it? Would that be okay with you?"

"Shit, Greg. Can't wrap my head around it. You'd raise my kid? I don't know." Mental images of Greg playing ball with Zach, going to games, barbecues, a family scene? He felt a twang of jealousy which disturbed him. His stomach knotted up and he finally blurted, "I don't think so."

"Well, actually asshole, if you put him up for adoption you won't have much to say about it." Greg was pissed that Josh hadn't jumped on board with the idea.

"Let me talk to Rach about it." He picked up the binoculars and continued tracing the ocean swells below him, then stopped abruptly. "Two o'clock. Something's there."

Greg turned, searching for a boat or submarine and finally located Josh's target. "Not a panga. Hot looking machine. Three engines. That has to be it."

Josh started the ATV. "Call it in."

"What cove are they headed for?"

"Has to be Silver Canyon Landing. Fuck. No roads. Keep your eye on 'em. Hang on." The ATV dug up a barrage of dirt as Josh made a sharp J turn and headed down the hill. He dodged the cactus and ravines, and was on high alert for any roaming buffalo. Passing the hiking trail he continued on the downward quest until he reached Silver Canyon Road. "You still see 'em?"

"Just lost 'em," Greg answered as he grabbed the sissy bar, "but they're headed to Silver Canyon. You know if we see them, they see us. Especially with the dirt cloud. Only a small beach there to land. Wanna wait for backup?"

"You fuckin' kidding me? They can unload that shit in a gnat's eye. Hang on, bump ahead."

Greg went flying and banged his head on the roll bar. "Slow down. Let me get some artillery from the back." He reached around, grabbed an AR-47, loaded it, loaded a shotgun and grabbed some extra ammunition. "You got your Glock?"

"Yeah plus my back-up." Josh maneuvered around a boulder.

"What's the plan?" Gregg clutched the roll bar as the ATV turned on two wheels.

Josh pressed on the brake and the ATV skidded four feet, finally digging into the sand. "For sure they have a crew waiting to unload. How many in the boat? Could you tell?"

"No but let's count on three. Probably wetbacks. Armed." Josh pulled on the bar and leaped from the ATV.

"Okay, the cove is about a half mile from here. Call in our position. We'll walk the rest of the way and surprise 'em."

Greg finished relaying the information, put on his Kevlar vest and loaded up. "Captain says to wait for back-up. Three guys would be okay to handle, but we don't know how many are waiting to unload."

"Okay, but let's get closer."

Marisa and Dred, sitting in their Jeep above Silver Canyon, spotted Josh as he maneuvered the ATV down the hill. "Not to worry, we've got 'em outnumbered," she said. "You take one guy with you, armed, and walk up to that ridge. Vantage point will be good." She checked her gun.

"If these guys aren't the Feds, well, the Feds'll be right behind. Make a call. Wave off the boat," pushed Dred.

"No." Marisa was adamant. "We can do this. I bought a present for you. Go over to the truck. Lift up the canvas." She continued searching the adjacent hills for more traffic.

"Sweet." A powered up Smith and Wesson M6P15 Magpul

MOE patrol rifle was resting under the tarp. A grin spread across Dred's face. He checked the magazine, shouldered the weapon and started up the hill.

"Now, get the fuck up there. We'll drop those guys in the cross-fire. They won't know what hit 'em." Marisa felt the power, loved the power.

As they neared the beach, Josh and Derek stopped and took cover behind a huge rock formation. "You go up that ravine, there, on the right, and I'll try to close in behind the truck. You okay with that?" Josh checked his weapon for the third time.

"Got it. Turn your radio down. Gimme the old SOS if you get into trouble," Greg whispered. "No shooting. There's too many of them. We'll have to wait for backup."

"Right." Greg scurried across the small opening and headed uphill.

Dred watched. He clicked off the safety, sited down the barrel and sent one bullet home. The man was dead before his head hit the ground.

Chapter 44

THE SMALL FISHING BOAT didn't have to leave Two Harbors before the search was over. Red hair, intertwined with green kelp, floated near Mooring 38, and as Sally's brother pulled closer, he recognized Stella's bloated body. Face up, with arms wrapped tightly across her chest, her grotesque smile looked down on a plastic doll nestled close to her breast.

"Whatcha' want me to do, Sally? She's tangled up in one of the moorings." He held the phone in his right hand, grappling hook in the left.

"I'll call the Sheriff's Department. Hell, I don't know. Any chance she'll sink?"

He tugged a little and the body moved. "Yup. She'll probably sink. I'll just tow her in to knee deep water and let them figure it out. Might want to clear the beach. Not that good for tourism."

Sally got voice mail again when she called Greg's muted phone.

Chapter 45

THE POWER BOAT IDLED DOWN and coasted into the sandy beach. The driver cut the powerful engines and sat back to watch the others work. Three men rushed to pull the boat further onto the shore, anchored it, and then began to toss the illegal contraband onto the sand.

Armed and ready for any type of fight, a branch of the Sinaloa cartel watched the activity on Silver Canyon beach. This site was a mile north of their regular drop off position. An informant had heard of a new dealer in town and relayed the information to the gang. Eager to squelch the intruder, the cartel's plan was to kill the newcomers and confiscate the drugs. From their vantage point they could see the ongoing activity. Two guys in a jeep, looked like cops, armed, plus a woman with a handful of armed men.

"Policia are walking into trap. Maybe they kill each other. Save us the bullets." The group of men laughed and then started down the hill as their leader motioned to them. The newly acquired HK-416's were strapped across their chests and they felt confident with their machine power. Their leader had a HK MR5566A1-SD with a thermal sight and special laser with a double point sling. He wore it proudly, but unknown to his men he wasn't quite sure how to use it.

When the bullet from Dred's rifle hit Greg squarely in the head, the sound ricochet across the valley and everyone dropped to their knees. The cartel leader motioned his men to spread out, Josh took cover, Marisa and her men crouched down and took aim, as the powerful boat took off with only half of the stash unloaded. Marisa peered around the corner of the truck and watched as a Coast Guard boat appeared from behind an outcropping of rocks to the west. It was performing its weekly sweep, looking for drug activity, when the shot was heard. They took pursuit. She knew it would only be minutes before the Coast Guard would catch up and the drugs would be history. As predicted the Coast Guard roared ahead, closing the distance and finally took aim and fired a shot across the bow of the drug boat. The driver slowed down and the men started throwing the remaining cargo overboard.

"Shit," Marisa yelled, "Find that other cop and kill him." She stood, readied her rifle and started toward the beach. "Get our men down there and load the truck. We've got to get the hell out of he…" Before she could finish her sentence the cartel started firing into the group and storming down the hill.

"Marisa." Dred yelled as he came stumbling down the slope. "Here. Come here."

She spotted him through the barrage of dirt that was being kicked up by the gun fire. He zigzagged across the open area, took a flying dive behind a boulder, knocking Marisa down on the way. "We've got to get out of here."

The FBI helicopters buzzed the beach as Marisa cowed behind Dred. When the cartel opened fire on the helicopter, Josh raced over to Greg and pulled him behind some boulders.

"No. The drugs. We need the drugs." Marisa was yelling as she ran for the jeep.

"Fuck the drugs. Let the cartel get caught with 'em. Come on." He tackled her. She sprawled in the dirt. They crawled behind rocks until they were out of range from the cartel's bullets. Headed up the hill. The jeep spit out a barrage of dust as they raced back toward their hideout.

Josh knew without checking for a pulse that Greg was dead. Bits of his grey matter, skin and hair combined with blood spatter dripped down the adjacent rock. The vest would have saved him, but the sniper knew that and aimed for his head. "Sorry partner. You didn't have a fuckin' chance." He sat with his friend and openly wept as the FBI and the rest of the Sheriff's Department emerged. More gunfire ensued and finally it was quiet. No cartel member survived.

Amanda confiscated a department jeep when she got the heads-up on the drug bust and headed toward Silver Canyon Beach. It was like a war zone when she located Josh. She found him sitting in the dirt, cradling Greg's head, a tortured expression veiled his face. She sat down in the dirt beside him. "Damn. So sorry, Josh. I know Greg was your best friend. I'm truly sorry." She had questions, but gave him a few minutes to come around. "Do you think this was the Sinaloa cartel? Did you see the drop?"

Josh sat back, leaned against a rock and wiped the drying blood from his hands. "No. Not exactly. It was a botched delivery." He described the whole scene, including the blonde woman and white guy who had escaped. "The guy was built like Derek, but it wasn't him."

An ambulance arrived and the medics attended to Greg's body. Josh silently stood as they put him in the body bag. "Stop. Let me zip it up." He looked down at Greg's distorted face and wept. "Love ya, man." He helped move the body onto the gurney, oblivious to the tears.

Amanda and Josh returned to her jeep. "I know it wasn't Derek. We've got eyes on him twenty-four-seven. He wasn't involved. But the lady. Blonde, you said?"

"Yeah. Bottle type. Built like a brick shit house and knew how to use her gun." He grabbed the roll bar and crawled into the jeep. His body was shaking.

Amanda nodded. "I met Marisa one time---Derek's and Elliott's sister---when she kidnapped mom and me. She was a brunette, but hair dye is cheap. I'm sure it was her. That would make sense. Wasn't sure she was on the island, but I think I have my answer now."

Josh fought to keep in the conversation. "Wasn't she supposed to turn state's evidence against Elliott's old team? Or work with Derek to take down the cartel? That Marisa?"

"One and the same. Do you think she knows that you saw her? We might still be able to salvage part of this."

"I'm sure the guy was the one who shot Greg. They were waiting to ambush us. Me? She saw me, but the cartel started shooting then, so she probably figured I got killed in the crossfire. Don't know for sure. I only saw her as she ran away with that guy."

"Okay. If we tell the paper to report that it was only the cartel, and that one officer was killed and one is in a coma, she might think she got away with it. Might try to continue on and we'll be ready for her then."

"Why not now? Get a warrant and let's go after her."

"We're not positive of her identity and have no friggin' idea where she is. There's still the chance that's she's going to cooperate with us. This blonde may be someone else. Marisa's been giving Derek mixed messages, but if today's blonde is her, that question's been answered. The cartel will be after her now, so she'll have to be more careful. But make no mistake. She's mine."

They drove back to Avalon with heavy hearts and drained bodies. "Anyone I should call about Greg?"

"No. There's only Aunt Sharon and Stella. I have her number and I'll call her." A lump constricted his speech. "Greg…Greg was going to adopt Zach…Damn."

Amanda looked his way. "I'm so sorry, Josh. I'll make the call."

"No. I'll do it, but I don't know how I'm going to tell her."

Chapter 46

RACHAEL RELAXED IN THE PATIO CHAIR, coffee in hand, absently staring across the house tops at the shimmering Pacific. Restless was hardly the word for her mood. She reflected on the last year, saw her life roll by in cinematic slides. She was still a detective with the Bullhead City Police Department, Josh had come to assist in the capture of Elliott but was shot and lost his memory. The next picture was Stella capturing him, raping him, and then the baby Zach appeared. She had been out of work for six months, sharing the house with Meg on Catalina, no job, money slipping through her fingers and a feeling of uselessness overtaking her.

Amanda had called and told her about Greg's death and Stella's drowning.

She stood, walked into the house and refilled her coffee cup. "Are you ever going to get up?" she yelled down the hall to Meg. Sitting and waiting again she realized how ineffective she was at the moment. Not allowed to participate in the search for Marisa, waiting to hear from the Conservancy about a job, pussy footing around Josh's emotions. Then she laughed.

Meg slouched through the door, her unruly blonde hair covering most of her face, coffee in hand, and plunked down across from her sister. "Geez, quit being so pushy. I was in a cart accident yesterday and a boating accident the day before. I need to heal." She shot a quizzical look toward her sister. "What's so funny?"

"Probably wasn't an accident and Derek brought you home with your pants off. How bad could that have been?" She smiled. "Just realized how pathetic I am. Feeling sorry for myself." She sipped her cold coffee and switched her focus to her Apple tablet on the table.

Meg peeked through sleepy eyes. She watched Rachael frantically typing, arrows going up and down the pages, names, dates scrawled in her own brand of shorthand. She turned the pad to Meg. "Okay. I have a plan and I might need some help."

"Holy shit. I've already got two jobs. Why don't you get one and help out with the rent?"

"You are such a brat sometimes."

Meg flashed a sarcastic smile her way. "Okay, what's all this writing about?"

"There is no way that the FBI or Catalina PD is going to let me work on this case. I'm supposed to check my Glock into the department, but that's not going to happen. With the murders and drug crap going on, Stella's death, Greg's death, everyone is stretched so thin and the disappearance of Zach is taking a backseat, so here's the deal." She outlined her case. "We both have reliable contacts on the island. I'll take the back side, Two Harbors, and up and down the island, and you cover Vons market and the town grapevine. Ask your buddy at Vons to look out for new babies in town or adults that are buying baby stuff."

"That's pretty vague. If Zach is still here on the island, the kidnapper is probably shipping necessities over on the Express every day. I don't think they'd be stupid enough to go to Vons for diapers."

"Maybe, but there could be a slip up and they might run out of something, like formula, or need baby aspirin or cough syrup. Just have the clerks make a mental note and call you. Any new baby purchases within the last ten days. Will you do it?"

"Yeah, that's not a problem. I'll start on it before I go to work at Catherine's. Got the noon shift. I heard they found Stella's body." Meg approached the subject carefully.

"Right." Instant guilt reflected on Rachael's face. "Of course, we need to help some way. With both Greg and Stella dead, there has to be some kind of service. Both were Island family. Josh's probably going to take over the funeral arrangements, or else Aunt Sharon."

"God, I was sick when I heard about Greg. Good guy. Family really. Josh has to be devastated." Meg bit her lower lip and glanced away. After a very quiet minute she continued. "I'll be happy to help. Just let me know what to do. Sad day." The lump that was forming got pushed down.

Rachael paused, not wanting to bring up the next subject, but knew it had to be addressed. "Someone needs to let mom know about the services. She was like a second mother to Greg and Stella. Want to volunteer?" Her focus changed from Meg to the corner of the room, waiting for the explosive answer.

"Are you kidding me? Grace here on the Island? She'll be all over our business. Derek and me? My paragliding accident? Murder at Catherine's? She'll have Duke bring over fifty guys from the CIA, launch drones, move the CIA satellite. Hell no."

When Meg stopped to take a breath, Rachael grabbed her chance. "I'll have Amanda handle it. Our sister with the voice of reason. She can make mom behave, maybe." She hesitated to say more, but felt Meg needed an attitude adjustment. "Since when did you start calling mom, "Grace?" Sure as hell doesn't show her much respect."

"Oh, maybe since she lied to me for twenty-three years about who my real father was? Start with that simple piece of truth," Meg blasted.

"You spoiled, self-centered piece of shit. Do you know the suffering mom went through to make your life perfect? Twenty years of denying her own happiness? Look at them. They adore each other and could have spent those years together except for you. You are one ungrateful brat, Meg." She grabbed Meg by the shoulders. "And don't you dare call mom "Grace" in front of me or I'll knock you silly. So will Amanda."

"She's always inter…"

Rachael shook her. "Don't. Don't say another word. Mom loves you with a depth none of us can fathom. I won't allow you to talk about her this way." She dropped her hands and glared at her sister.

Meg turned and left the room before the tears decided to erupt.

Rachael took a quick shower, worked through her own attitude adjustment, pulled on her white knee knockers and favorite blouse that hid her shoulder holster and Glock and headed out the door. "I'm taking the cart. See ya later."

"Oh, great. That means I walk to work." Meg picked up the couch pillow and threw it at her departing sister. Throwing pillows was their favorite way of saying goodbye.

The drive to Two Harbors took two hours. Rachael had a special pass, thanks to Josh, that allowed her to drive in restricted areas. Pulling up in front of the general store, she was surprised at the activity. Midweek vacationers who took off to the camping facilities were usually scarce. "Hey Sally, how's it going," she asked as she saw her old friend staring at her.

"Wow, Rachael, what brings you to this part of the island?" She walked around the counter and gave Rachael a warm, long-time-no-see girlfriend, hug. She was painfully aware of Rachael's historical romance with Josh.

"Monkey business, mainly." She wanted to skip over the Stella situation, if possible. "How's the family? I see you're expecting another rug-rat."

"Hope to hell this is going to be a girl. My two year-old son is driving me nuts." She massaged her stomach.

Since there were other clerks to help the patrons in the store, Sally poured two cups of coffee and signaled for Rachael to join her at the table. "Come, let's sit outside. We've got some catch-up to do."

After a few minutes of fill-in history, the conversation rolled around to Rachael's immediate needs. "I guess you heard about Stella drugging Josh and having his baby."

"Wow, the whole island heard about that. And now the little boy's missing." Sally stirred her coffee. "I was there when they pulled Stella's body on shore by the way. Tragic thing. I felt so sorry for her, for all of you."

Both women looked away. "I thought you and Josh would be married having your own kids by now."

"I wish. We were right there. He'd had the ring for six months while I screwed around trying to say yes, and then the amnesia and we had to start all over. Shit. Was a comedy of errors. Well, anyway, the disappearance of Zach is why I'm here. I need your help."

"Name it."

"Your store and the Vons store in Avalon are the only means of buying supplies like diapers, formula…you know, baby stuff. Has a stranger, a stranger to the island, been making such purchases?"

Sally didn't have to think very long. "There are five babies in town right now. Three of them are over the age of two. Then we have Ernie's newborn, a boy, but he's legit 'cause we all watched his wife grow to a gargantuan size. That leaves Ramon's sister's little girl, Emilie. Like I say, a girl."

Rachael leaned back, swallowed a huge sip of coffee and said, "Bingo."

"What?"

"Probably had a pink receiving blanket, pink onesie's and a pink bow taped to her almost bald head?"

Sally acted bewildered. "Ya, well, that's what moms do when they have girls."

"That's also what a kidnapper would do if he nabbed a boy. Perfect disguise."

"Oh, shit. How stupid am I?"

"Not stupid, you just don't think like a cop. Now, where does Ramon live, for how long, what does he do and how often do they come in here for supplies?"

"Slow down. Ramon's lived here for at least ten years. Works as a groundskeeper for the elementary school. Never did marry, but plays poker with the guys every Friday night. His sister, Lucia, brings the baby here in a makeshift car seat-stroller type rig twice a week. Should be today."

"Have you looked close at the baby?"

"Well, yeah. I pick her up if she gets noisy when Lucia's shopping. Cute little girl."

"Does she look Hispanic?"

"No, but Lucia said the baby's dad is a no-good gringo. So I figured. Well, you know."

"I need a DNA sample. Can you get one for me?"

"Like pull a plug of hair out of the kid's head? For God's sake, Rachael, she'd scream her friggin head off."

Rachael laughed spurting out a shot of coffee. She reached into her backpack. "No, silly. You swab the inside of his mouth. Here's all the stuff you need. Can you do it?" She shoved the kit into Sally's hand.

Sally looked at the vial holding the swab and raised her shoulders, moved her head back and forth, and said, "Yeah, I guess. Then what? Put it back in the tube?"

"That's it." Rachael jumped up, stepped behind Sally and gave her a huge bear hug from behind. "Oh, thank you, thank you. Now all we have to do is wait."

Sally started laughing. "Not for long. Your timing's perfect. Here comes Lucia now. Shit. Gimme that thing. Let's get this cloak and dagger crap over with."

Rachael moved from the table and went to the liquor department, hoping that would be one area that Lucia would ignore.

"*Hola*, Sally. How are you today?" Lucia boosted the stroller up the steps.

"Great. Business is a little slow but that gives me time to catch up on my reading. How's little Emilie?" She walked over to the stroller and tickled the baby's toes.

"*Bueno*. Did you get in those baby wipes I was talking about?"

"Sure did. I ordered three different kinds. Guess you'll have to read the labels. Aisle four, near the bottom. I'll play with Emilie while you shop. She's such a little sweetheart."

As Lucia walked to aisle four, Rachael moved to the refrigeration area and Sally performed her detective work, swabbing Emilie's mouth and replacing the sample in the vial. "Find what you need, Lucia?"

"*Si. Gracias.*" She placed four items on the counter and reached into her purse. "When Emilie is a little bigger, I'll pull her here in the wagon and we can buy more. Right now, I have to walk so far to get to Ramon's house that I have to make too many trips. Oh, well, I should be thankful that he took me in."

"Everyday blessings, I always say, come to good people." Sally rang up the purchase, gave Lucia her change and bagged the groceries. "See you next time. 'Bye, sweet Emilie. Thanks." Sally opened the door for Lucia and almost knocked down a male customer. "I'm sorry. I didn't see you there."

"No problem. What a beautiful baby. Mind if I hold her?"

Lucia scowled. "No, senior. No." She pushed the stroller forward and left abruptly.

Rachael stopped and stared at the stranger. Weird. Who would ask a question like that? A shiver instantly passed down her spine. Who, indeed? Once Lucia was out of sight, Rachael collected the sample, thanked Sally a million times and drove the cart like a madwoman back to Avalon. She grabbed an overnight bag, called her friend in Costa Mesa who worked at the Forensics Lab, left a note for Meg, voicemail for Josh and rushed to catch the Catalina Express back to the mainland with the DNA sample in hand. *Now we'll know for sure.*

Chapter 47

MARISA LEANED AGAINST DRED'S SHOULDER the last half mile of the ride to the bungalow. Her hair was matted against her head, blood had dried from her encounter with the cactus. Deep gouges were oozing blood down her arm and she was tired. Very tired. Dred practically carried her the last fifty feet to the house. "Let me help you," he said. Without waiting for an answer, he carried her up the wooden porch. He propped open the rustic door with his foot and helped her to the couch. "I'll get some water."

Marisa was tough and usually would tell anyone, including Dred, to piss off. But this close encounter with the cartel had drained her, both physically and mentally.

"Well, that didn't go as planned, did it?"

Being this close to the action was not to her liking. For the last six years she had been the accounting genius for all of Elliott's criminal activities, but now that he was dead, she had taken on the job of managing the physical aspect too. The thought of killing didn't bother her, but putting her own life on the line was distasteful.

"I might have to promote you to my number one man so you can deal with all the shooting business." She took a deep sip of the water. "A little too messy for me."

She decided to weigh the possibilities of dumping the drug business again or backing off and returning to Bullhead City. Maybe a clean start if Derek was still interested. She had millions that would cover her standard of living for a few years. Maybe?

"I thought I already had that title." He walked to the kitchen sink to wash blood off his hands and arms. As the rusty water circled the drain, he imagined circling Marisa neck with his hands to let her experience real fear and humiliation. Their relationship was chaotic, if anything.

Along the way, Marisa's need for sex overcame her professional relationship with Dred and they established a sordid affiliation, not love by any means, since both seemed incapable of that emotion. Not trust either. Just sex and now even that was not enough glue to make Dred want to stick to her arrogant persona. Overhearing the conversation between Marisa and Derek concerning the possibility of Elliott's surviving the fire pleased him. If Elliott were alive what would he be planning? Dred made up his mind to hang onto his present commitment for the time being. As long as there was money and sex, the position would be sustainable. *I'll play along and give the bitch what she wants for now.*

Chapter 48

AMANDA BARELY SLOWED THE JEEP, dumping Josh at his house, before she punched the accelerator and headed up the street to Derek's address. "Park it, brake, keys," she talked to herself as she flew out of the cart and stomped up the concrete path. She punched Derek in the chest when he opened the door. "You son of a bitch. How long have you known about this?"

"Hey, back off." He grabbed her wrists and held on. "What the hell you talking about?"

"Your sister, the cartel, the drugs. Don't act dumb with me, Derek. You've been playing us all along."

"Calm down, Amanda. Get a grip." He released her when he felt her tension dissipate. "I'd think you'd be a little more concerned about Meg's accident than this." He waited for it.

"Accident? What the hell you talking about?" Then it was her turn to wait.

Derek supplied a short version of the cart accident and watched Amanda's expressions change. "They loaned us another cart and I drove her home. A few bruises and scratches. Otherwise, you know Meg. She's tough as nails."

"Always appears to be, you mean."

"Okay, now that you've settled down, what's up? What's going on?" He walked into the kitchen and pulled two bottles of water out of the refrigerator. "Have a drink. Sit down and for God's sake, calm down." He didn't show any sign of frustration.

"Your sister and her gang just killed a Catalina cop, for God's sake. Greg. Stella's brother. He's dead."

Visibly shaken by the news, Derek leaned across the table to focus on Amanda's eyes, looking for the truth. "Amanda. I know nothing about this. Talk to me."

Amanda relayed the story of the drug bust gone wrong, how all hell broke loose with the cartel, Marisa's gang, and the Catalina Sheriff's department. She watched him carefully for any sign of recognition that he had already heard the story.

"You know I had nothing to do with this. Ankle monitor, remember? And I was with Meg all afternoon."

"You could have planned it, you could have known about it." Her flushed face was returning to a normal color, and while she felt spent from all the emotional warfare, she focused in on the problem.

"How do you know it was Marisa? Did someone see her?"

"She was ID'd by Josh. He recognized her picture that's been passed around the department. Has blonde hair now. No doubt, it was her."

"Blonde. Hmm. Hair color is cheap. So it was a drug bust? Give me the details."

"No, you don't get anything from me. She and her accomplice are now looking at murder charges. Not just drug running anymore. It's time to tell her you're ready to run. Call her. Tell her when you'll meet her and we'll end this matter. No more screwing around, Derek, or the deal's off."

Derek was mentally squirming. Splitting with Marisa was becoming a more realistic goal now that murder was involved. Whether to trust the FBI deal or not? That was the question. "Yeah, okay." He walked to the pantry and grabbed a bottle of Scotch for reinforcement. "Want a drink? Water isn't doing it for me." The look on her face told him no. He sat, drank the warm liquor, organized his thoughts and used the burner phone to dialed his sister.

"Hey you." Marisa's voice was tired. "I was going to call you."

"Thought you forgot me. How's it going?"

Marisa knew the FBI would be listening and had already made up her mind how many carrots she would dangle. "We might have to revise our thoughts about trading on the island. Our aerial drop went good, but the boat was stopped and boarded today. Shit, that was our most expensive boat."

"Are you okay? Did anyone see you?"

"I'm fine. There was a little gun activity."

"What?"

"Oh, the ass-kickin' cartel showed up with some heavy—I mean heavy—gun power. Fired on us. We got away though."

"We?"

"Dred and me. He had to pop some cop though. It's going to be a firestorm for a few days. We'll lie low." Marisa knew she was giving up a lot of information, but figured she might as well point the murder at Dred since the FBI was listening.

Time passed. No one talked. Amanda motioned with her hands. Palms up, palms down.

"Look, sis, with all this shit going on, let's take a step back. I've been thinking. It might be a good time to fold the tent. I'm ready to leave. I'm getting mixed signals from the FBI. Don't trust 'em." He looked at Amanda who gave him a nod of approval.

"Finally getting some smarts, huh?" Dred had been listening in on the conversation from the kitchen doorway, and mouthed the word 'careful' to her. She shook off the inaudible comment and continued. "I need two more days to wrap up some loose ends. Need to finish the distribution of drugs that we saved. Need to set up some contacts to see if heading back to Bullhead is a viable option."

"We might be able to work out of Oatman, or move down to Needles. Lots of places for our seaplanes to land on the river. Big empty areas of land with water access that haven't been developed yet. Or, are you thinking of going upstream? Maybe Lake Mead and bypass Laughlin? Head straight to Vegas?" Derek was pushing too hard.

Marisa paused.

Amanda shook her head. "Back off, you're spooking her," she mouthed.

"Not sure," Marisa continued. Which way to send the FBI? Encouraged to hear suggestions from him about a future, but knowing the FBI was listening, she pondered about how much of his encouragement was real? "I'll pencil it out. Still need the casinos to launder our money. Anyway, sit tight for two days and then we'll bust you out, so to speak. Can you keep the FBI from getting too close?"

"You know my penchant for speckling the truth with lies. No problem."

"Can hardly wait to see you."

"Me too, sis. Miss you."

"By the way," she whispered into the phone, "may have to dump Dred." She watched as Dred came in the room, and with a normal voice said, "I think I'll keep the blonde hair. Kind of sexy."

"You'd be sexy with a sack over your head. I'll act normal and play along with the FBI. Do you have anything for me to tell them? You know, a red herring or something?"

Marisa thought for a minute. "Sure. I found out the Sinaloa cartel drop their drugs by Black Jack Mountain. Due for another run tomorrow. That should keep the Feds busy for a day."

"How do you know that?"

"Got one of my guys in their camp. Been paying him big bucks but he sure as hell screwed up today. He's history. Okay, so we're set for now?"

"Yeah. I'll feed the Feds this info, wait, and then call you in two days so we can get the hell out of here. How do you plan on doing that, by the way?"

"Still working on it. Love ya."

"Back at ya," Derek said to a dead line.

Marisa gently closed the phone, concentrating deeply on the conversation, the innuendoes, the unspoken words, trying to sort out the truth about Derek. She had her misgivings. Was he going to set her up? What would be the benefit? A normal life for him. How much did he really want it? How much loyalty was there? As children they were inseparable. They clung together as Elliott would dish out the verbal and physical pain. They had always talked about running. It saved their minds and souls from total depression. But now with her taking up the criminal reins did he want to go along with the ride or jump off the galloping nightmare? And there's always the Meg chick. If he really loves her, what would he be willing to sacrifice? Me?

Dred interrupted her mental gymnastics. "You're not falling for that shit, are you? He's been turned."

Marisa didn't feel Dred was one hundred percent trustworthy but his instincts were usually spot-on. She raised her eyebrows, glanced his way and said, "We'll see."

———

Amanda knew the FBI had recorded the entire conversation and a meeting would be called as soon as she left Derek's house. But for now she spoke to him in general terms. "Fine. I don't believe that Marisa trusts you anymore. How do you feel about that?"

"She's no dummy. She should know that you're listening in our conversations, so she's feeding me what she wants you to believe. Convoluted shit. She did admit to the drug bust and murder of the cop. But she'll figure out a way to contact me when she wants to split other than the phone. She's not that dumb."

"You sure you don't know where she's holed up? If we could get her now at least we'd put her out of business. Save some bloodshed. Could catch the cartel later."

"Will my immunity still be good if that's the case?"

"Sure."

Derek didn't believe a word Amanda said. She'd say anything to catch Marisa's gang and he wondered if she still harbored hatred toward him for his participation in Meg's abuse. Probably. That sharp-edged sword just got a bit sharper.

Chapter 49

RACHAEL REACHED INTO HER PURSE, let her fingers search through the abyss until they finally located the vial. She relaxed for the first time in a week. The Catalina Flyer's magical rocking motion almost demanded that the passengers relax. Nothing else to do for the forty-five minute trip to the mainland. Arrangements had been made with Sarah, the DNA analyst at the Costa Mesa Police Department, to stay late at the office and perform a quick turnaround test on Zach's sample. Rachael was mentally jumping ahead, planning her next step to find Zach.

The sun was setting and the ocean swells were gently pushing the boat toward the coastline. Now the ever so slow, five-mile-an-hour zone was approaching, John Wayne's old mansion, the long row of multi-million dollar homes, and finally the boat dock for the Flyer appeared at the Fun Zone. While Rachael usually waited for the initial surge of people to disembark, this time she shoved her way past the masses and waded through the line of people waiting to board.

"Rachael?"

She turned to see Aunt Sharon in line.

Rachael didn't have either an inclination or time to stop for small talk, but good manners prevailed. "Hi Sharon. I'm in a hurry, but…what's going on? You going back to help find Stella?"

"You haven't heard?" Sharon's face morphed into instant sadness and she clutched Rachael's arm so tightly that Rachael flinched.

"Heard what? I talked to Josh before I left. He was on assignment and I think Meg was okay from her accident. There's no cell reception on the boat, but I just left the island an hour ago. What's going on?"

Sharon's eyes filled with tears. "Oh, Rachael. I'm so lost. There's been a terrible accident. Stella is dead. I'm going over to arrange her funeral."

"What?" Rachael couldn't find words. She grabbed Sharon and held on.

"Sally called me from Two Harbors. Looks like suicide. And Greg wants to adopt the baby."

The two women meshed by grief clung to each other, and Rachael supported Sharon until the tears subsided. "I'm so sorry Sharon. You've had more than your share of grief."

Sharon was being pushed along by other passengers boarding the boat and broke the embrace. "I'll call you when I get to the Island," she mouthed over her shoulder.

Rachael snapped back to the primary reason for the trip and took off running for the Uber she had waiting. "Costa Mesa P.D. and hurry if you can."

"Hurry isn't a word used much this time of day on P.C. I'll do my best."

It was after 6:00 p.m. when Rachael opened the glass doors to the police station, and while most of the employees had scattered for the night, there were two lab technicians waiting for her arrival. Rachael gave Sarah a quick hug and retrieved the vial from her purse. "Here ya go. I'm so nervous about the results. Are you going to start now?"

Sarah laughed. "Yeah, yeah. Hey girlfriend. Fill me in on this priority job. Must be really important for you to hand deliver." She started for her work station.

They had been friends since high school and even though they wouldn't see each other for months, or years, they were still best friends. Sarah knew about the serial killer history with Elliott and how the following year he had spread his mayhem across Catalina Island with his human trafficking scene, but she needed to be filled in on Zach's kidnapping and the drug war.

"I was wondering why I didn't get a wedding announcement. So. Josh was raped by Stella? Hmm. You believe that? My mind's eye can't quite grab hold of that scene." She tried to stifle a snicker, but failed.

"Of course I believe it. I was outside the window when it happened. He was tied down and drugged with all kinds of shit. He still doesn't remember." A mental picture of Stella, red hair flying, flailing around, naked, on top of Josh, brushed in and out of her memory.

"But he doesn't want his son? Wow. How does that sit with you? You've always wanted kids." Sarah took the sample and headed for the lab.

"You know me so well. As it stands, he may be coming around now that the baby is missing. And another thing. I passed Aunt Sharon a few minutes ago boarding the Flyer. She told me that Greg wants to adopt the baby if Josh doesn't accept the responsibility. I bet Josh really bristled at that. He probably envisioned Greg playing ball with Zach. Might've got to him. I think that mental image of a sane person willing to raise his boy made an impression. Hopefully, it's going to work out."

"Wow, his partner and best friend. Messed up, huh?" She sat back at her desk and took a deep breath, motioning to the other technician to join them. "Always were the positive one, weren't you. I hope it ends up in your favor for a change. Let's go grab a cup of coffee. Joe can finish up here."

They added sweetener to their coffee and plunked down into the straight-backed chairs.

Windowless and plain, the room added a touch of morbid forecasting. "Tell me about Greg,"

Sarah started. "How long have they been partners?"

"Eight years, like brothers. Now with Stella dead."

"What? When did that happen?"

"Aunt Sharon just told me. Looks like suicide."

"Say what?"

"Well, she drowned. Was by herself. I don't know if Josh even knows about it yet. He's out on assignment with Greg. This may be a game changer." Rachael paused and looked away, clouded up. "You know, Sarah, when we almost lost Meg, I had to overcome a new level of fear. Death was something that happened in other families, to other people. Even now, my stomach will retch and I freeze when certain things trigger me. Death is so damn final. It scares me."

"Wow. You live with death all the time with the police department. I'd think you'd be a little more hardened by now." A sad smile crossed her face.

"Not when it comes to loved ones. I'm worthless." Rachael swirled the coffee around in her cup and then started pacing, trying to shake off the emotion. "Should I wait for the results?"

"A preliminary should be done within the hour, so stay. Check out the magazines in the lobby and I'll start a new pot of coffee." She dumped the remnants of her coffee in the sink and tossed the foam cup.

"Do you have a computer I can use? I want to run a quick background on someone."

"Use my desk." She nodded down the hall. "You know where it is. My password is 'dogmeat.'"

"Charming."

Rachael typed in the password and immediately switched to her own police network in Bullhead. She could maneuver the screen faster. First she checked "Dred" then "Dave" hoping to find more intel on this mysterious character who was hanging around Meg. Without any observed tattoos or scars, sorting was a waste of time, so she switched her focus. She called the warden at San Quentin and after several minutes of elevator music he finally answered. "Warden, thanks for taking my call. This is Rachael Pennington, Bullhead City Police. I'm checking to see if you have put the death of Elliott Spencer to bed."

"We have, Rachael. The one tooth that remained after the fire gave DNA and was found to be his. So, as far as we are concerned, that concludes our investigation. You okay with that?"

Rachael decided to let the conversation sit until she had time to investigate her hunch. "That's really great news, Warden. I'll pass the word on to the authorities here in Bullhead and Catalina. Thanks again for your time."

"No problem. I know it's been haunting your family for a long time."

"Oh, there is one other thing. Would you check around with the guards that watched Elliott and see if he built any kind of relationship with a guy name 'Dred' or 'Dave'? Or possibly someone who visited him?"

"Will do. I have your number and I'll call with any update."

"Thanks again." She slowly put her phone down on the desk and searched back into her own memory cells. When Elliott reappeared in Bullhead to kidnap Meg, no one recognized him. He spent six months in Mexico and had undergone hours of plastic surgery, hair implants and weight reduction. It seemed as though Derek mentioned something important concerning all of the cosmetic work. She went down the mental list. That's it. He'd replaced all of his teeth with dental implants. How difficult would it have been to keep the old teeth? A perfect subterfuge for a later date to fool the police again? But what about the body—the incinerated body they found in his cell? If Elliott had paid another inmate to replace him in the cell and then incinerated him, the prison count would be short an inmate. She made a note to check with Amanda. She could rattle Derek's cage with the specifics. Rachael was so deep in thought that she didn't realize Sarah was standing in front of her. "Well?"

"I don't know if this will make you happy or sad, but…"

"But what?" Rachael held her breath.

"Blood type is a match. DNA will take a little longer, but this is good news. The baby you found on the island is probably Josh's son."

Rachael's eyes glassed over. Good news? What if crazy Elliott was behind all of this? Then what?

Chapter 50

ELLIOTT SPENSER'S SCHEMING EYES drifted across the lazy Pacific and then focused on the Carnival cruise ship anchored off shore. His pale skin exacerbated his newly coiffured black hair. After his successful escape from San Quentin he'd used his connections to sneak into Mexico. That was always the family escape plan. His physical appearance had been altered again in Cabo San Lucas where anything could be bought. The sharply pointed nose had been downsized, lips were thicker, fatty tissue added under the eyes. His new face was not nearly as interesting as his old one. Now he appeared plain, ordinary, older. No one would turn to look at him. This bothered him, but he knew that once he completed his mission on Catalina he would head back to Mexico for another facial transformation. Maybe more of a Brad Pitt look this time.

The suite at the Island Inn Hotel on Catalina met his immediate needs when he landed, but now he moved to the small house centrally located, unpretentious, comfortable, and most helpful of all, next door to Derek's house. Connected to the internet and with his new surveillance equipment running, his microcosm was complete.

Two weeks ago, while in Puerto Nuevo he'd located Marisa in

Mexico and contacted Gilbert to follow her and report all of her activities back to him.

"Senor. She sits under umbrella and drinks. No go out at night."

"She will. I have reason to believe she will be leaving very soon. Keep watching."

When Marisa called Gilbert two days later telling him she needed to fly to Catalina, Gilbert informed Elliott.

"Set up her flight tomorrow afternoon. I need to arrive in Catalina first and handle some business. We'll leave today. Is that a problem?"

"No, Senor. Let me know where you want me to pick you up. I need a little time to get some petrol."

"A little south of Rosarito, 1:00 p.m."

On schedule the seaplane landed near Rosarito Beach and transported Elliott to Catalina the same day. Everyone on his list of interested parties was returning to the island just as he planned.

Well, darling little sister, you were very lazy. Sitting in the shade and sipping Margaritas all day. Spending the money you stole from me. Seems it might be the perfect time for big brother to reappear and take care of you and Derek.

He changed his focus to the past. To the train ride. To his prize. To Meg. An immediate erection appeared.

Yes, dear friend. She is there on the island waiting for us. Our darling Meg, beautiful and vivacious as ever. But unfortunately she needs to pay for rejecting me. Yes, indeed.

He groaned, then smiled as the eruption came and went.

Elliott never put anything in writing and coded the phone numbers on his cell phone, erasing any messages and swapping out his phone on a weekly basis. The complexity of his new plan demanded notes, so he reviewed his master plan. He headed for the bathroom to clean up then left the house.

Now it's my turn, dear family.

He felt sure that Meg, Rachael and Amanda, each in her own space on the island, felt a chill.

Chapter 51

OLD AL WOKE UP WITH A START. "Where am I?" and then the hospital room came into focus. "Oh, yeah. Hospital." His head ached from the concussion. The bandages were too tight. His tired eyes moved around the space in little hops, in and out of focus, stopping at the shadow in the corner.

"Catherine? Is that you?" For fifty years he had been her guardian, but only witnessed her apparition one time. Ten years ago when she was mad because of new construction, she caused some mild chaos. But here she was again. "What's wrong, old girl?"

His skin exploded with heat. "You mad at me? Not me? Who?"

The shadow moved.

The door opened.

"Mr. James, you okay?" It was the night nurse on her ten o'clock rounds. "I thought I heard you talking to someone." She looked around the room.

"Hot. I'm hot."

She came to his side and checked his forehead, then reached for her digital thermometer.

"Nope. Everything seems to be fine." She checked the monitors and his IV bag.

A fire truck whizzed by, sirens blaring full bore.

The nurse went to the window and looked across the roof tops. "Oh, no. It looks like there's a fire on the edge of town. Lordy, I hope not. Last time we had a fire it almost burned the whole island up. Lack of water, and such." She started back to Al's bedside.

"Would you mind lookin' again, Missy? Could it be near Hotel Catherine?"

The nurse returned to the window and mentally walked up the street from the hotels on Crescent. "Let's see. That would be where the rental carts are, then the curve in the road, and…" She stopped abruptly. "Looks like you're right. Catherine's it is. What a shame."

Al rolled over and faced the wall. "Oh, Catherine. What have you done?"

Chapter 52

ELLIOTT RENTED A CART FOR THE WEEK and toured the island, gathering as much information as possible. Within one day of arriving he located his targets. Meg's working hours at Hotel Catherine and the ghost tour were marked down in his small tablet, along with her address on East Whittley Avenue. Likewise, Derek's daily breakfast at Jack's with Amanda, and his address were also noted in the tablet.

One seat remained at the counter at Jack's when he entered. Facing both Amanda and Derek would be the final test of his new identity. The diner was crowded and people were rushing through breakfast to hurry off to work.

Elliott pushed through the crowd aiming toward the single seat at the counter and quickly sat down. Amanda removed the used plates and wiped the area. "Good Morning. May I take your order?" She whipped out her pad.

"Coffee and a bagel with cream cheese." Elliott continued reading the menu, and only his eyes traveled upward to check Amanda's face. She showed no sign of recognizing his altered voice. He pushed a little harder and looked her square in the eyes, hoping his brown contact lenses hid his searing blue eyes. "No, change that to an English muffin."

"No problem, anything else?" Amanda's eyes checked him out and then glanced to the door as Derek entered. "I'll be right back with your order." She slid the order form under the cook's clip and headed toward Derek. "Hi, big guy. Saved your favorite table for you." She shot a beguiling smile his way and gave him a quick hug.

Elliott smiled and asked the man sitting next to him. "She's a cutie. That her boyfriend, or is she available? Might want to tap that."

His neighbor, an old timer and regular at the diner, took immediate offense. "Clean it up buddy. She's a local and needs to be treated with respect." He scoffed, picked up the daily paper and turned his back on the obnoxious Elliott.

"Sorry. Meant no harm." Not wanting to push his luck, he made quick work of his breakfast and left the diner.

Two sets of eyes checked him out as he left. Not a glimmer of recognition registered.

Elliott pretended to be window-shopping at the souvenir store next door until Derek appeared and headed in the direction of his house. Nothing interesting there. A quick call was made as he started for Catherine's to confront Meg with his new image. "Don't register any surprise. I'm here on the island. Go to Catherine's in ten minutes and meet me." The person at the other end of the call started to talk, but Elliott disconnected the call before any questions could be asked. He continued down Crescent at a brisk pace.

It was fifteen minutes before the beginning of Meg's shift, so Elliott ordered a beer and took a table next to the windows, watching the tourists shuffle by. A group of twenty thirsty passengers entered, taking all available tables as Dred entered. He walked to the bar, grabbed a stool and swiveled around, checking out the crowd. His gaze passed Elliott without breaking pace. Starting back a second time, checking the facial features more carefully, he took a closer look at Elliott, not because he recognized him, but because he was the only person not chatting with a group. He stood and walked to Elliott's table.

"Mind if I join you? I don't like to sit at the bar." He stood tall and waited, looking at Elliott's hands, posture, face, hair. He was ready to turn and leave. Nothing was familiar except… something.

"That's fine. I'm the same way. Have a seat, Mr…"

"Dred. Strange name, I know, but it seems to suit my personality." He was nervous and it showed. "Just kidding. My name is Dave." He pulled out the wooden chair and sat facing Elliott, searching for any sign of recognition. Nothing. He starting checking out the people in the room again, figuring Elliott hadn't arrived, feeling this stranger sharing the table was not his former boss. "Look, fella. I've changed my mind about breakfast. Have a good day." Dred stood and started for the door when Elliott grabbed his wrist and twisted it.

"Sit down, fool. It's me."

"Shit, man. You had me going." A bead of sweat formed on his forehead. "We thought you were dead, and then I got this call to show up here. Didn't sound like you, but who else would it be? What the hell's going on?"

"Retribution and murder. What else?"

———

Meg walked through the door at Catherine's and headed straight for the bar. She liked the noon shift. The cash was in the register, beer and hard liquor stocked, the tables ready and she didn't have to close. A quick exit after an eight-hour shift was easy and then she could find her Island buddies and party. She spotted Dred sitting at the table with some stranger and headed that way.

Dred panicked. "El Jefe. What'll we do?"

"Stay cool. Meet me tonight behind El Galleon at 11:00."

Meg was getting closer.

"If she asks who I am, tell her I'm visiting the island for a few days and asked you about available attractions. Keep it simple. This will be the perfect test to see if she recognizes me."

"What if she does, my God." He stood up and sent a smile her way. "Morning, boss. Right on time."

"Sure enough. My shift starts in five minutes. How's the traffic been?" She sent a happy smile Elliott's way.

Elliott's hand moved sharply to his lap to push down his erection.

"Kind of light 'til now. Carnival Line pulled in. Oh, speaking of visitors, this is…guess I didn't catch your name."

"Jeff."

"Okay, Jeff, meet Meg. He was asking about tours and stuff. Staying two days on the island. You're the authority. Any suggestions?" He didn't wait for her answer. "Look, I've gotta scoot. Got another job interview."

"Okay. Good luck." Meg eyed him with a suspicious question in mind---like the last time he had a supposed interview, but met with someone in the bushes. "I'll call you if I can't handle the bar. You be around?"

"Sure. Call me." He couldn't get out of there fast enough.

Elliott had watched every movement, facial expression, verbal exchange and knew she had no clue as to his identity. "So Meg. Any suggestions?" Saying her name out loud turned him on. She was only a foot away. He reached into his pocket and squeezed his growing penis again.

She twitched like something wicked ran down her spine and wondered why. Gave him a quick once-over. Nothing registered. "It'd be best to check in with the tourist information gang or the Conservancy. They could tell you when, where and times. I'd suggest the ghost tour." She smirked at that. "Cause I'd be your guide. Starts every evening at eight o'clock from the casino. You need to buy your ticket in advance though. Tips are welcomed."

"Hey Meg, I need a warm up on my coffee, if you're not too busy," an irate customer yelled.

"Right with you, honey," she said as she picked up Dred's cup and walked away from Elliott, thinking this Jeff guy's kind of creepy.

———

The El Galleon bar was still going strong when Dred turned the corner to the alley. Elliott was waiting in the shadows. "You're late."

"Meg's replacement didn't show up, so I had to close the bar. Sorry. This place is too public. Let's go somewhere else."

"It'll do for now. Here's a new cell phone. I've been watching Marisa's operation. What the hell's she doing? Crossing the cartel? She knows that's a suicide mission. And Derek. What's he up to?"

Dred liked living too much to try and play both sides with Elliott. It took only minutes to tell him about Derek's position of escaping with Marisa or working with the FBI and turning state's evidence against her.

"What's your gut feeling?" Elliott continued extracting the information from his old assistant.

"Seems like Derek wants out, even at the expense of turning his sister in. That's what I think. Marisa changes her mind daily. Wants no part of working with the Feds. She's really getting me worried. Making stupid decisions, always in a hurry to get the next dollar."

"And you. Where are you in all of this melodrama?" Elliott's piercing eyes shot a laser beam right through him.

"With you, now that you're back. Was with Marisa, but was beginning to pull away. Don't like messin' with the cartel. Figure I'd wait it out for another week and then decide."

"Is the baby still with Gilbert's wife? What was Marisa thinking?"

Dred's body snapped, like struck with a live wire, and then he stuttered around.

"What the hell is the matter with you?" asked Elliott.

"Well, Jefe. The kid was my screw-up. I was supposed to kill the occupant of room 230 but the bitch changed rooms. Killed the wrong person. Kid got noisy so I grabbed him." Dred stopped and stared at the man across the table. Unbelieving. The proverbial light came on. "You. It was you who hired me through the dark web. You wanted to get rid of Meg. That was supposed to be her room."

"Don't know what you're talking about," Elliott answered. "Your blunder may work to our advantage however."

Relief and reprieve washed over Dred. "Yeah, well, the kid's tucked away at Two Harbors."

"We need to change that first. You move the kid to another spot on the backside of the island. Cut Marisa out of the loop. Play innocent if anyone asks. Don't let Marisa or Derek know that I'm here or even alive. I need to know their real intentions---if their loyalty to me is still intact or if they're traitors."

"Move the kid? Why?"

One look from Elliott made Dred realized his mistake. "Sorry, boss. Yeah, there're a bunch of huts on the backside. I'll find a nanny and do it tomorrow."

"Use Gilbert's wife. She's trustworthy."

"Then what?"

"I save them or kill them."

Chapter 53

"FRED. YOU BUSY TODAY?" Rachael finished throwing her clothes into an overnight bag and raced into the bathroom of Motel 6 to grab her cosmetics. She stuffed the partial DNA report into the side pocket and urged–on Fred's answer.

"Just landing at the Fullerton Airport. What's up?" As usual his touchdown was perfect and he taxied the small Beech Bonanza toward his designated tie down location.

"Need a ride to Catalina ASAP." She slid the suitcase to the floor and started toward the door. "Have some vital information to get to the PD there. In a hurry. You can probably tell." She pushed the elevator button and hoped the phone wouldn't die.

"So what's new?"

Fred and Rachael had both graduated from Esperanza High School in Orange County and remained friends. He would land his seaplane on the Colorado River and spend a weekend with her in Bullhead City whenever he was in the area.

"Look, I need to replace a landing light, then a quick checkup, fuel her up and I'll be ready to go."

"I'll jump on the 55 Freeway and can be in Fullerton around 2:00. Work for you?"

"You buy lunch, and it's a deal."

"Done."

Rachael's car glided through the parking lot and she settled into the hour white-knuckle drive through horrendous traffic. She met Fred at the Fullerton airport, hugged him, and handed over a McDonald's bag along with a milk shake.

"Hmm. I was thinking more like Jack's in Catalina." He opened the bag and tossed a fry into his mouth. "This'll do, Cheapskate." Energetic as usual, he steered her to the plane and opened the door. They were airborne by three.

"Wanna tell me what's going on?" Fred shot a glance her way. "I've got a few days with no customers and maybe I can help." The clouds separated and Catalina came into view.

"Wow. What happened to the overcast? The clouds?" She glanced down at the landing strip. "Not much wiggle room for landing, is there?"

"Nope. First time I landed here I almost lost it. There's a katabatic onshore wind condition coming southeast from the mainland, close to the runway that causes a downdraft. Clouds clear up like magic. The fun part of landing here is that the runway is only 3200 feet long and it slopes up. You're also landing 1600 feet above sea level which fools a lot of novice pilots."

Rachael's eyes widened as the land appeared to reach up and grab her. "Oops. There goes my stomach."

Fred laughed. "Novice. But how about it? Need a right-hand man for your adventure?"

"Thanks for the offer, but I'm thinking no. It's a police matter."

"I didn't know you transferred your badge to the island." His facetious tone was not lost on Rachael.

"Smart ass. You know, as a citizen you can do a lot more than a cop can. If you're willing to hang around for a day or two, it might be helpful. The cops are involved with a murder at Catherine's Hotel, now Stella's suicide, so the disappearance of Josh's baby is on a back burner I'm afraid. I owe you big time for the ride." Rachael chewed on her lower lip as the plane landed and felt like saying a few "Hail Mary's" in gratitude for Fred's piloting skills. They taxied toward the hangers. "Excuse me for a sec. Gotta make a call." She quickly dialed Meg's cell phone as she unlatched her seatbelt and climbed from the plane.

"Meg." The call went to voicemail. "Listen, sis. We have partial results from the DNA testing. The baby's blood type is the same as Josh's, but we won't get a full profile for a few more days. It's enough for me. Can you go back to Two Harbors? To the store? My friend Sally will point out the baby when he comes in with the nanny and then you can follow her? Don't approach her. I just need her location. We need to be ready to move when the full report comes in. Can you do that? Call me back." She headed for the airport office.

"Wait up, I need a ride to town," yelled Fred. "Gonna meet a buddy for a beer. How about a lift?" Fred took two giant steps and caught up with her.

"Of course. Sorry, I should have offered." Rachael gave him a quick hug and apologized again for her dismissive action. After paying for the cart, they took off down the one way trail to town. She stopped long enough for Fred to jump out at the corner at Whittley. Meg hadn't called her back which was unusual. "You know, Fred, if you could hang around, it might be helpful. Meg doesn't seem to be answering and she's usually my sidekick. Might need a replacement if you're not busy."

"I packed my sleuth gear just in case." He laughed. "You know how to reach me. Later."

Rachael parked in front of the PD and stopped at the front desk. "Hi Lynda, is Josh around?"

Lynda looked shocked by the question. "No, God, Rachael, I thought you knew."

"What? Knew what? What's happened?" the fear in her voice was instant. "Is Josh okay?"

———

Rachael spotted Josh sitting behind the semi-closed curtain in the ER room. Head lowered, shoulders caved forward. The bed was empty. "Oh, Josh. I'm so sorry. Lynda tried to tell me what happened, but it was sketchy." She sat next to him, took his shaking hand and waited.

"God, Rach. How could this happen? We were supposed to grow old and retire together. Go out fishing every day. You know what he said to me this morning?" He didn't expect an answer. "He said he wanted to adopt Zach and raise him. I could be his uncle. Shit. I was so pissed. I hated him for saying that. What does that say about me? About him? I don't know what to do. He was my friend, my brother."

"I know. I know, darling." She knew sitting there would not help so she gently took his hand and pulled him up. "It's okay to cry."

As if he had been waiting for permission, Josh's body crumpled into a million pieces and shook from the eruption of tears. She led him out of the hospital and they settled into the cart. Processing the loss would be painfully slow, but Rachael knew they had to move forward to find Zach. She drove the cart to his home in silence.

Chapter 54

THE FBI SCHEDULED ANOTHER MEETING between Meg and Derek since the last meeting was cut short by the accident. Meg's job was to filter through his conversation and cement his intentions. Flee or cooperate. His ankle monitor was removed and a cart provided to pick her up. This would be Derek's last opportunity to demonstrate his allegiance to the FBI. Time was running out. Amanda was getting impatient.

Meg sat in her small living room, watching the carts drive past. She had changed her clothes three times, along with her earrings and sandals. Each time she changed she would scold herself. Dress up for that jerk? I think not, and yet her light makeup belied the underlying excitement of seeing him again. She heard the screech of brakes outside the house. Her nervousness was obvious. She needed the upper hand so she jumped up shook her arms, legs, hips and anything that would move to start the blood pumping for energy. By the time he knocked on the door, she was ready for him.

Derek was thrilled with the opportunity to see her again, to make her understand his motives and actions over the past two years. Realizing this was probably his last chance to make or break their relationship, he pressed forward. It had been two days since she listened to his forward speech about caring for her, a discourse that was interrupted by the cart accident. When she opened the door, all planned fetching remarks disappeared. He was speechless. She was motionless, frowning and breathtakingly beautiful. "Hi," was all he could muster.

"Derek." Icicles formed on each letter of his name. "Where are we going?"

A quick recovery brought the answer. "Thought we'd drive up to the Wrigley Mansion like last time, only with no accidents. Have a picnic lunch. That way no one will bother us."

"Well, don't get the idea that any of this is going to be easy. I have a lot of questions regarding our previous relationship that need to be addressed." Her snippy attitude was not lost on him.

They sat in silence as the cart chugged up and down the narrow streets finally up the hill to the mansion.

"How about here for lunch?" He stopped the cart under a lofty eucalyptus tree facing the picturesque harbor. "Spread the blanket, will ya?" He tossed it her way then took a wicker basket from the back of the cart. He remembered from their days at the river that Meg liked unpretentious food so he unwrapped a pastrami sandwich, chips and a Coors Light. "Lunch, my dear."

"What? Is this supposed to be a peace offering? Pastrami?" There was such a hate-love mash-up inside her that she couldn't be civil. *Don't lose sight of today's assignment. Knock it off. Settle down. Make him talk.* "Is this supposed to render me weak? Forgive you for assisting your brother in planning my demise? I think not." She hesitated and then decided to back off some of the hostility, but knew he expected some anger, so she minimized her attack. He deserved more than she could ever hand out, but that would have to wait. She plopped down on the blanket, facing the view, not him.

"Guess I deserve that, but since you're here I'd like to try and mitigate some of that anger. Meg, just listen while you eat."

She mumbled something that he couldn't decipher, and then grabbed the beer.

Realizing that this was probably the last opportunity he would ever have to express his side of their story, he started at the beginning. "When we first met at the Oasis it was a pure happening, not arranged by anyone. Your friends invited me over to talk at the bar and then you arrived. I was a goner the first time you laughed. I was practicing law in LA and the only friends I had were stuffy attorneys. Then you were there. Fun, gorgeous, articulate, ferociously athletic. What wasn't to love? Driving the boat, swimming naked in Willow Cove, those were the most memorable times of my life. My brother came to visit one weekend in Los Angeles and I told him that I was falling in love. Before I could tell him your name, he said he had moved to Laughlin and that he was also in love. The more he talked, the more I knew it was with you." He took a breath, and then swallowed some beer.

"Yeah," Meg said, "I know of all of this. If you had any balls, you would have told Elliott to back off. Fought for me or something. Not just roll over." A combination of hurt and disappointment poured forth from Meg. She had always wanted to tell him this. To chastise him. To punish him.

"It wasn't that easy. I owed him. Elliott raised me and my sister, Marisa, after our folks were killed. Paid for law school and paid for Marisa's education. I knew he lived on the fringe of the law, but he was also a respected business man in Laughlin. When he told me your name I didn't speak up. I owed him too much. That's when I backed away and told you and also Elliott that I was gay. It was the easiest way out."

"Well, turning your so-called love off that quickly sure was convenient."

"I led him to believe that I had found a male lover in Laughlin. It solved both problems. I had no clue that he was the serial killer until after he kidnapped you. I was devastated. I have never been a part of his vile business and when he grabbed you again, deploying his human trafficking venture, I vowed to save you which I almost did."

He stopped and looked at her. She munched away on her sandwich. No eye contact, no readable expression on her face. The only sound was that of children playing on the beach down below.

Meg's mind drifted back to the beginning days. She was falling in love for the first time, something more than puppy love. Seeing him, touching him was all that she dreamed of. And then on that night when they were walking, hand in hand on the river walk, it couldn't have been more romantic. She shook her head to replace the happy memories with bad ones. Elliott. The rape. Biting, painful intrusion of her body. Derek said he didn't know that Elliott was the serial killer, but she wasn't completely convinced of that. Derek did try to save her though. Her emotions were all over the place. There was too much personal stuff going on. His confession was tearing her apart. "Take me home. I don't want to do this anymore." She couldn't trick him now. Her assignment would have to wait. She needed time to think, process his words, reassess her own feelings.

"Since it's true confession time, let me explain my side." Meg's eyes demanded his attention. "I was in love with you. Not the shallow type of relationship that I have experienced, but the white picket fence kind. My heart was growing flowers until you sprayed it with Roundup. You tore me up. Aside from all the Elliott shit, you disappointed me, chewed up my heart and spit it out. I'll never—never—believe you again."

"Oh, Meg." He moved toward her.

"No, you don't." She put her hands up to stop him.

"What? That's it? No forgiveness?" Accepting that his tender outpourings had fallen on deaf ears, Derek bristled, stood, and pulled the blanket from under Meg. "Fine, get in." He was well aware of her stubborn side. A Pennington characteristic.

They didn't speak on the way home. Derek stopped in front of Meg's house, turned off the engine and took her hand. She flinched. He backed off. Meg, the interrogator was back.

"Don't tell me that just because you regurgitated your weak confession that you think it's okay to make a move on me." Meg turned sideways and glared at him.

Derek smiled his crooked smile that Meg used to find so alluring. "Was afraid this would be the last chance I'd see you, so decided to give it a shot. I thought maybe, well maybe, this would be the time —like forgiving the past transgressions?"

"I don't know where you got that idea. Transgressions? That's what you call it? There are a few items on the agenda that haven't been discussed." She finally looked into his blue eyes and felt an urge to straddle and kiss him. Damn, she thought.

"Go for it. Let's get it all out in the open. I'm tired of apologizing for caring about you."

Meg took a deep breath and started in on all the painful questions. "You know they all concern Elliott and a few about your sister Marisa." She paused to regroup. She had to get past the emotions and concentrate on the information that Amanda needed. "Yes or no answers, or possibly one sentence. No weaseling out. Tell the truth, don't embellish."

"Fine."

"Were you, or anyone you know, involved with the kidnapping of Josh's baby, Zach?"

"No,"

"When was the last time you saw or talked to Elliott?"

He mentally backtracked through the calendar. "Nine months ago at the trial I saw him, a year ago on the yacht when he shot me."

"Do you believe he's dead?" Meg didn't believe for a minute that Elliott had perished in the fire at San Quentin prison. He was much too rich, clever and connected not to have planned the perfect jail break. Derek's answer was pivotal in their relationship.

He took his time to answer since he too had reason to doubt. The gut answer sprang forth. "No."

An involuntary shudder ripped through Meg's voice. "Oh, God." The fear gave way to instant panic. Shortness of breath. "He's still out there. After me? Here, on the island? Probably responsible for my parasailing accident, and maybe the brakes on the cart?" This time when he took her hand she didn't pull away.

"Meg, I don't know for sure. With the ankle monitor on and only the FBI phone and no internet, I'm limited to investigate. I have no proof, but I know the spider web network he has with the underground. He's capable of anything, everything, and yes, if he's alive, you would assuredly be his target. That would include your family too. I'm so sorry."

She sank against his shoulder, rubbing the inside of her wrist where Elliott had tried to carve his initials. "What about Marisa? Have you talked with her?"

"Yes. Amanda set it up and has monitored all of the calls." He worried that someone knew about the one night he escape through the bathroom window. "I'm supposed to meet with her tomorrow night and make sure she's going to cooperate with the FBI in exchange for immunity."

"Does Marisa think Elliott's alive?" That wasn't on Amanda's list of questions, but Meg wanted to know.

"That's a tough one. We haven't talked about it very much." Derek instantly knew that his vacillating between a quick escape with Marisa or a new start with the FBI had to end. Immunity, betrayal, or escape? "I think not. From our conversations it seems she's intent on carrying on the family business. She's setting up a new route for the drugs. Decided to stay small, I think. The Sinaloa's frighten her. Wants me to join her."

"Does Amanda know this?"

"No."

"No what? You're keeping this from her? Are you going to run?" Meg knew that was a stupid question. Why would he answer yes? "You said you only talked to Marisa one time. What? Another lie?"

"Before we go any further, I have a question for you. Did Amanda put you up to sweet talking me into confessing some huge plot? Are you wearing a wire?"

Meg unbuttoned her blouse and faced him. It was nothing he hadn't seen before. "Do you see a wire?"

As much as Derek wanted to, he wouldn't look at her perfect body, he turned away. "When we undress next time, it should be because we care about each other. So, how about this? I have loved you since that first night at the Oasis Casino. If Elliott hadn't ruined everything, I believe we'd be married by now. That's how committed I am to you. If I knew for sure that Elliott was alive and on this island, I would hunt him down and kill him. I promise if I have one breath left I will protect you." He leaned back in the cart and finally looked at her.

Meg was overwhelmed with his moving words. Speechless. Silence. More silence until Meg finally uttered, "Thank you." There was no doubt in her mind that he was being open and honest with her. "Derek. You're in a terrible position. What're you going to do?"

"In my heart I know Marisa won't clean up her act. She wants the money, the thrill. She was actually a partner of Elliott's. Not a fearful accomplice like me. I'll speak with Amanda. I'll set up an escape plan with her so we can be captured. Along the way I'll find out if she or Dred know anything about Elliott."

"Dred?"

"Yeah, the guy that's been helping you out at Catherine's. I thought you knew that he's working with Marisa. I believe he was Elliott's right hand man in Bullhead."

"You mean Dave? That's the name he gave me. Was he the druggie that was hanging out with Stella? I thought he was a little strange, but no, I didn't know about his affiliation with Elliott or Marisa. Nor did Amanda. You gonna tell her or should I?"

"My job. I'll call her when I get home. I think she already knows though."

"Good, call her." Meg stepped out of the cart and paused. "You may walk me to the door." She was turning the temperature down on her emotions again.

Derek didn't hesitate. They walked side by side to the porch, both feeling like they were on their first date.

"Strange. For the first time in my life I want to ask a girl if it's okay to kiss her good night." He smiled and stood there. Awkward.

"It's a good thing you didn't go for it. I'm sure you remember all of the Krav training I've had. In fact I just got my black belt. I'd be picking you off the pavement."

He didn't move. "I guess that's a no?"

"A friendly hug would be in order, I suppose. After all we have known each other for a few years." Her pulse was racing. She wanted that hug, needed that hug.

The hug was long and passionate, filled with wonder and unrealized potential.

————

His piercing blue eyes froze on the embrace. The bushes stirred a little as the person's hatred grew. The bullet was meant for Meg but she moved as he pulled the trigger. The shattered glass crashed to the ground. So did Meg and Derek.

Chapter 55

ELLIOTT WASTED NO TIME implementing his next formidable plan. Missing the kill shot was a mere inconvenience now. He loved convoluted plots, building up the intrigue and suspense for all of the characters involved and also giving himself more opportunities to escape if the plans failed. "Gilbert's been contacted? Did his bitch wife move Josh's brat to another bungalow? Does it have an adjoining shack like I asked?"

"Just as you told me to do." Dred stood at attention.

"My darling sister Marisa will be unnerved to find the baby gone. More the better. Keep her on edge to make more mistakes. How she thought she had the ability to take over the physical aspect of the business is anyone's guess. Egotistical bitch. And I have plans for both Meg and Derek." He paused, started to chastise himself for missing the shot, but his narcissistic persona closed the door on the thought. "It's time for a family reunion."

"What's Meg got to do with all of this?" Dred was annoyed with all the personal stuff going on and felt Elliott's motivation was shifting. His mindset should be focused on drugs and money. "Drugs. That's where the money is. Forget this revenge shit. Marisa won't want to be a part of this Meg fantasy. How much of this does she know?"

"She knows nothing, not even that I'm still alive. I plan on surprising Marisa this evening. I've been watching her campsite and Gilbert has been informing me of her plans which coincide with what you said."

Dred shot him a fierce look. "You checking up on me? Don't trust me?"

"Calm down. I had my concerns about Gilbert, so I was matching his information with yours. Of course I trust you." Elliott's tone amplified his insincerity.

Dred was on instant alert, but didn't show any apprehension.

"Gilbert broke off relations with her now that we moved the baby. You are my only informant. Let me know her plans so I can stay one step ahead. Get her away from the camp tonight." He paused seeing a small loose thread in his tapestry of crime. "I don't know these new men she's hired. They might not be aware of my reputation and try to protect her." He looked to Dred for a response to the non-question.

"They work for me. No problem. Getting her away from camp may not be easy though. She thinks she calls all the moves."

"Imbecile. Don't bother me with your inept problems. Just handle it." His hand reached inside his sweat pants, searching. "I have plans for Derek and Meg this evening, a special rendezvous of sorts since today's plan didn't work. Tomorrow I may want you to follow Meg and abduct her if tonight's plan doesn't work. I want Meg and the brat out of the way. I'll tell you the rest of the plan later. Give me the burner phone that you have. I'll input my new number." Elliott fumbled with the phone and finally threw it back to Dred.

"Abduct Meg? What am I supposed to do with her?"

Elliott eyed Dred and wondered about his questions. His old submissive attitude had disappeared and was now replaced with an independent air.

"You'll be informed later if tonight's plan doesn't work. Take her to Gilbert's wife. Leave a guard. Keep Meg tied down. She's fast and strong. This is tentative but I want you to be ready for my call. I still want you to meet me at Fisherman's Cove at ten tomorrow night with Marisa. Now get the hell out of here. It's time I let my bitchy sister know I'm still boss."

———

The next afternoon Dred pulled the Jeep to an abrupt stop half a mile from Marisa's hideout. His life depended on his next move. Stay with Marisa and take down Elliott? Switch and join Elliott's insane plan to capture Meg again and take over the drug business? Maybe get immunity from the FBI and join Derek if that's the way he's headed? Or maybe start out on my own, he thought. I have all the contacts. Incapable of such a momentous decision he decided to let the next few hours decide for him. But for now, how to get Marisa to Fisherman's Cove?

"Marisa. I met Derek in town. He needs to talk to you right now. Something's come up."

Always suspicious regarding any immediate change of plans, Marisa walked to the window and scanned the exterior landscape of the house. She fell into a critical mind fog, mulling around any possible motive Dred might have to entrap her. Finally she landed on one potential problem. "What's wrong with the burner phone? Why do we have to meet in person?"

"How the hell should I know? I'm just your flunky, remember. You don't wanna go? Fine. I could give a shit." He turned and walked toward the door.

"Where and when?" Marisa yelled. She was comfortable with his answer.

Dred knew he had her. "Fisherman's Cove. Ten-thirty tonight." He kept walking, not willing to continue the conversation.

"Fine. Fire up the jeep. Bring along some extra ammo. And men."

"He said to come alone and pack a small bag."

"Small bag?" Marisa smiled. "It's about time he's decided to run. Thought maybe he was getting soft on me." She hurried into the bedroom to pack for the rendezvous. Delirious with the thought that Derek and she would be on the run. Just the two of them like old times.

Chapter 56

MEG, DEREK, AND AMANDA LEANED against the street guard rail as the forensics team finished their work. "Tell me again. What happened?"

Meg was angry, passing through the emotions of scared by almost being shot, through the questioning process and ending up feeling of course, it was Elliott, and turning scarlet mad. "That lunatic. This is it. No more Miss Nice Gal. I'm taking him down like the rabid dog he is."

"Calm down, missy." Amanda looked to the officers. "What happens now?"

"We'll take the slug to the department, run an analysis and then check our data bank."

"What caliber?"

"Forty-five. Whoever took the shot meant business." The bullet was placed in an evidence bag, a notation written, and the men said their goodbyes as they headed off.

"Let's go get the broom and finish up here. Rachael's got a lead on the baby that I need to follow up on. Derek, I have enough info from you, so hit the trail. I'll be in touch later." Amanda wanted him gone. "Wait. One other thing. The ankle bracelet is too damn visible to put back on."

"Thank God. It's been a pain," Derek said.

"Here's a ring with a GPS tracking devise installed. Less conspicuous. There will be a three to four hour delay in startup time, so don't do anything you'll regret."

"Marisa will know that I wouldn't wear this piece of crap." He looked at the brass monstrosity.

"Put it in your pocket when she's around, but always have it on you. Got it?"

"Yeah." He turned to Meg and took her hand. "You okay with me leaving? I can stick around for a while 'til you're comfortable."

Amanda didn't like the intimacy. Meg cooperating? Not good.

"Thanks anyway. I'm fine and I'll take my gun out of the closet and relocate it in the kitchen. I won't be caught with my pants down again."

Derek tried to stifle his laugh, but it bellowed out anyway. "Twice in the same week?"

"You jerk. Get out of here," Meg laughed as he headed to his cart. She tried not to feel the giddiness of his hug minutes before, but it still lingered. Big time.

"What's that all about? You were supposed to pump him for info, not let him get into your pants again. Damn it, Meg. If you're not going to take this mini assignment seriously, then you're off the case."

"Oh, cut the self-righteous shit. Nothing happened except…"

"Except what?"

"Except Elliott is still alive and here on the island with us."

Chapter 37

"LOOK, MEG. IS THAT TEMPORARY bartender a flake or what? With Al still in the hospital and the recent fire damaging the hotel, I had to cancel all registered guests for the rooms, but really need to keep the bar open. Can you handle both shifts for a while? Or, do you know of anyone else in town that can fill in?" The owner of Catherine's Hotel was sitting in his Brea, California living room, feeling old and useless. He needed the income from the bar until the escrow closed.

Meg hated to disappoint him but with everything else going on in her life she knew she couldn't handle it. "I'm so sorry, Mr. Schaner, I have to say no. I'll finish up this shift, but I think you'll have to shut it down." It was three o'clock.

"Damn. I don't know if you believe the ghost stories about the hotel or not, but I can guarantee you that if Catherine's beer is not waiting on her table at 5:00, there will be hell to pay." He was quiet for a minute. "Okay. If that's the way it is. I'll call the Conservancy and see if they can watch over the property until escrow closes next week. I'm going to Idaho on business, or I'd do it myself."

"I'm really sorry. I'll drop by every day and make sure it's not being vandalized. If I can, I'll set out Catherine's beer for her. That's the best I can do."

"I understand. Thanks, Meg. I know this sounds crazy, but I really worry about Catherine. I've seen the results of her rage before. No one will admit it, but I'm sure she was behind the fire the other day. Lucky, the bar is still intact."

"The fire department said it looked like faulty wiring," Meg commented as she tied her bartending apron.

"Oh, right," mumbled Mr. Schaner as he disconnected the line.

Meg replaced the receiver on the wall phone and thought about the conversation. What had Mr. Schaner meant? He'd seen the results of her rage? She'd heard stories, but scoffed at them. Written them off as Island fun. But? She shook it off. There were only two customers in the bar and their glasses were full. Within the next two hours she cleaned the kitchen, swept the floor, locked all the windows in the hotel rooms that weren't charred and put the cash in the tiny wall safe. At five o'clock she filled a mug of beer for Catherine, set it on her table and turned the key in the front door lock for the last time in Catherine's Hotel. She paused and said, "Now Catherine, behave yourself."

————

Two notes, allegedly signed by Amanda, were prepared and a local boy was paid five dollars to deliver them. Both notes were stuck in the door jambs of the rentals houses and were identical: "Go to the Casino, second level at 7:00 tonight. The ballroom. Change of plans. Don't tell anyone. Amanda."

The second floor of the historic building had been popular during the Big Band era. Harry James, Gene Krupa, and many other famous artists lured the public across the twenty-six miles to hear them play, but now the second floor stood idle. An apparition to the bygone days. Meg arrived first and, knowing the condition of the property, she brought along a flashlight. As she thought, the chandeliers had been removed and the only available light was from the sun or streetlights two stories below. When Derek arrived they were both a little confused by the surreptitious messages.

"Amanda sent you a note too?" asked Derek.

"Yeah. Weird. I tried to call her but got voice mail."

Derek walked around the huge ballroom, each step echoing across the empty room.

"Doesn't it seem strange?"

"What?" Meg was feeling giddy. In her fantasy world she often appeared as a famous ballroom dancer. Usually the swing era surrounded her senses, and sounds of "In the Mood" propelled her feet. She swirled around the room, dancing to the silent music of yesterday.

"Amanda's notes." Derek watched, enjoying her abandonment. "Why not call? Takes more time to deliver them."

Meg crossed to the window overlooking Crescent Avenue. "Maybe she thinks the phones are tapped. Paranoid FBI syndrome. Sun's going down. Good thing I brought along my flashlight." She reached in her pocket and pulled out her phone. "She probably had someone else drop off the notes. I'm usually the one with the conspiracy theory, but I'll call her again if you're nervous about being alone with me in the dark without Amanda to protect you." She loved making fun of him because of his usual superior attitude.

"Don't bother calling."

"Can't anyway. My battery's dead." She made an ugly face.

"Not the first time I imagine. Anyway, I left a voice mail for her saying I'd meet her. Didn't know you'd be here." He paused. "That's another thing. Doesn't seem right that she'd push us together in a vacant place. You know how she feels about any kind of relationship between us."

"You worry too much. Although, the last two times we've been alone, together, it hasn't ended too great." She let the worry pass. "She's probably hatched a new plan. I hope this meeting doesn't take too long. I need some sleep. Rachael asked me to drive to Two Harbors to follow up on some baby lead. Can't go until tomorrow." She walked to the wall next to Derek and slid down.

Derek didn't really care how long the meeting would take since he was delighted to spend more time with Meg. "Gimme your flashlight. I can make some really spooky faces."

"Dah. Who cares."

"What's wrong? Why the attitude?" Derek had a hard time following Meg's switch in moods.

"I just closed Catherine's doors for the last time. Makes me sad. The hotel's been such a huge landmark for the Island. Besides the historical value, I'm also losing one of my jobs. The ghost tour doesn't bring in very good tips and I really don't want to go back to Yorba Linda and live with Grace. That's what's wrong."

"Grace? Oh, your mom. How about your private investigator job in Bullhead? Thought you liked that." He put the flashlight under his chin and turned it on which brought a laugh from Meg.

"Idiot." Meg tried to analyze what was behind the meeting that Amanda set up. Couldn't be about Zach. Everyone had decided Derek wasn't involved with that, so… Must be something involving Marisa. Nothing else came to mind.

All light slipped from the room as the sun set. "Quick question, Meg. Say I'm exonerated from all charges, my attorney license is intact and I'm free to return to private practice. If I set up a law office in Bullhead, would you come to work for me? Take care of all the investigative problems?"

"I suppose you would expect side benefits? Ha! Not going to happen."

"No side benefits. I'm serious."

It seemed more than strange to sit in a dark room and talk about the future with Derek. "You're incredible. How did you ever come up with an idea like that? I don't like you, don't trust you and would never, ever work for you. You're one crazy dude." The room collapsed into black.

"Well, it might be a fantasy on my part, but…" he paused. "I hate redundancy, but truth is, I love you, trust you and would love to work with you. We'd make an awesome team. Then we could get married and have kids." Derek felt this opportunity to reveal his true feelings might never happen again. He waited, hoped, prayed that she would consider his offer. It was a now or never burst of commitment.

Meg's laughter filled the room. Derek still had the one flashlight. He turned it on and off in a second, just enough time to locate Meg's sitting position. Six feet away. He mentally measured his steps and approached her.

"I hear your breathing. You aren't going to be stupid enough to make a move on me, are you?" To her amazement, she hoped he would. She didn't move from her cross-legged sitting position. Her hands relaxed on her ankles. She could tell he was standing in front of her.

He leaned forward, his hand found her hand, then the second hand, and then he pulled her to a standing position. His hands ran up her arms, across the shoulders, up her neck and settled on each side of her face. "Escape with me this time. Be with me at the Willows. Love me as you did then. I love you Meg. I don't deserve you, don't deserve to have you love me, but for this one moment when the rest of the world isn't looking, love me back." And then he kissed her.

Five minutes after the two entered the ballroom, a figure silently scuffled around the exterior of the dance hall. All four entrances to the ballroom were now locked and chained from the outside, with towels stuffed under the door jambs. Meg and Derek, locked in an embrace didn't recognize the odor coming through the air vents until they did. Then it was too late.

Chapter 58

"HEY, SIS. WHERE ARE YOU?" Amanda reached into her desk drawer and pulled out her gun.

"Just landing on the island and heading to the house. Been to Costa Mesa with the baby's DNA sample. Looks like it might be good news," Rachael answered, busy with her own thoughts.

"That's great. But, listen. The reason I called is that I got a weird voice mail from Derek. Says he'll be at the meeting I set up."

"So?" Rachael didn't see the problem.

"I didn't set one up."

"Oh, shit. That's not good."

"That's not all. Someone took a shot at Meg and Derek yesterday."

"What? Are they okay?" Rachael did a U-turn and headed for police headquarters.

"Yeah, bullet missed. But, now I tried to call Meg and she doesn't answer. Went straight to voice mail. No one answers at Catherine's either. Do you know what she planned on doing today after her shift?"

"No. She's helping me out tomorrow. Going to Two Harbors.

That's all I know. Damn. You know how impetuous Meg can be. Can you track Derek's ankle monitor?"

"Took that off yesterday. Has a GPS ring as substitute. I'm pulling it up right now." The computer hummed with activity, and her cell phone buzzed an alert that he was away from his confined grid. "Okay. I found him." She was quiet as she analyzed the screen. "Strange. It shows that Derek's at the casino. Why would he break protocol? If he was going to run, that's a pretty feeble attempt. Stupid to go there. Gotta go, sis. I'll call you later."

"Like hell you will, see you in five minutes, east side of the building. Tell Josh if you see him."

———

Amanda arrived first, found the manager and waited for her sister. "Derek's inside. Hasn't moved in fifteen minutes," she mouthed to Rachael and Josh as they joined her at the top of the casino stairs. "This doesn't feel right." They drew their guns.

The smell of gas lingered in the hallway as they approached the ballroom. The chain stretching around the door knobs had a flimsy lock, so Rachael disposed of it in a hurry with the butt of her gun and kicked the towels away from the bottom of the door. All three turned on their flashlights. Amanda took charge. "Rach, go right, Josh, take the middle and I'll go left. Have no idea what we'll find. Heads up. Let's go."

"Clear" came from both Amanda and Josh as they stole through the room.

"Here, over here," Rachael yelled as the beam from her flashlight fell on the unconscious couple. "Oh, my God. Meg's with him." She reached for Meg's inert body, feeling for a pulse. "She's alive."

Derek moaned, "What's going on?" He was naked and a red marker line had been drawn around his penis.

Meg showed signs of life, moaned and contracted into a small ball. Her clothes were gone. Uncontrollable coughing started from both victims coupled with tears. Meg started to sit up but realized that she was naked. An 'A' from a marker was drawn on her forehead. "What the hell is going on?"

Rachael sank to the floor and covered Meg's nakedness. "Don't know, sis. Are you okay?"

The two victims sat in a confused state. "Why did you call us for a meeting, Amanda? Is this some kind of a weird FBI thing? "She tried to hide her nakedness.

"I didn't send the notes. Someone lured you here."

"That's crazy," uttered Derek. "Why? What did they hope to accomplish? They should know that you could find me. This stupid tracker thing and all."

Josh took off his shirt and tossed it to Derek. Meg turned away from the group and faced the wall.

Amanda rushed downstairs to the theatre and grabbed a robe from the wardrobe room for Meg and a pair of cargo pants for Derek. She overheard a conversation as she came back into the ballroom.

"If they wanted to kill you, they could have done that with no problem. So, it must be some kind of friggin' warning. Sick."

"By whom? For what? Derek and I were barely speaking before yesterday. What's the motive? Who the hell would care?"

"And why the A on Meg's forehead?" Derek asked.

"That's an easy one. Hester Prynne's 'A' for adultery," Rachael said.

With that revelation, no one utter a word until they did. It was as if they were waiting to answer on the count of three. In unison came the reply, "Elliott."

A man, sitting under the streetlight outside the Casino, watched and smiled.

Chapter 59

SALLY GRUMBLED AS SHE SCRUBBED the last fingerprint off the plate glass window of the store. *Dirty little buggers leaving their prints all over the place.* Tired from polishing so hard, she sat on the porch and watched the traffic snake through town. An Escalade flashed by, totally ignoring the stop sign. She yelled at the driver as the SUV ripped up the road toward Little Harbor. Typically rental cars and tourists didn't drive on this side of the island, especially at dusk. Their usual destinations went no further than Descanso Beach or the zip line next door. The passengers looked familiar. *Seems like I've seen that blonde lady before. Maybe she's one of the new owners here on the island. Haven't met them all yet.* She reached in her pocket for her notebook and added the time and date to the unusual occurrence. Rachael might be interested, she thought. Her diary was growing including the last visit from Ramon's sister, buying a bunch of baby food and camping supplies from the store. *Did she seem nervous? Am I being paranoid? Ever since Stella's body was discovered, I've been suspicious of everything.* With that, she walked inside the store and poured two fingers of scotch.

Chapter 60

DEREK PUT HIS CELL PHONE DOWN, disconnecting the call from Amanda. Amanda didn't appear surprised by the information he passed along regarding Dred. It seems he had been on her radar for some time. That was news to him. How did she know? He pulled the second phone from the loose board under the bathroom floor and dialed Dred's number. "What's up? I see you tried to contact me."

"Where you been?"

"Around." Derek wasn't inclined to answer to Dred but had to assume his role. "With that Meg chick. FBI put us together to work out some problems. Had to go along with it. Otherwise they'd know something was wrong. Just playing my part of the game."

"Yeah, well as long as you're not gamin' your sister. Speaking of Marisa, she's called for a meeting to cement the operation." Dred waited for a response.

"Well, shit. How does she plan on doing that?"

"Same way as last time. Through the bathroom window. Another dude will replace you in the house and someone will drive you to the meet up place. You'll be gone less than an hour. Is there a problem?"

"What's wrong with the phone?" Derek knew how sinister his sister could be and now with the added possibility of Elliott being around, he had to play it cautiously. Double whammy.

"Shit. I don't know. She doesn't tell me everything and I'm sure as hell not about to question her. Bring along this phone, but not your FBI one. It can be tracked. They took off your ankle monitor, right?"

"Yeah." He looked down at his hand to locate the ring. "When?" He knew he'd have to alert Amanda. She would be his only chance of survival in case anything went wrong. Anything go wrong? How about everything. The whole scene pointed toward chaos.

"Half hour. Do the bathroom exchange. A driver will be waiting in front of the other house."

"Gilbert?"

"No, he's gone missing." The phone went dead.

"Change of plans." Derek hurriedly called Amanda and regurgitated the last conversation with Dred and waited for instructions.

"Shit. This is escalating too fast. We aren't set up for this. Need more backup. What do you think is going on?" Amanda shouldered the phone as she holstered her gun and grabbed two extra clips.

"Who the hell knows? My conversations with Marisa have been so abrupt. A guess? Might be she's decided to make a run for it and will take me with her tonight. Other alternative is to join up with me and finish the island caper, resolve any drug issues with the cartel and head back to Arizona. Either way, I don't think she plans on letting me go." He paused and reassessed. "I really don't think turning herself in to you is a viable option anymore."

"I'm still concerned as hell with the whereabouts of Josh's baby. Pick up any hints about that?"

"None. Although…" He thought a minute. "If Marisa nabbed the child, Gilbert's wife could be caring for him. Gilbert and his wife always fly together." Derek tried to think through that scenario. With Gilbert out of the picture, what did that mean? No air transportation? Gilbert's wife missing? Is the baby missing again too? He decided not to share this guesswork with Amanda.

"Okay." Amanda pushed. "This is what you do. Cooperate. Switch with your replacement in the bathroom. Escape out the window. Wear the pinkie ring or hide it in your pocket if you think Marisa will question it. We'll follow you and make sure you're safe. If there's a problem, we'll be right behind you. Guess we'll have to wing it."

"And that's your plan?" His mouth was gaping.

"For now, we don't know if Marisa's intent is to run or cooperate. Just play along with her. And, oh, by the way, don't let Meg know what you're doing. You know she'll try to get right in the middle of it."

"Yeah, thanks a lot. We just took one giant step forward in our relationship. This'll screw it up again. I told her I wouldn't lie to her."

"You don't have to lie, just don't talk to her."

Derek was upset. "You know that I love her, don't you?"

"Yeah, so you say." Amanda felt a huge tug at her heart. She felt Meg loved him too and was willing to stick by him if he turned himself in. Meg had been in and out of love relationships but Derek was the only one who'd hurt her. If she hadn't cared so deeply, the hurt never would have happened. "Yes. I figured. But Derek, the best advice I can give you is, it's not going to happen. Too many open wounds to overcome. Do the right thing by Meg. Cut her loose." She felt sad at the honestly of the statement.

"We'll see. I'm way overdue for a miracle and still believe in them. Gotta go and get ready for the adventure." A thin veil of apprehension settled over him.

Amanda looked at the dead phone and smiled. Although she fought the instinct, there was something about Derek that she admired. Realizing that time was limited to set up the operation, she called Josh to rustle up a Jeep for her, grabbed the tracking tablet and headed out the door. "Is Rachael around?" she asked as she headed for the PD. "Thought I'd give her heads up on this."

"I think she's on her way to Two Harbors to meet up with Meg. They've got something going with the storekeeper. I'll drive, you've got shotgun. Bring some extra artillery just in case," Josh said.

"Already done. I'm on my way. Be there in five."

Chapter 61

"YOU DID WHAT?" Duke was finishing his morning coffee, trying to relax and pretend this was a vacation.

"I put a tracking device under the left tire well of Josh's jeep." Grace pulled on her jeans and searched around for her sneakers.

"Oh, great. Do you ever sit back and think about your actions? No wonder the girls are hesitant to call or text. You don't give them any room to breathe. If they get into real trouble, you know Amanda will call."

"Have you seen me do anything overtly crazy? Have I tossed anyone's apartment, slammed anyone up against a wall? No. I'm just watching as any good mother would." She knew Duke would be smirking at that one, so she didn't even look.

"Okay. I give up. So where are we going? And why, if I may ask."

"Well, yesterday I bought a Conservancy pass to drive on the back side of the island."

He laughed. "So now you're playing by the rules? A little late."

Her mouth twitched a little. Her tell. She had gone through the process of acquiring a card and sticker for the one day pass to roam the island at a minimal expense. She used a disguise and one of her fake IDs since revealing her identity to any official Island company was not going to happen. "Now we're going on a ride to whatever we find. Bring your guns and extra ammo. And hurry up, darling."

"Fine, fine. So much for hanging out on the beach today." Duke had made his own arrangements with his CIA buddies to monitor the satellite situation.

Chapter 62

ELLIOTT FINISHED HIS PHONE CALL and started pacing the floor of the rustic cottage. Finding this miniature compound on the backside of Catalina had fit into his plans perfectly. He glanced at the monitors showing the view from the exterior cameras installed around the perimeter of the two houses in the Eucalyptus trees and scattered shrubs. Inside the living room, kitchen and bedroom of the rentals, cameras and audio equipment were also hidden so a clear picture could be observed from his monitor. He smiled at his cunning. He had raised both Derek and Marisa to be guarded, cautious of set-ups like this and yet, here they were, rushing into the ruse so easily. The anticipation of pitting his siblings against each other was delightful and he wondered if they would talk of their sorrow over his death, their longing to be with their dead brother. Probably quite the opposite. Then thoughts of fondling Meg again before he killed her raced through his brain. Undressing her in the ballroom only whet his appetite for further exploration. His pants moved. The surge of anticipated power that would accompany his actions at the end of day was too delightful to ignore. His massive drug operation would start up again and once established, along with the Laughlin money laundering, everything would be perfect.

Like before. He felt sure that with the right amount of persuasion Marisa would transfer all of his off shore accounts back to him. She had been very clever in tracking his money. Elliott was a tad pissed off that he had not recognized her betrayal when they were in full operation. She would have to pay for that.

The month long trial and subsequent incarceration at San Quentin were now behind him. The pain of the plastic surgery was also gone. He rolled up all the frustration and pain into a small ball and tossed it out into his maniacal world. Only delicious sadism lay ahead. He checked the monitors again and headed to the bedroom, whiskey in hand, thinking, *let the rampage begin.*

Chapter 63

"MEG, WHERE ARE YOU?" Rachael's voice sounded jumbled on the cell phone. Transmission was poor and sometimes nonexistent on the back side of Catalina.

"On my way to visit Sally, like you asked. I don't have to work at Catherine's anymore so I thought I'd get an early start." She checked her watch. It was nearly sundown. "Well, not too early. Why? Where are you?" The sun was bearing down on her face and her sunglasses fogged up. "Shit." She swerved on the asphalt road to avoid a traveling tumbleweed.

Rachael grimaced. Meg had a penchant for screwing things up but this was a simple plan, so maybe, just maybe, there wouldn't be any wild repercussions "First. Are you okay? Any hangover from the gas?"

"Nope. I'm fine. Had a few coughing spells last night, but got some sleep. I'm good to go."

"Great. But pace yourself. There could be some residual."

"Got it." Meg yanked the wheel to the left to miss a pothole.

"I picked up Josh from the hospital and we're heading that way too. Sounds like a duplication of work. Why don't you have coffee with Sally and wait for us?"

"Sounds good."

Rachael wanted to discuss the possibility of Elliott, but decided to do that later, face-to-face. Meg's phone voice was often deceptive, but her face always told the straight story. "And, anything happen between you and Derek that you'd like to talk about?" Rachael worried that Meg might forgive too much history and fall for Derek again.

"God, you're nosey." Her long pause gave her away. "Actually, we had a good talk. He let me know what had really been going on in his life, you know, the struggle he and Marisa had with Elliott. I think he really likes me, sis. Dumb to even care one way or the other, but I do."

"Damn it Meg. I knew this would happen. Don't forget that he did nothing to help you until the very end." Rachael knew anything else would fall on deaf ears. "Anyway, when you get to Sally's wait for us. We're probably only twenty minutes behind you. Don't know how much we can do after dark, but maybe we can get an address or plate number from her this time. She's been keeping notes for Rachael and me."

"Yeah. Will do. I'm just pulling up now. Seems like a lot of traffic coming this way. Passed two cars on the way. Ha." A low battery alert showed on her phone. She closed the phone and parked in front of the store, low beams falling on Sally who smiled and waved to Meg.

"Hey, girlfriend. What's up?"

They sat on the porch and went through Sally's journal. A nagging thought kept racing through Meg's brain. "What's this notation 'Extra baby food and supplies purchased by Ramon's sister this afternoon'? Did she drop any clues about where they're staying?"

"I quizzed her about the extra supplies and she said they were thinking about moving. Also, some guy drove her to town this time, Mexican. That was also different. She usually pushes the baby in the stroller and only takes a few things, just enough to carry. Then there was that Escalade that ran the stop sign yesterday. Really seemed like they were in a hurry. Hey. Crap." Sally stood up and pointed.

"There's another idiot running the stop sign. Geez. Looks like the same one as earlier. I must've missed it if it backtracked. Damn it. Might be a different Escalade."

Meg jumped up and stood beside her friend. "Shit. That's Derek." She only got a glimpse of the man's profile, and while dusk was settling in she still recognized him and the Hawaiian shirt he had been wearing two days ago. "Get the keys to your Wrangler."

"Use your cart."

"No, he might recognize it." She jumped off the wooden porch and stared at the taillight of the departing car. She threw open the driver's door of the Jeep and yelled at Sally. "Hurry up. They're getting away."

"Here ya go." Sally threw the keys to Meg who thrust them in the ignition slot, cranked the old Jeep on, then put her foot to the medal.

"Christ, Meg. Don't wreck it. My old man'll kill me." Sally backed away.

"Tell Rachael when she gets here what's going on. My cell phone's dead again so I can't call." She threw the Wrangler in gear and ripped off after the Escalade. A huge billow of dust darkened the night.

Chapter 64

THE WINDS OF CHANGE swept across Catalina Island, swirling around the rustic cabin off Cottonwood Canyon. Inside sat Elliott Spenser, the nefarious brother. Smiling.

Just a little more time and all the Pennington women would be present to join in the fray. He steepled his bony fingers and then arranged the tidy gray wig. He took the makeup box to the mirror and applied a few more old-age lines to his forehead. He was an expert in disguises. Getting to this point in time, on the island and poised to remove all of his enemies, had not been easy. Choreo-graphing his death in prison had taken time and money but it was a successful venture. He knew the truth would come out, but it would take a while. A stupid prisoner volunteered to trade spots with Elliott. The poor sucker thought the five thousand dollars to sit in a cell overnight was certainly worth it. With that kind of money he could buy more drugs. Money he would never see.

Six months in Mexico was enough time to change his main facial frame. He started with dark brown contacts to cover his blue eyes, changed his height with riser shoes, and added a widow's hump. The most painful part of the surgery was cheek implants.

They had become infected and as a result his left cheek was disfigured. The surgeon's payment, expected in cash, came in the form of a knife through his heart.

During the makeover period he watched Marisa's bold attempt to manage his business, found she had confiscated sixty million dollars from the Swiss account, and found his Cayman Island account. Derek was still rusting away in custody and Elliott wondered how much he had told the FBI about the family business of money laundering, drug smuggling plus the new venture into human trafficking. *That pussy was never strong enough for the business. Well, we'll see tonight where his real loyalty lies.* A sneer crossed his lips then morphed into a sinister smile. *And Meg. Another mistake you made Derek, that you will have to pay for. You should never have touched her. Yes, my darling Meg will soon be mine again. It must be fate. I've tried three times to possess you, my impish tart, but you slipped through my fingers. Not this time. I will use you and then kill you and everyone you love.* His baggy sweat pants moved with his lecherous thoughts.

"El Jefe," Lucia said as she entered the room with the baby. "You stay tonight? El bambino is not good sleeper. He keep you awake."

Elliott glanced over at the bundle wrapped in pink, wondering how much longer he would allow him live. A truly noisy bargaining chip. While it appeared at first to be a nuisance, it ended up a stroke of genius for Dred to kidnap the brat. Leverage was always a good thing when dealing with sentimental fools. Hang onto the kid a little longer or toss him into the ocean? Elliott didn't like loose ends.

"I plan on leaving later tonight. Give the kid some knockout drugs. I don't want any of our guests to hear him."

Lucia hesitated but knew not to question El Jefe. "Si, Señor. I put him down now."

Car headlights flashed across the window and Elliott jumped to observe which of his two guests had arrived. A female figure got out of the car and headed to the main bungalow. The driver pulled the car forward and parked as another car pulled up. *Show time.* He moved from the window to watch the reunion on closed circuit TV.

The cameras and audio were well hidden in the house. They would never be found. *Which of my two stupid siblings will figure out my plan first? Let the carnage begin* screamed through his maniacal mind.

Chapter 65

THE TEAR-DOWN HOUSE on the backside of Avalon was dark except for a dim light showing through the small living room window. When Dred turned off the dirt road and came to a stop by the front door, Marisa tensed. "What is this place? I don't like the feel of it. Something's not right." She felt for her .22 and relaxed a little. It was loaded and ready.

"Lights aren't on yet. Come on. Don't get squirrelly on me." He turned off the engine but left on the running lights which added to the sinister feeling. Dred was also feeling a little spooked, not quite sure of Elliott's intentions. "Let's go in and check it out. Derek will be here anytime." He unfastened his seatbelt and opened the car door.

"I'm going to sit here for a while. I never like to be out in the open. You know that. In fact I don't like any part of leaving our camp." She stared him down.

Night had joined the dim shadows from the trees, but Dred didn't need to see her face, he could feel the pressure of her stare.

"If I find out you've been lying to me, that this is some kind of a trap..."

"Geez, Marisa. Trap? What's with you? For God's sake. Let's go in the house." He came around to her side of the Escalade and reached for the door.

Marisa leveled the gun at Dred's head. "Have you thrown in with Derek? Is this an FBI trap, you son of a bitch?" She unlocked the door and threw it open in one motion, catching Dred by surprise. He tripped backward and slammed into the dirt.

Instantly Dred reared up, brushing off the dirt. His temper flared but he managed to keep his composure.

"Stand still. If Derek doesn't arrive in the next five minutes, you're dead." Marisa's hand was steady as she pointed the gun.

Elliott, watching through the window, was pleased to see Marisa pull her gun. Knowing that Dred would also be armed fit into his master plan. He pulled back from the window as another set of headlights swept through the dark. Oh, yes, he thought.

Derek had been fidgeting ever since the Escalade had veered off on the dirt road. There was no way for him to contact Amanda and he was totally vulnerable. No weapon, no phone, just that tiny GPS ring. He rubbed it for good luck and then shoved it in his pants pocket. But could they pick up a signal in this deserted gulley? His future depended on his wits to handle his sister. He questioned the driver. "Man this still doesn't make any sense to meet Marisa here. What's up?"

The car turned into the narrow dirt road and skidded to a stop. The headlights flashed on Marisa holding a gun with Dred in its crosshairs. She momentarily diverted her attention. With lightning speed Dred grabbed the gun and disarmed her.

"You bastard." She lunged.

He had sparred with her before. Anticipating her move, he grabbed her arm, spun her and locked a dead man's choke on her. "There, there, sweet cakes. Calm down. I'm on your side."

Derek unhooked his seat belt but remained sitting, analyzing the situation. He knew this Dred guy was Elliott's sidekick in Bullhead, his accomplice. Where was his allegiance now? Marisa's new lover? Then why was she holding a gun on him and why did he disarm her? He sat. He watched.

Marisa finally stopped struggling and Dred loosened his grip.

"We okay now? Quite a reception for your brotherly reunion."

Marisa stared at the car and finally filtered out Derek's image. She smiled and headed for him. "Hey. Get out and give your sister a hug, won't you?" Their close hug was a little past sibling affection. He relaxed, she held on longer.

He whispered. "I don't like what's going on. You good with this meeting? Are you packin'?" Derek pushed off.

Elliott watched as the scene unfolded. The entourage stepped onto the porch. He smiled at his clever maneuvering getting all of the players into one tight location.

Two couches faced each other in the living room. A coffee table was set with turkey sandwiches, chips and a cooler with water and beer. Marisa's favorite brand.

"Derek. You're so thoughtful. My favorite beer." She grabbed a bottle and popped off the top, using the side of the coffee table as an opener.

Derek looked at the display of food. "I had no part of this."

"Well, you called the meeting, so I thought…"

Derek flashed a questioning look her way, and she knew…

Dred grabbed some food then started for the door, leaving the siblings facing each other. "Gotta take a leak," Dred said as he ducked into the black night. He spotted a clump of boulders and headed for them.

———

"Damn," Meg whispered to herself. When she saw the Escalade turn onto a side dirt road she decided to park and follow on foot. It was only two hundred yards before she spotted the dome light turn on and then off. Another Escalade was parked beside it. She watched as Derek and some lady entered the house. Caution never her strong suit, so she decided to get a peek inside the window. The moonless night helped as she moved closer.

Dred shook off the remnants of pee and as he started to zip up his pants he noticed some movement by the house. *What the hell?* He squinted through the dark. *What the hell was she doing here?*

Chapter 66

DRED WATCHED MEG MOVE from boulder to boulder creeping closer to the main house. *Damn. I'm sure this wasn't part of Elliott's plan.* Since there was no way to contact Elliott, he decided to step up and take care of the problem.

In a loud whisper he said, "Meg. Is that you?"

Meg froze, then reaching behind her back she touched her gun.

"What the hell you doing here?"

"Back at you." Meg took a defensive stance, ready for any aggressive move on his part.

Dred improvised. "I've been driving for Uber since I've been here on the island. Couldn't find a bartending gig. This chick called from Avalon and wanted a ride to Two Harbors. I just let her out of my car."

"Why are you hiding in the bushes?"

"Taking a leak." He laughed. "It happens you know. That's my reason, but what the hell you doin' back here in the bushes?"

Meg was unconvinced. "I thought I saw an old friend drive by when I was in town so I followed him. I was curious about what he's doing on the island. Why he hadn't called." She relaxed and starred back at the house. "Did your passenger go into that house or the bunk house behind?"

"The house. You want me to go and knock on the door with you?"

Impetuous Meg hesitated, thinking back on all the times she had screwed up an FBI operation. "Yeah, maybe. Let me call someone first." She started to dial Amanda's number but stopped. "Oh, yeah. My phone's dead. Lemme borrow yours."

"I would but there's no cell reception on this part of the island."

"Damn." She stepped on the porch and looked through the window.

———

Inside the main house, Derek and Marisa smiled at each other, waiting for the other to start the conversation. "Come on over here and sit with me. I need another hug."

When Marisa pulled away from the brotherly hug, she tried to look relaxed and positioned herself on the end of the couch, sliding her hand behind her back, moving her gun behind a pillow. From the hug, she knew Derek wasn't hiding a gun. "I was surprised when Gilbert said we had to meet in person. Are you ready to leave with me? What's going on? Why couldn't we do this without the cloak and dagger shit?" Marisa's radar was whirling.

"Me? This Dred dude came by and told me you called a mandatory meeting. What gives?" He tensed and his eyes searched around the room. "Oh. Right."

In unison they realized their meeting was a setup, a trap of sorts, but why and by whom?

"You packin?" Derek headed for the adjoining bedroom for a quick search.

Marisa checked the other bedroom and bath. She was quick to accuse. "What. You working with the FBI? You turn me in? They outside?" She headed for the window.

"No, I swear. This isn't my doing." And then he stopped and whispered, "Elliott."

"What?" Marisa rushed to the couch, retrieved her gun and pointed it at Derek. "What did you say? Elliott's dead."

"Never proved."

Marisa wasn't ready to consider such an absurd thought. "You're crazy. Making shit up 'cause I caught you."

Derek slumped into the only chair in the cabin. "No."

The pounding on the door stopped the conversation. When Meg entered with Dred another layer of confusion fell on the group.

Chapter 67

MEG STUMBLED OVER THE THRESHOLD, bumped into Derek's chair and went sprawling. Derek caught her before she ended up on the floor. "Derek. What are you doing here?" She accessed the room, spotting Marisa. "What's she doing here?" Meg had only met Marisa once three years ago in Yorba Linda where she thought Marisa was Derek's girlfriend. Meg did, however, know that Marisa was totally invested in Elliott's crimes. She pushed away from Derek and stood by Dred.

"Well... because..." Derek didn't have a ready answer. Things were moving too fast.

"Well, what?" Meg's emotions were flying all around the room.

"I invited him," answered Marisa.

"How damn cozy. All we need now is for Elliott to show up. Nice little family reunion and maybe you can draw straws for who gets to shoot me." Meg was too enraged to be frightened. Her mind reeled, trying to fit together the pieces of the puzzle facing her.

"Meg, you've got it all wrong." Derek's gaze shifted to Dred. How did he fit in this scene? He saw Marisa's hand move behind the couch pillows and noticed the glint of a gun as it passed behind her back. Dred, more than likely had a gun stashed somewhere and Meg, of course was packing. He was the only unarmed person in the room. Sides were being drawn.

Chapter 68

THE TRACKING DEVICE Amanda had implanted in Derek's ring led her directly to the bungalow. When she noticed the signal wasn't moving anymore she stopped, turned off the engine and walked the last quarter mile. She grabbed her two-way police phone. "Rachael, where are you?"

"Just leaving the store in Two Harbors. The clerk said Meg took off in a Jeep after she spotted some guy she used to know."

"What the hell? I told her to wait. God, how that girl can get mixed up in my stuff so easily. Josh with you?"

"Yes."

"Extra ammo?"

Josh leaned forward. "We've got enough for a medium sized shootout. What's up?"

"Listen, continue tracking my signal. I don't like the feel of this place. There are two buildings here. I'm going to check out the smaller bunk house in back and then wait for you to join me. I see movement in the main house. Okay?"

"You by yourself?"

"Yeah."

"Look around, but don't get involved. Wait for us. Josh'll call for backup."

"Ten-four. See you in a few."

Amanda drew her gun and headed for the small bunk house. She peeked inside and saw an old man staring at a monitor. He looked harmless enough so she holstered her gun and knocked on the door.

"Excuse the interruption sir. I'm Agent Pennington with the FBI." She showed her creds. "Do you have a minute?"

"Of course, Agent...Pennington, is it? What are you doing way out here in the wilderness?" He slurred her name and inwardly smiled at the irony of their meeting. Last time was in court when she testified against him and sent him to San Quentin for life. He liked the addition to his plan.

"I wonder if you might know who's living in the other house?" She glanced around the room, taking inventory. Was that a TV he was watching or CCTV?

Elliott was enjoying the subterfuge. "FBI? Out here in the back-woods? Am I in danger?"

Lucia entered the room, holding Zach in her arms. "Senor, the baby——" She stared at Amanda.

"I hope I didn't wake the baby." Amanda moved toward Zach, questioning the age of the old man with a small child. *Could it be?*

Elliott took over. "Oh, no problem, my granddaughter has a hard time going to sleep. It's okay Lucia. I'll help in a minute. This lady is going to leave." He tried to block the bedroom door but Amanda pushed through.

"So this is your granddaughter? " Amanda tried to take the baby from Lucia, but Lucia put a shoulder between them. "Do you mind if I hold the baby? A girl is she?"

"Of course, I mind. In fact, just leave. I don't like your snoopy attitude." Elliott shuffled across the room and opened the door. "You're a pervert."

Amanda leaned toward the baby, trying to snatch a glimpse of the features, but Lucia quickly pulled the blanket over his face. "Sorry to have bothered you. My apologies."

Elliott mouthed some obscene phrase and slammed the door as she left.

Amanda's antenna was up and her mind was vibrating with questions. She retreated to the vacant area between the two houses and tried to call Meg again. No signal, so she tried her other sister. "Rachael. There's an old man, housekeeper and baby in the bunk house."

"Baby? Oh my God. Is it Zach?"

"The old geezer said it was his granddaughter, but I think he was lying. I was pushy as hell and asked to hold the baby to check its diaper, but he kicked me out."

"Geez. I wonder why?" The phone was on speaker and Josh grinned.

"Gotta go. I'll call in for a search warrant and wait for you. Ten minutes back or so?"

"Wait. One sec. Have you seen Meg yet? She was driving Sally's jeep. She should be there by now. She left over an hour ago." Rachael's concern poured through the phone.

"No." Amanda's eyes searched around in the dark. "There are three cars next to the main house and I passed one about a fourth a mile back. Don't tell me she's right in the middle of this, messin' everything up again?"

"The store clerk said she took off after she spotted a man she knew who flew by in an Escalade."

"Well, the Escalade's here. No sign of Meg. Is she packin?"

"Probably yes. God, Amanda, take care of her."

Chapter 69

The satellite tracking coordinates were changed by Duke. Being the assistant director of the CIA had its advantages. After much prodding from Grace, Duke finally relented and ordered the temporary change supposedly to watch on international drugs trafficking appearing on Catalina.

Grace was following Josh's jeep, via the tracking device she had placed under the fender well. She hadn't seen the vehicle leave town, but was notified of its travel direction by an alert. "Is your laptop fired up?" She pushed Duke. "Are you getting any thermal images? We're way the hell out in the boondocks. Two Harbors has to be ten miles back there." She steered around potholes.

Duke ignored her prattle and focused on the screen. "Looks like there's a party going on ahead. First there's nothing, and, shit, there's a grouping of cars, buildings, people. In fact there's another vehicle pulling up now. Someone's getting out and walking around."

"How many people?" Grace sideswiped a cactus and jerked the wheel back.

"Well, shit-howdy, partner. Hold 'er steady. Looks like two houses. Three people in the back house, one is really small. The center house has two with another two going in. Another person's wandering around outside."

Grace pulled the car to a stop. "Josh's Jeep just stopped." She turned off the lights and told Duke to cover the light from the computer. "Shhh. Be quiet."

"I'm not the one talking," he whispered. Duke took out his night goggles and handed them to Grace.

"That's Amanda with Josh. What're they up to, I wonder." She handed the goggles back to Duke and watched as he surveyed the scene.

Duke handed the night goggles to Grace. "You take these. I've got another pair in the back. I'll take the person hiding out, you start with the back cabin." They separated.

Chapter 70

ELLIOTT, NOTORIOUS FOR HIS CONVOLUTED PLANS, reveled in his intricate strategy. The elaborate setting. All arch enemies would shortly be in the same room, all armed with artillery, but not armed with the most important thing, knowledge. Rigging the room with a projector had taken more time than he anticipated, but the mission was accomplished. Surveillance cameras were hidden along with microphones and amplifiers. Every movement was being recorded and heard. He returned to the monitor and watched as the dialogue continued.

Meg was surprised at how betrayed she felt. *Get over it. Derek has betrayed you again.* With that insight she lashed out at him. "Great, Derek. You played me for a sucker again. A little smoozing and you think you have my forgiveness. Well think again, asshole. I'm outta here. Enjoy your family reunion, you pervert." She turned and stomped toward the door.

"Hold up, Missy," said Derek. "How do you figure?" He caught her elbow and jerked her around.

"Well, since you don't have your ankle monitor on and you're here with your sister, it looks and feels like you decided to join the dark side. Too bad your crazy brother isn't here to delight in the moment. Do I have a chance of living through this decision of yours?" She was near tears of disappointment.

Marisa broke in. "Well handsome brother. Is your old girlfriend right? Is that why you called me here? You decided to ditch the FBI and we can get started on our new drug adventure?"

"I didn't ask you to meet me first of all. Dred gave me the message about the meeting. He said you insisted I meet you tonight. It was all planned by you. Don't pull a switch on me now. What's going on?"

The emptiness and disappointment within Meg was staggering. "You know what, Derek. You owe me an answer. Who's it going to be? Marisa or me?"

He turned pale. "If I thought for a minute that the "me" meant a future for us, I would jump at that." He paused, took her shoulders and glared into her eyes. "You've given me no encouragement and I don't trust the FBI. No written assurance has been given that I would get my attorney privileges reinstated, that I wouldn't end up in jail, and add to that, the woman I love skips out on me." The despair in his eyes was apparent. What to do? Stay or run to freedom?

Before he could utter his final decision, the lights went out, a voice boomed through the black room and a projected image of Elliott appeared on the living room wall.

"Family." He paused, a dramatic moment to let the reality set in. His voice boomed through the amplifiers. "Yes, it's your amazing brother, alive and well. So nice of you to join me. I've assembled a collage of our lives to entertain you. After you watch the slide show, we'll have an opportunity to establish our future plans. Sit back and enjoy. This is your life."

A wooden bar dropped across the only door to the cabin. Gilbert waited for his next instruction.

The three guests instantly rushed to the door to escape and pushed against it to no avail. "What the hell's going on?" Marisa screamed.

"It's our sick brother getting his pound of flesh. Meg, where are you?" Derek searched around in the dark.

"Over here," she whispered as the first of twenty slides appeared on the wall.

The first five pictures were of the three siblings, playing in a rundown neighborhood of Los Angeles. Next came Derek's graduation from law school, Marisa's graduation from business school and Elliott's first job in the broadcasting world. Then the dark side appeared. Six women—dead---with their hearts carved out. Three from Santa Cruz, three others from Bullhead City. The narrative broke through. "Oh, yes, the lovely women I thought would be perfect. Sadly they didn't live up to my expectations, but they had good hearts, so I saved them in formaldehyde." A row of jars appeared with an excised heart in each hiding behind a label indicating name of the victim and date of death. Then remnants of human body parts for sale, human trafficking victims, and finally a picture of the baby.

"Derek we have to get out of here. He's insane," Meg whispered.

Derek felt along the wall, holding onto Meg's hand. As he felt toward what he thought was the door, he whispered, "Marisa. Come on. Follow my voice."

Dim light from the projected pictures disappeared. And then, there it was. Elliott's singular maniacal obsession. Meg. Naked, bound, tortured.

"Damn you, Elliott," screamed Meg.

Psychedelic lights flashed around the room, shooting weird images into space. Elliott's voice exploded. "Yes, I have had a very prolific life, with large sums of money to show for it. Well, I did have money until you got greedy, Marisa, darling." The screen turned off and the lights came on. "This is your only chance family. Make your decision now my little siblings. Oh, sorry, Meg. You don't get to decide. You will be dead in five minutes. No one gets away from me."

Marisa answered first. "Of course, Elliott, I'm with you. Let me out of here."

The door opened and Dred motioned for her to leave. She darted outside into the night air as the door slammed shut. As she jumped off the porch Gilbert grabbed her and pushed her toward the back cabin.

"Let go of me, you shithead." Marisa wrestled with him.

A man appeared in the darkness. "Marisa, darling. Good choice."

"Elliott?"

He slapped her across the face, added a punch to her midriff. "Tie her up, Gilbert, leave her in the dirt. Go behind the house now. Let's finish the job." He stumbled over some rocks but maintained his balance, aiming for the front cabin, a portable microphone in hand. "Derek, are you ready to run?"

Derek responded to his voice and dropped Meg's hand. "Sorry Meg. I wish you would've chosen me. Okay, Elliott, I'm in."

A mini-explosion ripped through the back of the house and a burst of flames engulfed the bedroom. Instant inferno. Dred opened the door for Derek. He rushed forward, leaving Meg behind. As Derek stepped through the doorway he tackled Dred. They grappled on the floor.

"Run, Meg!"

Chapter 71

AMANDA WATCHED AS THE OLD MAN LEFT THE BACK CABIN and headed for the main house. "Where are you, sis?" She waited for a reply from Rachael, but nothing.

As Marisa staggered from the main house and approached Elliott, Amanda pulled her gun and moved forward. Realizing the girl involved in the scuffle was not Meg, she backed off to watch.

A noise in a nearby bush drew her attention and gun.

"Don't shoot," a woman's voice pleaded. "It's your mom."

Duke heard a Jeep engine as he moved toward the main house. He stopped abruptly and used his night goggles to identify the newcomers. With a muffled voice, he called to them as they got out of the Jeep. "Over here. It's Duke."

In a crouched position, Rachael sidled over. "What the hell's going on? Is Mom with you? Where's Meg?" Duke spieled a short synopsis of events and they moved toward the front cabin, guns pulled.

———

Meg ran for the door, but Dred tripped her as she passed him. He delivered a knockout blow to her chin, grabbing her as she fell. Gilbert jumped up on the porch and saw Derek turn to help Meg. He rushed forward and cracked him over the head with the butt of his Glock.

"Pull his body into the cabin. Let the fire get rid of 'em," yelled Dred. Smoke engulfed the small room as the two men slammed and barricaded the door.

Amanda and Grace were moving toward the cabin as the fire erupted. "Meg might be in there," yelled Amanda. "Call for backup, I'm going in."

As she ran toward the cabin Elliott stepped out of the bushes, gun in hand, aiming at Amanda. Grace looking through the night goggles, pulled her gun and fired three shots. The man fell. Grace ran to his side, kicked the gun out of reach and felt for a pulse.

Amanda stopped to see her mother seize control of the situation and then ran full speed. She lifted the bar securing the door and burst into the blazing room. "Meg, Meg. Answer me. Where are you?" Visibility was nil. Amanda tripped over a body and fell. "Thank God. I got you, sis." Fire licked at her feet as she dragged Meg toward the door. Now Duke was beside her. Flames were close to engulfing the entire cabin.

"I've got her," yelled Duke as he lifted and carried Meg the last ten feet into the fresh air.

"Is she okay? Is she breathing?" pleaded Rachael as she appeared.

"Looks like smoke inhalation only. She'll be okay in a few minutes."

Meg stirred, trying to focus. "Did you get Derek out?" She whispered, choking through her smoke-filled lungs.

All eyes turned to the cabin as two of the walls fell. Duke ran full out, rushed through the living room and found Derek, passed out on the floor. He threw Derek over his shoulder and bound out through the smoky opening. "He's not breathing." Duke immediately started CPR as Amanda ran to help.

Rachael called for backup and EMT support on Duke's two-way. "Anyone see where those other two dudes went?" She stood, pulled her gun.

"You'll find both Elliott and Marisa behind the main house. I put tuff-ties on both of 'em to keep 'em out of trouble for a while. Elliott might be dead." Grace joined the group.

"What?" Rachael stared at her mother as if seeing a ghost.

"Well I shot him three times, but it was dark, so I didn't kill him. Didn't have time or desire to stop the bleeding."

All eyes turned in Grace's direction with smile lines beginning to show around the mouth of the sisters.

Rachael was the first to break away. "I'll check the cabin."

"I'm coming with you," yelled Josh.

Chapter 72

Dred and Gilbert peered through the underbrush, observed the house go up in flames. Light from the fire illuminated the area and they watched the drama unfold. "They'll head for the bunk house next. We'll make our stand there." He punched Gilbert's arm to get him started.

"No, Señor. They have many people. Let's run." Gilbert didn't like the odds for survival.

Dred weighed the choices and decided Gilbert was right. "Okay. We'll split up. The keys are in the Escalade. Here's my extra gun. They're busy right now. Two will have to handle Marisa and Elliot, some with Meg and some will go to the back house. It's a perfect time. Head uphill and double back to the car. Be there in five minutes."

Gun shots resounded four minutes later when Gilbert crossed paths with Duke. "Put your gun down, man. We've got you outnumbered."

Rather than face jail for murder, or deportation to stand for his crimes in Mexico, Gilbert pulled the trigger and Duke responded. One down.

Hearing the shots, Dred rushed even faster toward the Escalade.

Seeing no one around, he slipped into the driver seat, cursing the overhead light and reached for the ignition.

Amanda smiled broadly as she set her gun site on Dred's head. "Sorry, buddy. You lose."

Dred held on to the steering wheel and slumped forward, knowing there was no chance of escape. "How's Elliott?" he mumbled.

"Dead, I hope."

Amanda held the button down on the two-way radio and told everyone that Gilbert and Dred had been neutralized. Even with that welcomed information, Josh and Rachael approached the back cabin with caution.

"I'll go first," said Josh as he raised his gun and turned the handle of the front door. Lights were on in the living room and Lucia was sitting in the rocking chair, holding a bundle.

"Anyone else in the house?" He motioned Rachael to enter and started for the back bedroom. Amanda searched the kitchen and bathroom. "It's clear."

Lucia's head was lowered and she mouthed a small whisper to the child in Spanish. Her hands were visibly shaking. "Do not hurt me, Señor. I take care of bambino for El Jefe." She held the child up for someone to take.

"I got this," said Josh in a quiet voice, as he held his son for the first time.

Chapter 73

WHEN THE FIRE DEPARTMENT ARRIVED they found the house in ashes. It looked like a football stadium all lit up with lights from the emergency vehicles. Besides the fire truck, the ambulance had arrived along with the coroner and another squad car. Elliott's gunshot wound was dressed, an IV started, and he was pushed into the back of the ambulance.

Meg talked to the driver. "What's the prognosis?"

"Lost a lot of blood. Will be touch and go. Probably need some surgery."

"Well, won't hurt my feelings if he doesn't make it."

The driver gave her a knowing look since he had been told the story.

When Lucia saw Gilbert's dead body, her wailing drenched the air. She was cuffed and pulled away from the bunk house. Dred was shoved into the backseat of the patrol car next to Marisa who continued her tirade, cursing out loud. "Derek. I'll get you for this, you son-of-a-bitch. If Elliott dies, then I swear to God, I'll put the hit out on you. You're a dead man." The officer pushed Lucia's head down and shoved her into the front seat, attaching the cuffs to the overhead bar. Gilbert's body was stuffed into a body bag and shoved into the coroner's van.

"Joe, you good to handle these three without help? Man, we're so shorthanded." Josh glanced into the patrol car making sure all of the prisoners were tied down.

"I'm good. Straight to jail they go." The seasoned deputy stuck his head in the window and yelled, "Shut up, woman. Settle down." He replaced his shotgun on the rack, and turned the ignition key, not looking forward to the two-hour drive back to Avalon with the loud-mouthed woman.

Grace took over the baby-rocking duties. Josh radioed ahead for another car to meet up at the airport and separate the prisoners. He knocked twice on the top of the squad car as it left.

The moon decided not to appear, so the drive over the dirt road was hazardous. Joe was well acquainted with the terrain and after ten minutes of slow, cautious driving, flat asphalt appeared in his headlights. He accelerated.

Marisa continued her outburst, with Dred shoving her, banging his body against hers, and yelling at her to shut up. The officer turned to yell at her but noticed a slightly higher pitch in her voice as she screamed, "Watch out. Buffalo." He yanked the steering wheel to the right, too late. The car careened to the right, went airborne, and flipped over three times, landing upside down in a ravine.

The wheels continued spinning but nothing else moved. The driver's air bag had deployed. Steam rose from the engine. Lucia's face was twisted into a grotesque mask. Blood mixed with saliva dripped from the open slit that once was her mouth. Her eyes stared ahead. Not blinking.

"You okay Marisa?" Dred didn't know how long he'd been unconscious. "Marisa?" He shifted in his seat to look at her. A limb from a Eucalyptus tree stared back at him. A branch had sheered through the top of the car, finding its way through Marisa's fore-head. Blood and gray matter dripped down through the wound. "Oh, my God. Lucia, you okay?" His eyes drifted to the driver. He couldn't tell if he was dead, but knew he was unconscious. Silence.

The door Dred had been manacled to was split in half. While still handcuffed, he was not attached to anything. Sliding out of the seat and locating the key in the officer's pocket took a minute. He collected everyone's money, cellphones and guns and limped into the night. By his calculations he had an hour to get back to his old camp, pick up the electronic equipment and split with a handful of men. There might be room for a small number of leftover drugs.

Chapter 74

A FIREBALL SPREAD ACROSS THE NIGHT SKY, along with an undeniable sound of a crash. Everyone standing by the cabins froze. "Shit. That has to be the patrol car." Duke was getting ready to drive off. He turned off the cart and ran to the Escalade. "Who's got keys?" Grace was right behind him.

"Meg. You and Derek take the baby." Amanda took charge. "Rachael, you and Josh get in my Jeep. Hurry." The two cars took off in a flurry of dirt.

Moments later the vehicles pulled up behind the sheriff's patrol car. "Amanda, get the fire extinguisher. I'll get Joe out first," Josh yelled as he leaped from the Jeep.

Duke ran toward the burning car to assist. It took a second to see that Marisa, Joe and Lucia were dead. He struggled with the caved-in door, finally jerking it loose, unsnapped Marisa's seat belt and tried to pull her out. The tree branch piercing her skull jammed into the metal structure of the car. He couldn't move her.

Josh grabbed his flashlight and followed the beam through the tangled metal, searching for Joe. "Oh, God. No." He desperately tugged on Joe's seatbelt, but then backed off, realizing that rushing would be to no avail. He leaned over and closed his friend's vacant eyes. He searched the rest of the car. "Damn. Should have been Elliott instead of Joe. He's got a family. Three kids." Josh straightened and shot a look around the chaos. "Where the hell is Dred?"

"Gone," yelled Amanda. "Shit."

"Dispatch?" He grabbed the mic through the cruiser window. "Yeah. This is Josh. We need the coroner back here. Three dead. Near Catalina Harbor. One prisoner got away. Get a BOLO out. Dred...last name to follow...Male, Caucasian, brown hair, 37, 6 foot 2 inches, last wearing jeans, black t-shirt, armed and dangerous. FBI will stay here with the victims and I'm heading back to Avalon." He turned to Amanda. "Anything else?"

Amanda nodded. "Yeah. When Elliott gets to the hospital in Avalon post a guard outside his room. Dred may show up there."

"Right. Look, are you okay waiting for the coroner by yourself?"

"Absolutely."

"We've still got Dred out there. Probably has Joe's gun."

"Right, but I'm fine. Bus'll be here in no time. Go. Get back and pick up Meg, Derek and the baby. Get the baby settled down for the night. We'll straighten this out in the morning. Shit load of paperwork."

"What should I do with Derek? Can you trust him not to run?"

"He won't run now. Both his sister and brother dead in one day? Guess it's your job to tell him. Sorry."

"Great." He headed back to the Jeep

———

Meg and Derek were sitting in the back cabin watching the baby take a bottle. "Oh, good you're back. What happened?" Meg was startled by Josh's expression. "What?"

He sat next to Derek. "Meg I need to talk to Derek alone. Would you mind?"

Before Meg had an opportunity to argue, Derek spoke. "She can stay. What's going on?"

"I've got some bad news."

"Meg sat down on the couch next to Derek and listened as the tragic events of Marisa's death were exposed. She took Derek's hand and squeezed it.

The room gave way to silence as the three people let the tragic news sink in. Finally Josh pushed forward. "I don't want to sound insensitive Derek, but Dred did get away and we need to get him before he leaves the island. Any idea where Marisa's hideout is located? We need to move fast."

Derek had a hard time switching. "The house behind mine is where she was in town. I don't know where the rest of her crew is hiding out. With Gilbert dead and Elliott unconscious, Dred'll be short of help." He thought for a minute. "Probably on the back side of the island, near water. Because of the seaplane." He stopped, sifting through images. "There's a computer in her house, maybe get some info off it." He stood and walked to the window.

Meg took Josh aside. "Hey. What're you going to do with the baby?" Meg glanced around at the crib. When Josh didn't move, she picked up Zach cautiously placed him in Josh's arms. "Probably time to make a decision." She turned and walked away.

Chapter 75

AL HOBBLED FROM THE WHEELCHAIR to the waiting cart. "Thanks for picking me up at the hospital, John. Guess you know I'll be staying at the Island Inn from now on."

"Sure 'nuf. You know Al, folks in town wonder what's happened to Catherine." With a very mischievous tone in his voice he continued. "Did you have to negotiate with the hotel for a special price to have Catherine stay in the room with you?"

Al nodded. *Poor sucker. Thinks he's kidding.* "Didn't cost anything extra, but there were some strings attached. I had to keep her happy."

"You know, everyone thinks she started the fire at the hotel." He muffled a laugh.

"Well, she did, but we talked about that yesterday. She apologized for it. Still a tad pissed off at the Conservancy for deciding to tear it down."

"Ever wonder what's going to happen when you kick the bucket? Where the hell will she go?"

"No. That's been covered. She took a likin' to a little baby boy that spent a night at the Hotel not too long ago. Says she'll float on over to his house when I'm not around. Fact is, think she has plans on trying it out tonight."

John stifled a laugh. "What? Catherine's turned into a cougar?" This time he laughed out loud.

Al slumped a little as he reached for the car door. "Catherine has her ways. Shouldn't treat her with disrespect."

Chapter 76

TWENTY-FOUR HOURS PASSED. Elliott was transported by Medevac to the LA County Hospital, placed on life support with around the clock security outside his room. Surgery was planned for the following morning. With Dred missing, Amanda was taking no chance on Elliott escaping again. Both FBI and Sheriff's department would share the shifts. Marisa and Gilbert were chilling out in the L.A County Coroner's cooler with appropriate tags hanging from their big toes. Dred was in the wind. Josh and Rachael took the baby to his home on Sumner Road and fell into heated discussions about everyone's future. Amanda negotiated with the FBI and Derek no longer had a tracking device and was allowed to make funeral arrangements for his sister and brother.

———

Renting a nurse's uniform was easy. Cash only.

Purchasing the narcotics took a little finessing, but a cash transaction was completed through a Mexican Pharmacy.

Entering through the Emergency entrance of the hospital went unnoticed.

The night nurse nodded to the FBI agent sitting outside Elliott's door. He had watched her enter and exit two other doors down the hall and she smiled as she entered Elliott's room. Her hospital ID was where it belonged. IV lines dangled from their stand, heart monitor was whizzing away and the crash cart stood guardian over the unconscious patient. Duct tape was spread across the CCTV so the nefarious activity would not be observed. The nurse took the syringe loaded with potassium chloride from her uniform pocket, injected it into the saline line and watched as the mixture entered his body. She put a hand over his mouth in case a last minute exhale of life decided to get noisy. Then she waited. She turned the volume down on the heart monitor, not wanting a siren to interrupt the exquisite moment.

"Karma's a bitch, Elliott. Time for you to leave my family alone." She sat through his last breath and was amazed at how good it felt.

She walked unnoticed out the front door of the huge hospital. The trustworthy security cameras recorded her exit, but her long blonde hair and glasses were a perfect disguise. After she got into her rental car and headed down the 5 freeway, she made a call. "I'm on my way home darling. Probably be forty minutes or so unless you want me to stop for take-out. Chinese?"

"No. Just hurry home, I miss you. Everything go okay?"

"Oh, yes. Just taking care of some loose ends. Probably best the girls don't know."

"Of course." He paused. "Don't you think they'll figure it out?"

"Probably."

The morning nurse found the deceased patient and a notation of 'patient succumbed to a heart attack' was posted on the computer. The FBI was notified. No investigation followed.

———

Meg and Derek spent the next few days trying to sort out all the drama. The one-time almost lovers sat in a back booth at Jack's restaurant and waited for coffee before they leaned back and relaxed into the moment. Meg's impetuous nature took over. She couldn't stand any more of the silence. "So, how did you sleep last night?"

"Alone."

"Okay, smart ass. Is that how it's going to go?"

"What?"

Meg decided two could play the one word answer game and transferred her focus to the crowded diner.

They each placed their order and then Derek decided to exacerbate the problem by whistling 'Love Walked In and Drove the Shadows Away' under his breath. He knew Meg's love for old movies, Fred Astaire, Ginger Rogers, Gershwin, Ella Fitzgerald and the like.

Meg laughed out loud. "You are such a shit. Talk to me." She knew she had no choice but to love him.

"Sleep was welcomed with no ankle monitor on and no surveillance cameras to duck. Only one problem. Sexy dreams appeared."

"Oh, yeah. Want to elaborate?" thinking he was going to further woo her. She did a number with her eyelashes.

"Well, she was a voluptuous redhead."

Meg reached up and touched her long, blonde wavy hair without realizing it.

"We were in Maui on a beautiful sandy beach. West side of the island. By ourselves."

Since Meg had never been to Hawaii and the conversation was not going her way, she interrupted. "Okay, Romeo. Let's not wallow in your perverted dream life. What are your plans?"

"Easy. To marry you."

Typically Meg was never surprised. She was too smart, too alert and astute, always positioned for the other person's replies, in fact she was capable of maneuvering the conversation so there were no surprise questions or answers. Ever. And yet, here she was. She regrouped. "Interesting. And how do you plan on accomplishing that?"

"Simple, I say Meg, will you marry me, and you answer yes." He spread some cream cheese on a bagel and took a bite.

What to say? Meg decided to follow suit and attack her breakfast. "Well, we'll see about that." *Holy moly. Sure wasn't ready for that.*

Chapter 77

THE SISTERS PLANNED A FAREWELL DINNER at the Descanso Beach's restaurant two weeks later. The evening cooperated with a seventy-five degree temperature and only a slight breeze. Amanda talked Fred into flying her back to the Island for the party and he joined the family for dinner. Attired in a flowered summer dress, Rachael arrived holding hands with Josh, while Meg and Derek strolled along the shoreline, not at all worried about being late.

"Hi, gang." Meg waved to the group as she and Derek trudged across the sand to the gathering. He held her chair while she sat. Damn, she thought, sure like it when he does that. After a sumptuous dinner of lobster they took their wine and settled in the lounge chairs lined up, side-by-side on the sandy beach. All was quiet. The ocean cooperated and only light waves lapped the shore. Everyone was enjoying that long awaited moment in time where life was good.

Amanda breeched the silence. "Okay, ladies. What's on the agenda starting tomorrow?"

Rachael was first to break the reverie. "I'm heading back to Bullhead. Captain called and said to get my butt back there by

Monday or there won't be a job waiting for me. Josh's staying here with Zach. Needs to find a permanent babysitter." She leaned on Josh's shoulder. "We'll finish with the funeral arrangements for Stella and Greg before I go." She hid the tear that was forming.

Amanda chimed in before the whole group reverted to tears. "I feel like a yo-yo, popping back and forth between here and the mainland. I still have some wrap-up to do here. Probably take a week or so with all the friggin' paperwork. FBI's set up a file on Dred. Already started the manhunt. I may be assigned a new case on a cruise ship. Sounds intriguing. Next?"

"That would be me," Meg said, "But Mandy, what about Derek? You didn't mention him."

"Oh, I thought you wouldn't notice." She grinned. "He's still mine. We'll be going back to the LA office in a week or so to sort out his status. Hopefully, with time spent incarcerated in L.A., wearing the ankle monitor and helping us with this case, he might skate by with time served."

"What about my record?" Derek asked. "If it shows a felony I won't be able to practice law anymore. Any chance of sneaking by that?"

"No promises, but you have great character witnesses. I'll do what I can."

Meg squeezed his hand. "Well, the Conservancy is tearing down the rest of Catherine's Hotel so it looks like I'll be job hunting. Think I'll join Rachael and go back to Bullhead. Maybe dust off my PI license or go to work at the Dam again."

"Mom keeps suggesting that you get your real estate license and sell property in Yorba Linda. Town is booming."

"No thank you. Really love Grace, err, Mom, but don't want to live with her. Besides she has Duke. Can't imagine them making out in the kitchen when I come home. EEK."

Amanda raised a hand to stop the conversation. "Speaking of mom, I just got an interesting text."

Rachael and Meg yelled in unison, "What does she say?"

Amanda laughed. "Sorry I had to miss the party but I had to

take care of some loose ends. Love you girls." She flopped her phone down on the table in case anyone wanted to read it.

Her sisters laughed and said, "Got it," while Fred, Josh and Derek sat with a puzzled look on their faces.

"Any romance in the wind for you two?" Rachael decided to change the subject before the men got too inquisitive. She had mixed emotions while waiting for an answer.

"What are you talking about?" said Meg as she plopped down on Derek's lap and kissed him.

The End